Agoraphobia

Copyright © 2018 by Justin Finley

All rights reserved. This book or any portion thereof may not be reproduced or used in any manner whatsoever without the express written permission of the publisher except for the use of brief quotations in a book review.

Publisher's note: This is a work of fiction. Names, characters, places, and incidents either are the product of the author's imagination or are used fictitiously. Any resemblance to actual events, locales, or persons, living or dead, is entirely coincidental.

Printed in the United States of America
Edited, formatted, and interior design by Stephanie Lomasney Levert
Cover art design by Emily Johns

First edition published 2018
10 9 8 7 6 5 4 3 2 1

Finley, Justin
Agoraphobia / Justin Finley
p. cm.
ISBN-13: 978-0-9991639-2-4

For you,

For believing in and
continuing on this journey with me.

Agoraphobia

A novel

Justin Finley

Wednesday

Chapter 50

Eight days following his first and only meeting with the man simply known as John, Tyler Bennett once again stood in the investigator's lavish office. Just as it had done during his first visit, the *Starry Night* painting hanging behind the thick glass before him incited questions about its authenticity. *If it's real, why would he display it in such a way that he could get caught? But then again, maybe he has it in plain sight because it's a fake. Or, it's so blatantly out in the open that no one would suspect it's the original painting.* He finally concluded that he couldn't come to a conclusion.

Tyler took to one of the tightly-bound leather chairs in front of John's desk. He found it to be not only comfortable, but also a stylish piece of furniture. *This chair and a matching couch would look great in the living room.* Tyler was in the process of renovating the house in which he had lived between the ages of six and eighteen. His late parents' house (built in the seventies) was in dire need of some updating, especially since he was once again residing in it. The idea of selling it never became a thought in Tyler's head, as he didn't want to part with memories of his family. Just the façade of the house had been completed so far. Gone was the termite-infested wood exterior, giving way to stucco and brick. Next to be remodeled was the living room. He stood, lifting the cushion until locating a tag. *Restoration Hardware. I'll stop by tomorrow morning.* Upon returning to the chair, his phone vibrated. The number on the screen belonged to his ex-girlfriend, Sophia. He placed the phone back in his pocket.

For the past week, Tyler's cell phone never left his side. While working out, it rested in his pocket on vibrate mode. When he showered, it sat next to the bathtub with the ringer set on the loudest setting possible. Whenever he awoke during the night, he glanced to see if he missed a call from the person whose leather chair he currently occupied. He experienced disappointment every time he checked his phone—that is until 8:05 in the morning, when a text sent by John instructed him to go to his office at exactly noon.

It was the Fourth of July. Tyler didn't have family to spend the day with. Both of his parents were deceased, and three time zones separated him and his sister. Two barbeque invitations were extended his way from friends, yet Tyler was much more interested in receiving information about Christina than eating a hamburger and potato salad while sweating in the Atlanta heat. After reading the text from John, Tyler jumped out of bed like a kid on Christmas morning. He couldn't wait to hear what had been discovered about his former girlfriend.

Over the past three years, Tyler had great difficulty imagining why Christina broke up with him out of the blue, when everything seemed so perfect between them. The one reason he kept coming back to was that she had met someone during her trip to New Orleans. Despite telling John that he doubted another gentleman was involved, part of him wondered if she in fact did meet someone else, and if so, if she was still with him. Given the peculiarity of her actions upon her return from New Orleans, it was plausible. The excuse she gave him—that she was moving to California to start a new life—didn't hold an ounce of truth to it. Christina never once mentioned going to California during their two-year courtship. No matter what the situation may have been, Tyler strongly believed John would bring the two of them together again.

Floorboards outside the office door creaked. Tyler was certain he was just seconds away from discovering the truth about Christina. He could hardly contain himself as the bronze handle turned. Once the door opened, the nervous smile on his face waned as the person he thought he was about to see was instead said person's secretary.

"Mr. Bennett," stated the sixty-something-year-old woman, whose right hand was hidden behind her back. "John is still on assignment and will not be joining you today."

The excitement and optimism that had snowballed inside him over the last four hours quickly transitioned to disappointment. "Then why did he send a text telling me to be at his office for 12:00?"

The secretary's right hand came into view. "He wanted you to see this." She handed him a thin, slick piece of paper that appeared to have come from a fax machine.

The view of the woman in the black and white picture was taken from the side. She wore oversized sunglasses and had hair that was darker than Christina's dirty-blonde locks, yet Tyler had no doubt that the pronounced cheekbones, the cleft in her chin, and the pouty bottom lip belonged to his former girlfriend. She looked to be in the lobby of a hotel, about to board an elevator behind a man and a woman pushing a stroller. He read the writing beneath the photograph.

I found Christina. I know where she lives. I know her relationship status. I know her every move over the past few days. Congratulations, Tyler. Christina will be yours again. Be patient.
- John

Tyler's excitement and optimism once again returned. He stood from the leather chair. "Do you mind if I make myself a drink?"

"Help yourself, Mr. Bennett."

While pouring Jack Daniel's single-barrel whiskey into a glass, Tyler couldn't stop smiling as he envisioned Christina, her eyes brimming with joyous tears upon seeing him again. "I can't believe he found her. He's good."

"You have no idea, Mr. Bennett." As Tyler took the first sip, the secretary approached him, grabbing the paper from his hand. She then held a cigarette lighter to it. Once the paper caught fire, she dropped it into a metal wastebasket next to John's desk.

Tyler didn't ask the secretary why she burned the paper. It was quite clear. John was meticulous at what he did, and didn't want to leave a shred of evidence behind. "What do I do now?"

She handed him an unsealed envelope.

"What's this for?"

"You'll find out soon enough. Go home and enjoy the holiday, Mr. Bennett. John will be in touch very soon."

Chapter 51

I awoke from my nap. The backseat of a Mustang wasn't the most relaxing place for a seventy-two-inch-long body to rest, and three days in the backseat was almost more than I could take.

"Is it okay to sit up?" I asked my driver.

"Hold on." We slowly decelerated. I could hear a car passing on the left. "You're clear."

I stretched my arms while sitting upright. My neck was stiff and my lower back was even tighter. "It's so uncomfortable back here."

"Well, if I wasn't in a rush to secretly escort you across country, then I would have visited other rental agencies to see if they had anything bigger than a sports car." The sourness in Caroline's tone was followed by a sarcastic smile.

"I'm sorry. I didn't mean to complain."

She let out a lengthy yawn before saying, "I'm sorry too. I'm just a little tired, thus cranky right now."

"I'll take over if you want me to." I had offered to drive at least a dozen times since leaving Delain's house on Monday morning.

"You can't. If anyone sees you, we could both end up in jail." Her reply was identical to the previous twelve answers. One thing I discovered about Caroline in the last few days was that she was meticulous when it came to executing the plan the three of us had devised.

"I doubt anyone is going to know the two of us out here in..." A plateau and several mountains were visible in the distance, while red clay covered much of the land around the road, "where are we?"

"Arizona, close to Scottsdale. By the end of the day, your face will most likely be on every news channel in the U.S. We can't take the chance of someone telling the police or the F.B.I. or C.I.A. or anyone else that can incarcerate us that they saw you with me. We have to be—down!" I quickly reclined. "We have to be very careful. No mistakes, Jackson."

I grew more apprehensive as Caroline reminded me that I was just a few hours away from lying to the police and/or federal agents about my whereabouts over the last few days. The story was sure to make headlines—a young man got cold feet before marrying his fiancée, and let another person take his place on a plane that crashed and killed everyone on board. I was petrified by the ensuing chaos, and the feeling only increased as we grew closer to our drop-off point. Several times over the last few days I imagined myself wearing an orange jumpsuit, enclosed behind the walls of Angola Prison after being incarcerated for either the murder of Davis Melancon or Cliff the demented truck driver. I needed reassurance that I wouldn't see the inside of a jail cell. "Do you think our plan's going to work?"

She nodded. "Yes. Do you?"

"I hope so."

"Keep telling yourself it's going to work. It's a very believable story. Just stick to what the three of us discussed and researched over the internet. We'll be fine."

"You're right. It's going to work." I still wasn't convinced.

"The car passed. You're clear."

I sat up, scooting to the middle of the backseat. Our eyes met in the rearview mirror. Caroline subtly smiled before returning her gaze to the road. For the last few days, the backseat wasn't the only uncomfortable subject in the car. Neither of us had yet to mention what happened in Denver, but I was certain it was on Caroline's mind just as much as it was on mine. Another subject matter that occupied my thoughts all morning was the fact that someone's fiancé had yet to be mentioned since we left New Orleans.

"How's Brock?" Caroline didn't offer a reply. I assumed she didn't hear me. I leaned closer to her left ear, again asking, "How's—"

"He's okay."

It was apparent she had heard me the first time. "Have you talked to him in the last couple of days?" Except for Caroline's bathroom breaks at gas stations (mine were less private as she made me urinate in plastic bottles in the car), we had been by each other's side every moment since we left New Orleans. The only person she spoke to over the phone was Delain, but perhaps she had talked to Brock while I was in the motel shower or napping in the car.

"No."

Her answers were short. I also found it odd that she and her fiancé hadn't spoken to one another in at least forty-eight hours. Something seemed wrong, but I didn't want to pry. "How much longer until we arrive in Scottsdale?"

An unusually quiet Caroline appeared to be in a daze, so much so that she didn't notice a car passing us on the left. I ducked.

"Jackson, what did you think of Brock? And please be honest."

My first impression was that he was the kind of person that men wanted to look like, as well as live the life he had. Most women, I imagined, would trample over their best friend just to talk to him. "Let's just say that if he and I were competing for the same girl, I would be prepared to lose. Can I sit up?"

"Yes. Why do you say that?" We again made eye contact in the rearview mirror.

"He's got it all: success, good looks, a body that belongs in Greek lore. What more is there?"

"How about honesty, compassion, and trust?"

Her question, along with the sudden realization that I couldn't recall seeing an engagement ring on her left hand over the last few days, incited a peek over her shoulder. Nothing shiny rested upon the ring finger of her left hand. "Where's your engagement ring?" She didn't answer me. "Caroline, are you still engaged to Brock?"

She intently stared at my reflection in the mirror, squinting before telling me, "No."

Even though I was shocked by the news, a part of me found enjoyment in her answer. "What happened?"

The car began to decelerate before Caroline pulled onto the shoulder of the road. We came to a stop next to a cactus that stood taller than the roof of the Mustang. Caroline turned around. She lifted her sunglasses, and then straddled the center console, resting her forearms on the front seats. Her head grazed the roof as we sat face to face. Moderate bruising was still visible on her left cheek from where Davis had slapped her, as well as both forearms from where he had pinned her to the bed. "I told him I needed some time to think about things. I don't know if he's the one I want to be with forever."

"Why?"

Caroline slightly tilted her head to the left and raised her eyebrows, as if expecting me to know the answer. "During the three months I was working next to you, I rarely thought about Brock. When I left to go back home to San Diego, I missed you so much that I made myself sick. When Al called to tell me you had died, I wept for hours. It was the saddest few days of my life—even more so than the days following my encounter with 'Mickey the rapist'. I may only be twenty-three and not know all there is to know about how love works just yet, but I do know I have feelings for you that I can't turn off. Believe me, I've tried. When I awoke on Delain's couch after being drugged, and finally realized you were alive, I had to control my emotions big time. I wanted to hug you and never let go, but I held back because of Delain. As for Brock, I can't marry him when I am constantly thinking about someone else. The only reason I accepted his proposal was because you were engaged. Besides, I know you have feelings for me as well. I haven't forgotten about our first night in Denver."

Even though I was drunk, I remembered everything.

"The way you looked into my eyes that night, Jackson, is something I will never forget. What were you thinking while we were in each other's arms?"

"Caroline, now isn't the—"

"I know it's not the best time to have this conversation, but let's be honest—what if I'm wrong and we don't see each other again for a while once you get out of this car? God only knows the shitstorm that's about to transpire. I'd rather ask you now than never get to know the answer to that question."

I glanced out of the window at the cactus, wishing the conversation wasn't taking place hours before I was about to lie to those that had the power to send me away for a long time. As she pointed out, though, our conversation may in fact be the last time we talked face to face for some time. "I care about you in—"

"Down."

From a slouched position I told her, "I care about you in a way that I can't really explain right now."

An eighteen-wheeler passed, rocking the car as Caroline said, "Try to. Up."

Over the course of three-and-a-half months, I imagined what life would be like once Delain ditched me at the altar. I wondered if I would be moving to San Diego, starting over with Caroline. I pictured waking up next to her every morning, and how beautiful she would look walking down the aisle in a wedding dress. I wanted to tell her those things, yet I couldn't since Delain was still in my life. I loved my fiancée, and was hopeful she felt the same way towards me. However, Caroline mentioning that we may never see one another again didn't sit well with me. "Did Delain tell you everything that happened while we were together?"

"She told me a lot, but I don't know if it was everything. Why?"

"Did she mention that I knew she was going to dump me on our wedding day almost five months before it was supposed to happen?"

"I don't remember her saying that." Caroline then squinted her mismatched eyes before saying, "Wait; that was the 'plan' you hinted at last week in Denver; wasn't it?"

I nodded. "On Valentine's Day, I found out she was going to leave me at the altar. I started taking antidepressants the same day. I then told her my dad had cancer, so she wouldn't ask why I seemed depressed. I was at the lowest I had ever been. Then, you walked into the clinic, and things weren't so bad."

With a dead-pan stare and a hint of a smile, she told me, "That's funny you say that. I was also depressed when you and I first met because of what happened with 'Mickey' back home. After a couple of days of hanging out with you, a lot of the sadness and anger melted away. I'm not saying being raped was by any means a good thing, but if it didn't happen, then I never would have moved to Louisiana for my internship, and you and I would have never met. Something good came out of something horrific in my life." Her knee-weakening smile fully surfaced.

"There's more. As the wedding grew closer, I took a liking towards you—"

"You do realize that's three days from now—the wedding?"

I had nearly forgotten about it due to the anxiety over the many laws I had broken over the last five days. "I forgot how close it was."

"And today's the Fourth of July. Happy Independence Day."

"Not how I thought I'd be spending the Fourth of—"

"Down," she commanded. "It's not how I planned it either, but at least we get to spend time together. Sit up and finish what you were just saying please. You took a liking towards me…"

I sat up. "I took a liking towards you because Delain was certainly going to leave me, and I wondered what life would be like with you." Once the words crossed my lips, I wanted to take them back. In my head it sounded different.

"So," any semblance of a smile vanished as she exhaled, "you only took a liking towards me because your fiancée was dumping you? That's good to know." She looked off to the side.

"That came out wrong. I meant to say I took a liking towards you especially because Delain was going to leave me."

"Still doesn't make me feel tingly inside, Jackson." She looked none-too-pleased.

"You want to know what I was thinking in Denver?"

She shook her head. "It doesn't matter anymore."

I didn't like that she appeared upset, and it wasn't until she turned to face me that I saw how upset I had made her. "Caroline, don't—"

"Thinking that I may never see you again or that you may still marry Delain this weekend makes me realize that it's not a crush. I love you, Jackson." The floodgates opened.

I grabbed her hands. "Please don't cry."

"I can't help it. I don't want to drop you off."

I hated seeing women cry, especially one I had strong feelings towards. "What I was thinking in Denver, Caroline, while we were embracing one another, was how much I wanted to kiss you. You looked so incredibly gorgeous that night, by the way."

After wiping at her eyes with a Dairy Queen napkin, she said, "I did look pretty hot that night. I wanted to kiss you too, but I didn't want to cross the line."

"The only reason I didn't kiss you was because I've never cheated on a girlfriend or fiancée."

Caroline subtly nodded. "And I respect that about you. You're a good person, Jackson. Delain is an incredibly lucky woman."

It then dawned on me. Sitting directly in front of me was a beautiful, caring, compassionate, young woman who had no problem expressing her feelings towards me. She even broke off her engagement to someone I considered one of the most handsome and successful men I had ever met because of me. Unless she was an Oscar-winning actress who could cry on demand, I was certain she was telling the truth. Delain, on the other hand, couldn't even tell me she loved me when I left her house two days earlier. While staring into Caroline's eyes, I began to second guess Delain's feelings towards me. For all I knew, she could have still been using me just to get her son back. "Not only did I think how incredibly gorgeous you looked that night, but I also wanted to tell you how much I cared about you."

She perked up on the console. "And how much is that?"

"Caroline...I love you too." It just came out. Perhaps it was because she mentioned I might never see her again, or because I wanted to lift her spirits, or maybe I was terrified about ending up in jail. Or, perhaps, I was subconsciously telling the truth.

Caroline's face lit up in a way that could best be described as someone who just experienced their 'eureka' moment. She squeezed my hands before turning around and sliding into the driver's seat. "That's what I needed to hear, Jackson. Things are going to be okay now. I'm certain about that."

At least someone thought so. Not only was I a few hours away from lying to police officers, federal agents, and everyone in the United States, but I had also inserted myself deeper into a love triangle with two women I cared immensely about. My stress levels were multiplying by the hour. As we drove off, I felt a peculiar tightness in my chest. Not long after, it began to dissipate.

Chapter 52

Scared, confused, yet determined, Delain sat in her parked car across the street from the entrance to the JW Marriott, hopeful she would catch another glimpse of her son. In her lap sat the brown teddy bear that fell out of Caleb's stroller the night before. For the past eighteen hours, every waking moment was spent focusing on a strategy to gain custody of her son. Because nothing she came up with yet seemed plausible, she grew discouraged, causing many tears to be shed.

While holding the teddy bear to her chest, Delain momentarily closed her eyes, picturing Caleb's angelic face smiling back at her as he sat in his stroller in the elevator. The thought of him calling someone else 'mommy' made her stomach turn. At two years old, the window for Caleb to accept someone else as his mother was quickly closing. Delain was well-aware time was a concerning factor. She opened and then wiped at her eyes while returning her gaze to the hotel entrance.

Uncertain if her son's adopted parents were still in the hotel, Delain called information from her cell phone before being connected to the hotel concierge.

"JW Marriott New Orleans. This is James. How can I be of service?"

"Scott Melancon's room please."

"One second while I check, ma'am."

Delain's anticipation grew exponentially as she waited to discover if the man who had been raising her son for two years was still in the hotel. She needed to see Caleb again, and would stop at nothing to do so.

"Ma'am?"

"Yes?"

"I'm now connecting you to Mr. Melancon's room."

"Thank you."

Delain hung up before the connection could be made. She reached into a bag in the back seat containing the wigs and accessories she and Caroline wore into Davis' restaurant three nights earlier. Since she had already worn the red wig in the presence of Davis' brother the night before, she opted to go blonde. After a quick check in the mirror to make sure her hair was hidden beneath the wig, she slipped into her oversized purse an item she thought she would never own. Hours earlier, she purchased a Rossi .357 magnum revolver from a sporting goods store. Recent events, along with the realization that she may need protection in the near future, prompted the purchase. Still, she found herself anxious about owning a gun. *I hope I never have to use it.* Just before renting the Mustang on Monday morning, Delain and Caroline retuned the 'borrowed' gun from Al's house back to its original location. Since neither Al nor Betty were home, the return went smoothly. Delain placed the heavy purse onto her shoulder, and made her way towards the hotel entrance.

Delain sat on a couch in the hotel lobby with a direct line of sight to the elevators. After removing her laptop from her purse and powering it on, an older gentleman sat on the adjacent couch with newspaper in hand. Delain's only intention was to once again see her son. Beyond that, there was no further agenda. She killed time by surfing the internet—reading local news stories about Davis' death—between glancing at guests exiting the elevators. The developing news in his death, said one online article, was that he died alone in his garage, and a heart attack was believed to have been the cause of death. Relieved that she, Jackson, and Caroline were still in the clear, she glanced upward upon hearing a 'ding'. A lone bellboy emerged from the elevator. She returned to the article. Within seconds, another of the elevator doors opened. Walking towards her, wearing a dress shirt and slacks, was the man she had been waiting to see. He was alone. Scott Melancon glanced at his watch while briskly walking down the long corridor leading to the Canal Street entrance. Wherever he was going, he appeared to be in a hurry. Delain closed her laptop and shoved it back into her purse. Without the slightest hesitation or trepidation, she stood and followed him.

She watched from the other side of the carousel door as Scott attempted to hail a taxi. *I can't let him out of my sight!* Delain walked through the doors and to the left of Scott, hoping not to gain his attention as a taxi continued past the hotel. Once she arrived at the corner of Canal and St. Charles, half a block from the entrance to the hotel, she glanced over her shoulder to see a taxi slowing as it approached Scott. Even though the pedestrian sign flashed 'don't walk', Delain ignored it, hastily jaywalking to her car. Upon unlocking the door, she watched as the taxi drove off. *Shit!* She started the car and merged onto Canal Street. A quick u-turn and some shifty maneuvering put her three cars directly behind

Scott's taxi at the first traffic light. Her heart was racing and her right hand trembled while grabbing the teddy bear from the passenger seat. *I'm doing the right thing. Caleb needs me.*

Within minutes of leaving the hotel, the taxi came to a stop in front of 'Chick-ory'— a coffeehouse in the heart of the French Quarter. Delain watched Scott walk into the establishment she had visited once before, during the brief, miserable time she dated Davis. Davis was friends with the owner— a woman about the same age as he—and had introduced her to Delain. While parking her car down the street, Delain tried to recall the woman's name. It was that of a southern city or state: such as Charlotte, Savannah, or Virginia. Whatever her name, Delain was certain the woman wouldn't be able to recognize her behind her oversized sunglasses and blonde wig.

    Delain, ignoring the uneasy feeling in her stomach, entered the coffeehouse and immediately spotted Scott shaking hands with a man at least a decade older than he—if not two. The rotund man, wearing a traditionally Southern seersucker suit, removed his straw hat before directing Scott to a table in the corner of the coffee house. The man's thick beard, along with the full head of hair on his head, was as white as a fresh blanket of snow—with the exception of a small area above his lips, which had a yellowish hue. Delain took a seat at the table next to them. Her back was less than three feet away from Scott's and the mystery man's table.

    "Happy Independence Day, Scottie," spoke the man in the deepest Southern drawl Delain had ever heard. "I apologize for dragging you away from your family on this spirited holiday."

    "Not a problem. We didn't have much planned today anyway."

    "How are you holding up?"

    "I'm okay," Scott dismally answered. "I'm still a little shocked by his death; a heart attack at fifty-two. I'm only a few years away from that age."

    "You're in excellent shape, Scottie. I wouldn't worry about any health concerns on your end. How's Bridgett and little Thomas doing?" Delain waited to hear his reply, but was interrupted.

    "Can I get you some coffee and chicory, sweetie?" asked a woman with Auburn-colored hair tied back into a ponytail and eyes the color of cinnamon. Delain recognized the middle-aged woman as the owner.

"Um…" Delain pretended to read the menu above the counter while awaiting Scott's answer.

"Thomas is growing so fast. He's walking everywhere and getting into everything. He's a handful."

"I hear those terrible two's can be more than a handful," the man spoke before laughing at himself.

Delain kept her composure while turning her attention back to the waitress. "A large coffee please—black."

"Is that all?" asked the woman.

"Yes." As the woman wrote onto a pad, Delain asked, "Do you have an extra pen I can borrow?"

The waitress handed Delain the pen in her hand before removing another from her apron. "One large black coffee coming up, dear." The woman smiled before walking to the table behind Delain.

"Mrs. Georgia, I must declare that you look as lovely as a peach from the state in which your name is taken," spoke the older gentleman.

"Charlie, if that was coming from anyone else I would find that flattering. But I've heard you compliment every woman that has walked past you for the last five years you've been coming here, so I'll just chalk that up as another one of your many lines."

Delain grabbed a napkin from the holder on her table, writing onto it the name 'Charlie'.

"Mrs. Georgia, you know I'm being truthful when I say those things to you. Besides, when are you gonna leave your husband and run off with me, thus making me the happiest gentleman in the great state of Louisiana?"

"On the day that you start acting like a gentleman, which if I'm correct, will never happen."

Charlie let out a roaring laugh, which was soon followed by a series of heavy coughing.

"And on the day that you stop smoking those nasty cigars," Georgia added. "You better quit or Maxine is gonna leave you for good this time, Charlie Guichet."

Delain added Maxine to the napkin then drew a line to Charlie's name, adding the word 'wife' above the line. She then tried to spell his last name. Still a novice with French/Cajun spelling, she wrote 'goo-shay' on the napkin.

"I'm trying to quit. By the way, Mrs. Georgia, I'd like you to meet Scott Melancon—our late friend, Davis', younger brother."

Delain turned her head to the side, watching from the corner of her eye as Georgia wiped her right hand on her apron several times before extending it forward. Scott stood while shaking her hand.

"I'm so sorry to hear about your brother, Scott. Davis was a great man and did a lot of good things for this city. Not only was he one of the nicest men I had ever met, but he's also the reason I was able to open my coffee shop five years ago."

Delain clenched her jaw as compliments were being given towards one of the vilest men she had ever had the pleasure of knowing.

"He was a great man, and an even better brother. He will be sorely missed."

"That's the God-honest truth," Charlie added. "He was by far my favorite client, and the dearest of friends."

Delain added the job titles 'financial planner' and 'lawyer' under Charlie's name, followed by question marks.

"I hope it's not too soon to ask, but what will happen to his restaurant?" Georgia inquired. "I see that it's been closed for the past few days."

"That's what Scott and I are discussing this afternoon."

"Are you planning on taking it over?" she asked.

"Perhaps. I've been looking for a reason to come back home. This may be what gets the wife on board. We'll see what happens."

"Well, if it makes any difference, I've heard a lot of people in the last two days saying how much they already miss eating there."

"The Fleur-de-Leans is as much a part of New Orleans as Mardi Gras, jazz music, or Napoleonic law. I'm confident its doors will open again very soon," Charlie spoke with great authority.

"We'll see," Scott added.

"Well, I hope so. While you gentlemen decide on that important decision, can I get you some of our delicious chicory?"

A flush of optimism overcame Delain. Scott moving back to New Orleans meant that Caleb would be closer. She placed the napkin in her pocket before her coffee arrived. While continuing to eavesdrop, a plan started to come together; a plan she had no intention of sharing with anyone else.

Chapter 53

I stood on an empty highway, about half a mile from the isolated gas station Caroline and I had passed minutes earlier. There were no buildings, cars, or people anywhere in sight— just a few bushes, cacti, and a cloud of dust slowly moving past me as the Mustang began to fade in the distance. In the direction of the gas station, the highway looked like it was melting beneath the July sun. Humidity, something I was accustomed to back home, was nearly nonexistent in the desert. My skin felt as if it was splitting apart, like the cracks in the pavement beneath my feet.

Before beginning the walk to the gas station, I shut my eyes. It was quiet. Not even a gust of wind could be heard. I'm not sure why, but Tiffany immediately came to mind. I envisioned her grieving over the loss of her father as she stood next to his coffin. I grew curious to know if she was saddened by my death as well, or felt that justice had prevailed because of my actions at the wedding. Tiffany may have been spoiled, controlling, unfaithful, and moody at times, but I didn't consider her to be a horrible person. I was hopeful that she was upset by my passing. I then wondered how she would react knowing I was the catalyst for her father's death. If she were to ever discover the truth, I imagine all hell would break loose. I tried to push that notion out of my head to focus on the monumental task ahead. I opened my eyes, took a deep breath, and began to walk.

Ten minutes later, I stepped into the chilled gas station. From behind the counter, a slender, pale-complected man wearing a black Nascar t-shirt and a red mesh hat with the number '3' printed on it nodded at the profusely sweating Caucasian who was about to reclaim his existence into the world inside a desolate gas station. The man looked out the windows facing the empty gas pumps before glancing back at me.

"Did your car break down?"

After wiping sweat from my forehead with my t-shirt, I stepped closer to the counter. I noticed a blonde, pencil-thin moustache on the man that looked to be around my age. "No."

He stared me up and down. "Then how in the blazes did you get out here?"

"A truck driver dropped me off just a short walk from here. I was hitchhiking. I don't know if that's illegal around here or not."

"It's legal in these parts…I reckon. Would you like a cold beverage? You look like you could use one."

"Please." I removed my wallet from the back of my jeans' pocket.

He grabbed a lemon-lime Gatorade from a small cooler next to the counter before tossing it to me. "It's on the house."

I downed most of the twenty-ounce bottle in one sip, gasping as I told him, "Thank you."

"You don't look like the hitchhiking type."

The gentleman's comment, identical to the line Cliff told me in his rig just before confessing to murder, had me further doubting the alibi I would be telling authorities in a short while. I finished the remainder of the drink before asking, "What exactly does the hitchhiking type look like?"

"I don't know—someone with a duffle bag, a Vietnam veteran jacket, ragged clothing, and/or a beard."

"I lost my duffle bag."

"Why were you hitchhiking?"

"I was trying to escape something."

A concerned look appeared on the man's face. I watched him slowly reach his right hand beneath the counter. "You mean like the police?" I suspected he was reaching for a gun.

I shook my head. "A marriage. I got cold feet." His right hand remained hidden under the counter as I asked, "Did you hear about the plane crash outside of Salt Lake City last Friday?"

He casually nodded. "I did." A mirror on the revolving sunglasses display behind the counter disproved my theory of a gun in his right hand. I was on the right track, however, as another form of weaponry was being gripped. My eyes remained fixed on the reflection of a baseball bat in the mirror.

"I just heard about the crash. I was supposed to be on that plane."

"Are you serious?"

"Yes."

"And why weren't you?"

"I'm getting married this Saturday, but I got cold feet and decided before I got on the plane in Denver that I was going to run away for a little while; kind of clear my head and do some thinking. I switched tickets with someone else, but we didn't tell the airline we were doing so. I'm afraid people think I'm dead."

"Like loved ones?"

"Yes. I didn't talk to anyone while I was doing my…soul-searching."

I watched as his hand let go of the bat. He next removed his hat, running his left hand through his eyebrow-length, dirty blonde hair before returning the hat to his head. "That's crazy. I bet they're gonna be happy to hear you're alive…except for maybe your fiancée." He then chuckled.

"You might be right."

"Where did you go?"

"I've basically been wandering around the west for the last five days, staying in cheap motels. I was riding with a truck driver. She just told me about the plane crash. I had no idea what happened until a few minutes ago. Once we saw your gas station, she slowed down and dropped me off. And now here I am. I didn't go to a police station because I didn't know where one was. By the way, where am I?"

He folded his arms against his chest as he leaned against the back counter. "A few miles outside of Kirkland, Arizona. Basically, the middle of nowhere. I think we may need to call the authorities. What do you think?"

Even though it was part of the plan, my stomach tightened. "That's probably a good idea."

The man picked up the phone behind the register, dialed, and then spoke into it, "Harold, its T.J. Are you close to my store?...Good. Get over here right now." He hung up.

There was no turning back and no room for error. "Is Harold close by?" I assumed Harold was the lone sheriff of the town of Kirkland.

"He's gonna be here soon," T.J. told me while walking to a nearby closet. After grabbing a bucket and a squeegee, he handed it to me. "Do you mind giving me a hand?"

"With what?"

"Cleaning. If you're telling the truth—and I think you are—then this place is gonna be on every news channel across the country. Hell, it just might be all over the world. I can't have it looking like this." T.J. was practically beaming.

Imagining something happening on a national level was one thing. Realizing it was about to happen was harder to fathom. I instantly felt sick, doubting the plan yet again.

"You okay? What's your name, by the way?"

"Jackson. I'm fine, just a little…nervous."

"I'm T.J. Why would you be nervous?"

"I like keeping a low profile."

"There's no need to worry, Jackson. Just tell the truth and you'll be fine."

"Yep."

T.J. smiled. "Why don't you start outside with the windows while I get everything in here straightened up? Now, I would imagine the news people are gonna be swarming in here in an hour or so." T.J. walked off as he continued talking to himself. "They're gonna be hungry, so I should clean out the hot dog oven and put some new ones in there. It's hot out too, so I'm sure they'll be thirsty as well…"

Grime and spider webs covered the ten-foot-high windows that looked like they hadn't been touched in years. While spraying and scrubbing, reality started to set in. I, Jackson Fabacher, had killed two people. It could be argued that both men were killed in self-defense. It could also be argued that I committed first and second-degree murder. Regardless of whether or not I was tried in a court of law, I was guilty of murder—plain and simple. I had to repeatedly convince myself that both deaths were justified. I then wondered if convicted murderers felt their crimes were justified as well, and if they considered themselves to be a 'good person' while being strapped to a chair before being lethally injected. I began to second guess if I was a 'good person'.

Upon completion of my chore, I walked back into the station. "All done."

"Those windows look immaculate." T.J. next placed a broom in my hand. "Do you mind sweeping?"

"Do I have a choice?"

T.J. grinned, shaking his head side to side. "You sure are handy to have around, Jackson. Do you mind if I ask you another question?"

"You want me to mop the floor afterwards?"

T.J. laughed. "That's a good one. But on a serious note," his smile lessened, "you said a trucker dropped you off. I don't recall seeing a truck drive by in the last few hours, so I'm still trying to rack my brain around how you ended up out here. I saw a black Mustang drive by about thirty to forty minutes ago, but no truck."

And just like that, the first error in the plan was brought to light. I didn't have an honest answer for T.J., so I took a shot in the dark. "Maybe you were in the bathroom and didn't see us drive-by."

"I haven't gone—" The sound of squealing tires diverted our attention to the windows. "There's Harold."

I made sure the attention stayed diverted from a question that could land me in hot water. "Who's Harold, by the way?"

"My best friend."

"How long have y'all been friends?"

"Since middle school. He married my cousin, so we're pretty much family now too."

Harold stepped out of a baby blue Ford pick-up truck that looked like it rolled off the assembly line sometime in the mid-eighties, which, coincidentally, was about the same time Harold purchased the clothes on his back. His snug pair of stone-washed jeans (ripped and covered in holes) looked as if they had been washed with razor blades, while his sleeveless ZZ Top t-shirt showcased the classy barbwire tattoo encompassing his left arm. A pair of sunglasses that used to adorn the faces of professional baseball outfielders in the early nineties covered his eyes. He ran his hand through his blonde mullet before rubbing the five o'clock shadow on his face. I could almost hear *Bad to the Bone* being sung by George Thorogood as Harold—whom I no longer believed to be a sheriff—walked into the gas station, pushing both doors open as if he had just entered a Wild West saloon. I was momentarily distracted from the stress brought about by the pandemonium that was about to ensue.

Harold removed his sunglasses, placing them on his forehead. "What's the situation?" He flashed a badge while staring intently at me.

"You're a cop?"

"I am a police officer," a proud Harold declared with authority.

"You're a mechanic who happened to get deputized when a peeping Tom was on the loose in your neighborhood," T.J. blurted out. "There's quite a difference."

"I am an officer of the law, Thomas Junior."

"Can you arrest anyone?"

"What does that matter?"

T.J. propped himself onto the counter next to the cash register. He grabbed a stick of beef jerky while appearing to make himself comfortable. With a smirk, he asked, "And where is your gun?"

"I don't need one."

"You don't need one? Or did it get apprehended when you got drunk and shot all four of my cousin's tires a few weeks ago because you thought she was cheating on you?"

"That's neither here nor there. I have a walkie-talkie and a badge, so I would advise you to not make fun of me anymore. I don't care if you're my best friend/cousin-in-law or not. Mocking an officer is a criminal offense."

"You sure about that? What's the police code for mocking an officer of the law? And by officer, I mean deputy."

Harold gave T.J. a sour look before turning his attention back to me. "Now, if we can get down to brass tacks for a second— why'm I here?"

T.J. spoke before I could. "This fella' was supposed to be on the plane that crashed outside Salt Lake City last week. No one knows he's alive except for us and whoever he hitchhiked here with. This is gonna be a big story—a man who people believed was dead is actually alive, and he's got cold feet about his upcoming wedding."

Harold approached, and then stood only a few inches from my face. I grew uncomfortable as someone I didn't know stood so close to me. I tightly clutched the broom, ready to strike in case he tried to hit or apprehend me. "Are you telling the truth, citizen, or are you pulling our chain?"

I got the impression Harold was a hall monitor when he was in high school, and took the position very seriously. "Yes. I just heard about the plane crash about an hour ago."

Harold continued to uncomfortably stare me down while subtly nodding his head. "You're telling the truth. I can tell. So…" he began to walk around the store with both arms behind his back, "why do people think you're dead?"

His questioning was good practice for when the actual authorities arrived. "Because I swapped tickets with someone else, and we didn't tell the airline workers what we did. Plus, I haven't contacted anyone since the crash."

"Why didn't you contact anyone?"

"He was doing some soul-searching," T.J. blurted out.

"Interesting." Harold then whipped his walkie-talkie from the side of his pants, speaking into it, "This is Officer Harold P. Simmons. Come in command base."

"*Deputy Harold. Please switch to channel 4.*"

Harold adjusted his walkie-talkie. "Come in, command base."

"*I thought we took your walkie-talkie away, Harold.*"

"I got another one. We have a situation here, command base."

"*What now? Another suspicious person in blue attire is on your doorstep? Is the mailman on your porch again, Harold?*"

"I'm gonna hurt him, I swear to God," Harold spoke under breath before pressing the button on the walkie-talkie. "My 10-20 is T.J.'s gas station, and we have a case of…mistaken death."

"*What are you talking about?*"

"A man standing right in front of me was believed to have been on the airplane that crashed in Salt Lake City on Friday."

"*Is this for real, Harold?*"

"Yes, command base."

"*Stop saying command base, for one. And, two, if I send some real police officers out there and you're lying I swear I'm going to beat you.*"

"This is the real deal, Don!" He then walked towards and placed the walkie-talkie in front of T.J.'s mouth. "Tell him it's the truth, cousin."

"Don, it's T.J. This is real. Harold's not making this up."

"*You I trust.*"

"Don, I mean command base, switch back to channel two now." Harold adjusted channels before speaking. "Command base, we have a citizen here that was supposed to be on the doomed flight from Denver to Salt Lake City last Friday, but he changed flights with another passenger without telling the airline. He's believed to be dead, but I'm talking to him. We're gonna need the media at T.J.'s gas station. Over and out." Harold turned down the volume before placing the walkie-talkie back on his belt. "You see what I just did?"

"How you said 'command base' about eight times?" T.J. asked.

"The police don't always alert the media, but they're usually listening to our police scanners. Now, they know what's going on, and they'll be here shortly, maybe even before my fellow officers arrive. We're gonna be famous. Who says you gotta graduate high school to have smarts?"

"I'm gonna nominate you for deputy of the year," T.J. said before biting into the beef jerky.

"It's gonna be about fifteen to twenty minutes 'til they get here." Harold grabbed a few items from the toiletry aisle on his way to the bathroom. "I gotta take the browns to the Superbowl, then freshen up. I'll be out in a few minutes." He shut the door behind him.

I looked at T.J. while letting out a deep 'I can't believe this is about to happen' breath.

"I know you're nervous, Jackson, but try not to be."

"My parents, my brother, and my friends all think I'm dead. They're about to find out I'm not. It's a lot to take in."

"If it makes you feel any better, I'd be nervous too." T.J. jumped down from the counter. "Don't forget about your fiancée. She might be upset with what you did to her, but I'm sure she'll be glad to know you're alive; right?"

"Fiancée—yes, her too."

"Got another question for you if you don't mind, Jackson."

"Ask away."

"For the five days you were thinking about things, you didn't try to contact her? I know you said you were trying to clear your head, but not even a phone call to tell her you were okay?"

"No. I should have. I realize that now."

"Well, did you miss her at least?"

I nodded. "Yes."

"I don't mean to get up in your business, but are you still going to marry her?"

I was certain the wedding would not be taking place in three days. "I don't know. We'll see."

"Well, whatever happens, I'm sure she and your family are all gonna be grateful that you're alive."

"Yes, they will. I can't wait to see them. I'm just really anxious about talking to the police or F.B.I. or whoever I'm gonna have to answer to."

"Alcohol might help with that."

He was right. "I need to buy some." I began to look around the station. "Where is your liquor?"

T.J. looked at me as if I just asked him the square root of 867. "Liquor in a gas station?"

Because Louisiana was the only state I had ever lived, I thought it normal to purchase liquor in a gas station. "Sorry. I forgot about the laws out here."

"Where you from anyway?"

"New Orleans."

"No shit. I've always wanted to go there. Is it true women flash their boobs for beads?"

"Some do."

"Man, I gotta get down there."

"And I need to get my hands on some alcohol."

While reaching under the counter, T.J. flashed one of those sneaky, up-to-no-good grins. "Look no further, my friend." He held a bottle in his hand.

Ever since alcohol first crossed my lips, whiskey had always been my preferred spirit. Whether it was in a mint julep or combined with Coke, I loved the taste of it, and the way I felt while it was circulating in my body. In fact, I was the same happy drunk whenever I drank vodka, gin, scotch, rum, beer, wine, or champagne. There was one spirit, however, that brought out the Mr. Hyde in me. On the three occasions in which I drank it in excess, I became mean, belligerent, and someone my friends didn't want to be around. The word best used to describe how I acted while under the influence of tequila was 'asshole'. It had been about six years since I last drank tequila. I swore I would never drink it again. "Do you have anything else back there?"

"Nope. Good 'ole Mexican tequila is all I got in the store." He extended the bottle towards me. "Don't you want to settle your nerves?"

I did, but I also didn't want to get arrested for trying to fight the police or T.V. reporters. I convinced myself that just a few sips would be okay. As T.J. placed the bottle in my hand, I noticed a worm floating at the bottom. I made sure not to swallow it while placing the bottle to my lips. The first sip was God-awful. Warm tequila, in my opinion, was the worst-tasting spirit in the world, even more so than the black licorice taste of Jagermeister. "You drink this stuff at room temperature?"

T.J. smiled while nodding. "Real men drink it that way."

"I must not be a real man then."

T.J. laughed. "You said it, not me." His stare was then diverted to the windows. "What do we got here?" A cloud of dust kicked up as an automobile approached the gas station.

"Is it the police?"

"Possibly."

"They got here pretty quick." I took a second sip, nearly gagging in the process.

"Nevermind. It's just a customer filling up."

"You don't seem to get too many of those out here."

"Ever since the new highway opened up in the spring, it's been pretty dead out here. I've been praying every day and hoping that something will happen because I sunk all the money I had into this place. I figured I got another couple of weeks until my money runs dry. After that," he shrugged his shoulders, "who knows what I'm gonna do?" A smile then appeared as he continued. "But, if what you're saying is true, this place just might get the attention it needs." T.J. grabbed the broom from my hand and began sweeping.

"I'll do that," I told him.

"I got it. You just relax, drink up, and get ready to come back from the dead."

I adhered to T.J.'s advice. Next to the ice cream freezer, I sat, occasionally taking a sip of the tequila. T.J. kept to himself as he swept the floor. Harold remained in the bathroom. Except for the continuous buzz softly echoing from the freezer to my right, and the arrhythmic sound of bristles grazing the linoleum floor, the gas station was awfully quiet. It created more apprehension as it gave me time to think.

T.J. approached the windows. His eyes appeared to have been fixated on more than one moving object. "Jackson, you ready to come back from the dead?"

My breathing grew heavier as my heart began to race. Still seated, I turned around to see an enormous cloud of dust in the distance. I could see at least six vehicles heading towards the gas station. Still unable to feel the effects of the alcohol, I took several long sips before handing T.J. the bottle. With the last swallow, I felt a lump in my throat. I glanced at the bottle as he walked towards the register. The worm was gone.

"There's a lot more cars than I expected. There must be nothing going on today," T.J. said.

Upon standing, I had to reach for the freezer to regain my balance. Mexico's finest had infiltrated my liver and coursed through my bloodstream in what felt like milliseconds. "Shit."

"You okay, Jackson?" T.J. asked. "The tequila got 'cha?"

The anxiety of what was about to occur was amplified by the sudden feeling of drunkenness. I then remembered the only food I had eaten all day was a breakfast burrito about eight hours earlier. "I haven't eaten much today."

T.J. hurried to one of the refrigerated cases. "This might help." He tossed a plastic triangular container towards me.

While devouring the egg salad sandwich, I asked, "Is it necessary to have their sirens on?" Three police cars lead the way, followed by a news van, an unmarked car, and another police car in the back.

T.J. cupped his hands over his mouth while facing the bathroom. "Harold, it's time to be on camera!"

The bathroom door squeaked opened. Harold emerged. His face was freshly shaven, and his hair had about triple the volume from before. "How do I look?"

"Like the king of the trailer park," T.J. told him. "How much moose went into that hairdo?"

"Enough to make it look this damn good."

T.J. grabbed the sandwich container from my hand, placing it into the trashcan before returning the broom to the storage closet. After positioning himself behind the counter, he tucked his shirt into his pants and removed his hat. "Time to look good, boys. I think we're about to be on every news station across the land."

The convoy pulled into the parking lot. My heart felt like it was about to pop out of my chest. I took deep breaths as the driver's door opened on the first police car.

The first officer to walk into the gas station pointed at me with his right hand while removing his sunglasses with his left. "This must be our man."

Harold stepped forward, walkie-talkie in hand. "This is the man I radioed about, Karl."

"It's Officer Smith," he sternly told Harold.

"Yes, sir."

"What's your name, son?" the actual police officer asked me.

"Jackson Fabacher." As I answered, three more police officers and a woman holding a notepad and microphone entered the store.

Officer Smith repeated my name to someone on the other end of his radio. The woman and other officers all stared at me in silence. Officer Smith then asked me, "What's your story, son?"

During the car ride from New Orleans, Caroline repeatedly asked the same question Officer Smith had just asked. I reiterated my answer somewhere in the neighborhood of about fifty times. "I was supposed to have been on the airplane that crashed outside Salt Lake City last Friday. Instead of boarding the plane, I gave up my seat to someone I met at the gate. He was in a rush to get home, while I was beginning to have cold feet about getting married. We didn't tell the airline that we switched. I didn't call anyone after the plane took off. Instead, I've been doing some soul-searching for the last couple of days. I just found out about the crash, so here I am."

"None of your family or friends or acquaintances know that you're alive?"

"Not that I'm aware of."

"Do you have anything to validate this story?"

"Yes, sir. I have something in my wallet. I'm going to reach for it. Please don't shoot me." The "asshole" effects of the tequila were in full effect. I removed Brad's boarding pass from my wallet. After unfolding it, I pointed to his name. "This is the guy I switched tickets with. He was on the plane. He's dead."

The female walked to the door, where she signaled to someone inside the van. Seconds later, a man entered the store with a giant camera on his shoulder. An excited look appeared on her face as the camera light flashed in my eyes.

Chapter 54

Andrew Fabacher III flipped through one of the many Fabacher family photo albums while seated in his office chair. Even though pictures of Jackson brought upon an even greater sadness, he couldn't pull himself away from them. His wife could no longer bear to look at the photo albums. She, instead, spent most of her time in bed, heavily sedated. It was nearing seven o'clock in the evening, which on a typical Wednesday night meant that Cecile would be placing one of her delicious meals onto the dining room table, along with a glass of wine and an old-fashioned. The two would then talk about their day before discussing ideas of where they should travel on their next trip, or when they would throw their next get-together with friends and family. Andrew suspected those typical nights would be few and far between over the next couple of months, if not years.

Andrew set the album on his desk before leaning back in his swivel chair in silence. He tried his hardest to not think about it again, but upon shutting his eyes, he imagined the agonizing last moments of Jackson's life. He envisioned the look of horror on his son's face as the plane descended, along with the shrieks of terror coming from the other passengers just before impact. The realization that he would never see or talk to Jackson again prompted Andrew to weep, while a few of the tears shed were for the guilt that came from withholding the truth to Jackson about the past. It was a secret Andrew wasn't sure Jackson would ever learn, even if he were still alive. *I'm a horrible father.*

He turned on the television, mostly to allow noise to fill the room that had been silent for hours. A twenty-four-hour news network was often the channel he watched while in his office, and it was that channel being broadcast as he placed the remote back onto his desk. As a commercial for a pill that treats depression aired, Andrew thought of his wife, as she was currently taking two anti-depressants. Neither he nor his wife had ever taken an anti-depressant prior to Jackson's death (not even during the tumultuous few years earlier in their marriage), but Andrew believed she would most likely be on them for quite some time. Cecile had yet to leave the house or eat much of anything since the funeral. Andrew hated to admit it, but he wasn't sure if his wife would ever recover from the recent tragedy. Cecile, he feared, may never be herself again. He wasn't quite sure if he would be either.

Andrew walked into the kitchen to grab a few crackers from the pantry, along with a couple slices of cheese and turkey from the refrigerator. He set the food and a bottle of water on a tray before bringing it upstairs. Andrew gently pushed the bedroom door open. Cecile being asleep was no surprise to him. He set the tray next to the collection of prescription bottles on the nightstand, and then kissed his wife's forehead before heading downstairs.

While passing his office on the way to the kitchen, a female news anchor's voice spoke, *"And now we go to Arizona for a breaking news story that is sure to bring happiness to a family in New..."*

The voice trailed off as Andrew returned to the kitchen. He sat on a stool at the island while snacking on crackers and what was left of the turkey and cheese. Unlike his wife, Andrew didn't sleep much when he was depressed. Since Jackson's death, Andrew averaged about two hours of sleep at night, whereas his wife was getting around sixteen hours per day. The lack of sleep produced a few ill side-effects for Andrew. Earlier in the evening, he saw an eight-year-old Jackson standing on the bookshelf ladder in the study. The hallucination was so strong that Andrew talked to him. Following a few exchanges of dialogue, the image disappeared.

After returning to his office, it came as no surprise for Andrew to see Jackson on the television. A reporter held a microphone to his mouth as police officers and a man with a sleeveless ZZ Top t-shirt surrounded him. Andrew turned off the television with the remote, sinking back in his chair. "I need some sleep." After rubbing his eyes, a book he had ignored over the last few months caught his attention from the shelves behind his chair. As he opened the King James Version of *The Bible*, his cell phone rang. He ignored it, picking up where he last left off.

Proverbs 4:10: *Hear, O my son, and receive my sayings; and the years of thy life shall be*

many. I have taught thee in the way of wisdom; I have led thee in right paths.
He shut *The Bible* nearly immediately after opening it, setting it atop his desk. The words hit too close to home. While staring despondently at the leather-bound book, Cecile's cell phone rang in the kitchen. The desire to answer her phone had escaped him. It wasn't until

the house phone rang seconds later that he thought someone, perhaps Marcus, may have been desperately trying to reach him. Since his office had a separate telephone line, he walked to the kitchen. "Hello?" There was only a dial tone. As he hung up, the floorboards squeaked overhead.

The ringing, he imagined, had awoken his wife. He walked to the bottom of the stairs to greet her. The floorboards soon creaked again, following a return path to the bed. As Andrew made his way back to the office, the sound of keys rattling outside the front door startled him. The front door swung open. His oldest son moved hastily through the cloakroom, barely using his cane, as he hopped on one leg into the hallway. It was the quickest Andrew had seen Marcus move in decades.

"He's alive!" Marcus exclaimed. His grin was nearly as big as his eyes.

"What?"

Marcus embraced his dad, lifting him as if something momentous had just occurred. "Jackson's alive! It's all over the news!"

Andrew came to the sad realization that his son was starting to go crazy. "What are you talking about?"

"Jackson's not dead!" Marcus let go of his father before hopping into the parlour. Andrew followed. He walked in to find Jackson's face on the television screen behind the bar. "See!"

"I'm hallucinating again. I need some sleep."

Marcus pinched his dad's forearm. "Did that hurt?"

He very much felt his son's pinch. "Yes."

"Then you're not hallucinating or dreaming. Dad, he's alive!" Marcus' bug-eyed smile was one he had never seen on his son's face before.

Andrew glanced at the television, and then back to his eldest son. "What is going on, Marcus?"

"He didn't die! Isn't this amazing?!"

A smile slowly emerged on Andrew's face as he no longer believed Jackson's image on the television to be an illusion. "But…how is this possible?"

"He never got on the plane. He swapped tickets with someone else and never told the airline."

When Andrew first kissed Cecile, he felt an almost out-of-body experience; a feeling of tranquility he expected one might experience as their soul transcends into heaven; a feeling one experiences when they find their soul-mate. He once again felt the same type of surreal sensation as he hugged his first born and stared at his second son on the television. Someone else needed to hear the revelation. "We need to go tell your mother."

Marcus was the first out of the room. He hopped up the stairs like a jackrabbit, yelling along the way. "Mom! He's alive!" Andrew was right behind him.

Marcus swung the bedroom door open, creating a thunderous crash as it slammed into the wall. Cecile quickly sat up.

"Honey, he's alive!" Andrew told her while Marcus grabbed the remote from the nightstand.

"What?" she asked, her eyes barely-opened.

"Jax!" Andrew shouted. "He didn't die!"

"What's wrong with you?" she spoke, on the verge of tears. "Why would you say something like that?"

Marcus flipped through the channels until Jackson's face appeared. "Because it's true, Mom. Look!"

Cecile opened her eyes fully, adjusting to the light from the T.V. Upon recognizing the image on the television, she covered her mouth with both hands as tears brimmed her eyes. "Oh my God! He looks like Jackson!"

Marcus placed his arm around his mom. "That's because he *is* Jackson. He was never on the plane."

"Is this really happening?" she asked. Her cheeks began to lift. "He really is alive?" She then looked to her beaming husband.

"He's alive, sweetie. He's still with us."

With outstretched arms, she lifted her head upwards. "It's a miracle! Thank you, God! My baby's alive!"

"Do you have anything to say to loved ones back in New Orleans?" the reporter asked.

Jackson leaned closer to the microphone. *"I'll be home real soon."*

Chapter 55

The light on the camera shut off, prompting the reporter to lower her microphone. "How'd we do?" the brunette woman, wearing lipstick as red as a maraschino cherry, asked her cameraman.

He gave her a thumbs-up. "Perfect."

While glancing around the bustling gas station, she said, "It's about time we got a real story."

Dozens of police officers and a few of what I assumed to be locals looked on, as did a handful of reporters that arrived too late to get in on the breaking news. T.J. was busy ringing up customers behind the counter, while Harold tried to mingle, unsuccessfully, with the officers on duty. Also in the store were two men I had an uneasy feeling about the moment they walked in. The men, one white and the other black, were dressed in dark suits. They stood next to the entrance, as if bouncers at an upscale nightclub.

"I'm assuming those gentlemen are here to talk to you, Jackson," the reporter told me.

"F.B.I.?"

"Judging by the suits, earpieces, helicopter, and lack of enthusiasm on their faces—yes."

"Fantastic." I was hoping to at least make it back home before they got to me. Their continuous staring in my direction only furthered my already heightened sense of trepidation, while the tequila still circulating in my bloodstream helped to create a bit of irritability. There was no sense in putting off the inevitable. I approached the door. As expected, the men stepped in front of me.

"Jackson Fabacher?" asked the white gentleman with not a single strand of hair upon his head. He was just barely shorter than me, and wore glasses that looked too big for his narrow face.

"'Tis I," I answered, staring between the two men at the helicopter sitting in the parking lot.

"My name is Agent Parker and this is Agent Williams. We're with the F.B.I. I'm afraid we need a few minutes of your time."

"Absolutely. Right after I see some identification, of course." My gaze shifted from the helicopter to Agent Parker's I.D. It looked legit. "I'm going to need to see yours as well, Agent Williams."

The response time of the quieter and much taller of the two agents as he reached for his identification was significantly slower than his partner's. Agent Williams' expressionless gaze and the leisurely pace in which he grabbed his identification made it seem as if he was insulted that I asked to see it.

"Take your time. I'm in no rush to get home to see loved ones," I told the towering man with broad shoulders and a well-trimmed goatee, whom I already disliked immensely. Once he held his I.D. out to me, I opted not to look at it. My eyes were instead focused outside. "Is that helicopter for us?"

"Yes," Agent Parker answered.

"How romantic." After stepping between the two men, I pushed my way through the glass doors.

Once we were airborne, I was told we were heading to Phoenix. Besides that one line of information, the rest of the helicopter ride was quiet. It gave me ample time to go over the answers to the questions I was anticipating from the federal agents.

Less than thirty minutes after take-off, we landed on the roof of a five-story building. After a short elevator ride, I was directed to sit at a table in a concrete-lined room. There were no pictures on the wall, no windows looking outside, and no glass mirror with men on the other side observing what was about to ensue. I still assumed, however, there was a camera or other type of recording device hidden somewhere in the room.

A good fifteen minutes passed before I had company. The same two agents that accompanied me in the helicopter entered the room. Agent Parker sat across the rectangular metal table with a blue folder in hand. Light from the fluorescent bulbs overhead refracted off his shiny head. Agent Williams stood behind me, out of sight. I could smell his pungent cologne. It wasn't an aroma I would have chosen.

"Jackson, thank you for joining us this evening."

"Did I have a choice?" The tequila was still very much with me.

Agent Parker smiled. "We want to make this quick. I'm sure you're ready to get home to your family." He seemed sincere.

"Yes, but can I ask why I'm here in this secluded room talking to the F.B.I.?"

"Of course. We have some questions that we need to ask you regarding the flight departing from Denver to Salt Lake City last Friday afternoon."

"Don't I have the right to an attorney?"

"Would you like one?"

I always felt that someone wanting their attorney present was a sure sign of guilt. "Nope. I don't need one."

"Good. Let's get right to it, shall we?"

"We shall."

"You, Jackson Fabacher, by all inclination boarded flight number 4479 on Friday, June the 29th heading from Denver to Salt Lake City, en route to New Orleans. That plane crashed and killed everyone on board. You, however, are very much alive and well. Tell us, please, why the airline assumed you were on the airplane."

Through numerous movies, television shows, and literature over the years, I learned various traits and mannerisms people showcased when speaking an untruth. I didn't remember all the telltale signs of a lie, but managed to recall a few. A lack of eye contact was one, so was a change in voice, and fidgety feet or hands. With that in mind, I clasped my hands together on the table while staring into Agent Parker's eyes. "I'm engaged to a beautiful woman named Delain Schexnaydre. We're supposed to be married Saturday."

"As in three days from now Saturday?"

I nodded. "I love her with all my heart, but this isn't the first time I've been engaged." As I continued, Agent Parker opened the folder in front of him. "I was engaged to someone else named Tiffany Melancon. I thought she was the last girl I would ever be with, but a couple weeks before we were to get married, she slept with her ex-boyfriend. I found out about it just hours before the ceremony. Long story short, I managed to let everyone in the cathedral know about her infidelity seconds before we were supposed to say 'I do.'"

"How did you let your wedding guests know about Tiffany's infidelity?"

"I played a video of her confessing to cheating on me."

Agent Parker lowered his head, peering at me from above the chocolate-colored, outdated frames resting upon his nose. "During the actual ceremony?"

"As I said seconds earlier—yes, during the actual ceremony."

"That was a very…brazen thing to do to someone you love, Jackson."

"She cheated on me. I wanted everyone to know what she had done. I hate cheaters."

Agent Parker lifted his head, readjusting his glasses. "Please continue."

"So, flash forward to last Friday. I was in the airport thinking about my upcoming nuptials when a young man sat next to me. He, also from New Orleans, started talking to me about his girlfriend and how he was proposing to her when he got home that weekend."

"What was this man's name?"

I unclasped my hands as I looked downward and to the right at the tiled floor. "Something with a B. Brian, Bob..." I was well aware of his name, but tried to act as if I hadn't rehearsed my alibi several dozen times in the last two days.

"Bradley?" Agent Parker asked.

Subtly nodding, I shifted my gaze back to Agent Parker. "That's it. Bradley Boudreaux. I remember seeing it on a business card he gave to me."

"Do you still have this business card?"

"It's in my wallet in my back pocket. May I grab it, or should I ask Agent Williams to retrieve it since he's closer to it than me?"

Agent Parker looked above my head. "Agent Williams, do you mind giving Jackson some breathing room?"

Agent Williams stepped to the side. I leaned to the left to retrieve the wallet. "What kind of cologne is that, Agent Williams?" He didn't answer. I was certain I was getting under his skin. After glancing at the business card, I handed it to the friendlier of the two agents. "Bradley Boudreaux, DDS."

Agent Parker examined the card, jotted something down in his folder, and then set it on the table. "And what happened after Bradley told you he was proposing to his girlfriend?"

"It got me thinking…" I made sure to continue staring into the agent's eyes, "that maybe I was rushing into marriage too soon. I love my fiancée, but another marriage less than two years after the first failed attempt to get married had me second-guessing that I was moving too soon. Bradley was desperate to get home early to prepare for his proposal, while I wasn't sure I wanted to go home just yet. Since neither of us checked our luggage, we decided to exchange tickets."

"You didn't think to tell the airline about what you were doing?"

I made the same unpleasant face I would if I had just sucked on a lemon. "Screw the airline. First of all, he was at the bottom of the standby list, so someone else would have gotten my ticket. Secondly, if they would have let us swap tickets, they probably would have charged some ridiculous fee to do so."

"Did it ever occur to you, Jackson, that swapping airline tickets the way you did may have been illegal?"

"Nope. I don't see why it would be."

"Jackson, another man boarded an airplane pretending to be you. That is a federal offense."

"I didn't know, but at the same time, I don't regret what I did. It's horrible that Bradley and all those passengers and crew members died. However, if I didn't do what I did, I'd be dead too."

Agent Parker nodded. "That is true."

"Are you going to arrest me for exchanging tickets?" I had a hunch he was bluffing about the ticket swapping being a crime.

"No. At least not right now," he spoke with a grin and a wink. "What happened after you swapped tickets with Bradley?"

"I did some soul-searching."

"Can you elaborate on this 'soul-searching'?"

"I placed my luggage in a locker at the airport, and then walked out. The battery on my phone was drained, so with no working phone I hopped on a bus and contemplated whether or not I would go back to the airport for my later flight. I eventually decided not to. My fiancée and I…" I paused, letting out a lengthy exhale while glancing at the ceiling. I never partook in an acting class, but felt I would excel in one.

"Your fiancée and you…?"

"Let's just say I have trust issues with women. I can thank my last fiancée for that. My current fiancée had, or has, a relationship with a male friend that I'm a little uncomfortable with."

"May I ask why?"

"Sure, Chief. She is friends with a guy that I'm certain has strong feelings for her. She says I'm being paranoid. I don't think I am."

"Can I ask this gentleman's name?"

When the three of us discussed our plan early Monday morning, it included a fictional male friend of Delain's with whom I was jealous. We came up with a name and how Delain knew him, but I wasn't ready to divulge that information. "I'd rather not give his name. I don't want him knowing that I'm jealous of him. If he were to find out, I'm sure he'd be doing backflips."

"Fair enough. So, you got on a bus. Where did you get off?"

"I don't know exactly the name of the city, but I think it was on the outskirts of Denver. I saw a restaurant and I was hungry. While eating, I tried to come up my next move. I didn't want to talk to Delain because she—"

"What was the name of the restaurant?"

During the discussion with Caroline and Delain early Monday morning, I spoke of the actual restaurant I dined in located by Scott's house. Caroline feared that a little bit of homework by the authorities might have them questioning why I ate so close to my ex-fiancée's uncle's house. An internet search on Delain's computer provided the perfect dinner location. "I don't remember the name, but it's located on Washington Street; it was connected to a truck stop." We also discovered that it was on the bus route and several miles away from Scott's house.

"Washington Street," Agent Parker said while again scribbling. "You didn't want to talk to Delain because…?"

"She went out the night before with some girlfriends. Her male friend just happened to be at the same bar. She didn't call me when she got home. It upset me. I felt that a few days without communication would maybe make her come to her senses and realize I was more important than her friend. So, before I left the diner, a trucker struck up conversation with me. He was an older man and he seemed harmless—married, three kids, a Christian. I asked where he was going. He said California. He asked where I was going. I said I didn't know. He then asked if I wanted to tag along. I at first declined, but after thinking about it, thought why not."

"You hitchhiked with a stranger?"

"Doesn't everyone who hitchhikes do so with a stranger?"

"Good point. What I meant, though, was that you hitchhiked with someone without letting anyone know what you were doing. Don't you find that a little risky?"

"I can see how one might think that, but this guy seemed like a good person to me."

"And the truck driver's name?"

"Bobby."

"Did you get his last name?"

"Smith. Bobby Smith."

"That's a pretty common name."

With a shrug of the shoulders, I told him, "That's the name he told me. I'm not sure if it's right or not. I didn't ask to see his damn driver's license."

Agent Parker leaned back in his chair. "Jackson, you seem a little…defensive."

"I'm sitting in a room with two men asking me questions like I've committed a crime when I'd rather be on a plane heading home to see loved ones who think I'm dead."

"Well, you did swap airline tickets with another gentleman whose girlfriend reported him as missing Monday morning."

"About the ticket exchange—I've been thinking. I never pretended to be Bradley Boudreaux and he never pretended to be me. Neither he nor I showed an I.D. claiming to be someone we weren't. The airline never asked to see identification before boarding the flight, so you can blame them for that mishap." I leaned back in my chair, confident about my claim. The tequila was making me feel confident and almost invincible in the presence of the federal agents; so much so that I felt the need to reconsider my stance against consuming tequila.

"Another good point, Jackson. We'll have to review the guidelines to see if you did or did not commit a crime. Now, getting back to the story—to where did you tag along with Bobby Smith?"

"California, just outside of Bakersfield. We got there on Saturday afternoon."

"Where did you sleep Friday night?"

"He drove through the night. I dozed off for about an hour or so. Once we got to Bakersfield, I thanked Bobby for the ride and checked into a motel."

"Which motel?"

"Super 8."

"And for how long?"

"Until Tuesday."

"And during that time, you never once learned about the plane crash?"

"Nope. I didn't turn the television on, I didn't read the newspaper, and I didn't have a working phone."

"Then what did you do for three days?"

"Sleep."

"That's it?"

"Pretty much. I guess you could say I was depressed. I took sleeping pills the first night, woke up, and then took them again. I repeated the process until realizing what day it was. After checking out of the motel, I walked back to the truck stop where Bobby dropped me off. There, I met a driver who was heading east and was looking for company."

"And what was his name?"

A popular childhood movie from 1985 containing a 'ghostly' female truck driver was the inspiration for the second driver's name. "Marge. I never got her last name. She's the one who told me about the plane crash just as we passed the gas station where I met you two. She dropped me off, I walked back, and now here I am."

Agent Parker set his pen down. "Yes, you are." He then again leaned back in his chair, crossed his arms, and grinned. "The runaway groom. Isn't there a movie called that?"

"You're thinking of the 1999 hit *Runaway Bride*, Agent Parker, starring Julia Roberts and Richard Gere, directed by Garry Marshall." Agent Williams finally spoke his first words in my presence. His voice was deep.

"So, he's not a mute." I turned towards Agent Williams. "Julia Roberts fan?"

"Isn't everyone?" Agent Williams grinned, revealing a spacious gap between his two front teeth.

"Well, she is one of America's sweethearts," I quipped back, naming another Julia Roberts film.

"And a pretty woman."

"Yes, she is, Agent Williams. I had a discussion about that recently at my best friend's wedding." I was starting to like our little game. I wasn't losing to him.

"Sounds like the discussion was something to talk about," he said after finally taking the seat next to his partner. "Tell me, Jackson, when you were with your ex-fiancée, did it feel like you were sleeping with the enemy?"

I smirked while trying to recall more Julia Roberts movies. "What can I say, I love trouble."

Agent Williams stopped grinning as he leaned towards me. "This sounds like one big conspiracy theory to me."

"And that sounds like confessions of a danger—"

"I wasn't naming a Julia Roberts film with my last statement, Mr. Fabacher. This whole thing sounds like a conspiracy theory."

I crinkled my nose and smirked while asking, "How so, Williams?"

Agent Parker put his hand in front of Agent Williams, speaking on his behalf. "Jackson, your ex-fiancée is Tiffany Melancon."

"Thank you for the reminder." I anticipated what the next question would be.

"Are you aware that her father was found dead two days ago?"

I purposely dropped my jaw and showcased a mildly shocked look that included squinting my eyebrows together. "I am now. How?" My heart was pulsating.

"Carbon monoxide poisoning was believed to have been the cause of death, but a massive heart attack may have also been to blame. We'll know for sure when the autopsy results are in."

I leaned back, placed my hands on the table, and subtly shook my head back and forth "Wow."

"Are you saddened by his death?" Agent Parker asked.

Despite my tequila buzz, I was still careful as to what I said. I didn't want them to know the truth (that I despised Davis and wished he was dead before it actually happened), but I also didn't want them to think that I considered him to be a great specimen of a man. I tried to keep my thoughts on Davis somewhat in the middle. "At the wedding, after I played the video of his daughter confessing to cheating on me, he tried to attack me. My friends stood in his way. He backed down before attending to his daughter. After I left, he got into my mom and dad's face, telling them they were horrible parents. He then tried to take a swing at my best friend after he tried to restrain him. Am I shocked that he's dead? Yes. Am I deeply saddened by his death? Not entirely. Why are y'all breaking this news to me?"

"We just thought you'd want to know about the passing of the man who was almost your father-in-law."

I pointed to Agent Williams while continuing to look at Agent Parker. "And why did he mention 'conspiracy theory' a second ago before you told me about Davis' death?"

Agent Parker shrugged his shoulders. "You'll have to ask him."

I slowly turned my head to the left. "What sounds like a conspiracy theory to you?"

"Everything you said. First, you never once turned on your phone after you left the airport? You didn't bother to check your voice mail or text messages? I find that hard to believe."

Delain and I have the same type of cell phone. During the few hours I spent in her house before Caroline and I began our drive out west, we went over every possibly detail, including depowering my phone. While the three of us worked on my alibi, I placed my battery in Delain's phone, and then set it in her downstairs bathroom, which rarely receives service. The continuous roaming caused the battery to drain. I then placed it back in my phone before going to bed. "Do you?" I removed my phone from my pocket, attempting unsuccessfully to turn it on. "As I stated earlier, it's been dead since Friday. Check my phone records. Next conspiracy theory question please, super-agent."

"The places you dined—did you use a credit card?"

I shook my head. "I paid with cash."

"How convenient. What about the motel in Bakersfield? Cash or credit card?"

"Cash."

"Of course you did. And the two truck drivers— Bobby Smith and Marge No-last-name; any idea how we can get in touch with either of them?"

"Phone book."

Agent Williams grinned while counting on his right hand. "No alibi, no credit card purchases, no contact with friends or family, and getting around by hitchhiking. Sounds like you lived off the grid for about five days."

"And your point?"

"And it just so happened that your almost father-in-law died of," he lifted both hands upward, using air quotations marks, "'carbon monoxide poisoning' during the time of your absence."

I was convinced that I had covered my tracks meticulously, with the only exception being my fingerprints in Cliff's truck—which I was beginning to believe would never be searched for fingerprints after all. It felt like Agent Williams was throwing a Hail Mary by suggesting I had something to do with Davis' death. The idea was so out there that I don't think he even believed it was possible. I smiled subtly. "First of all, who still uses air quotes? Secondly, you're absolutely correct, Agent Williams; my crystal ball told me that the airplane I was supposed to board was going to fly into a flock of geese and kill everyone on it, so I made it appear as if I were on the plane. I then carefully snuck all the way to New Orleans, killed Davis in his garage via carbon monoxide poisoning or possibly a heart attack, and then snuck all the way back here to Arizona where I," air quoting seemed like the appropriate thing to do, "'resurrected' myself." I then remembered we were in Phoenix. "Oh, and we just happen to be in the city named after the bird that resurrected itself. How apropos!"

Agent Williams slowly shook his head side to side. "We never said he died in his garage."

I didn't become alarmed. I knew he was down to his last swing. And I was throwing a fucking strike. "Everyone who dies of carbon monoxide does so in their garage. Where else can it happen?"

Agent Parker glanced at his partner, grinning before looking back at me. "Mr. Fabacher, how about we get you to the airport, so you can get back home to your loved ones?"

"That's about the only sensible thing I've heard since I've been in this room. No offense to you, Agent Parker."

Agent Williams gave me a look as if he wanted to ram the butt of his gun against my skull. I flashed him a wink as I stood. Truth be told, I was intimidated by him, and I'm sure I wasn't the only person to feel that way in his presence. Like a hiker that's told to appear stoic and brave during an encounter with a grizzly bear, I didn't back down or show fear to Agent Williams. Hopefully, it would be the first and only time I would be in his and Agent Parker's presence.

As we exited the room, Agent Parker asked, "Are you okay with flying home, considering what happened to the last airplane you were supposed to have boarded?"

"I'm fine. Lightning won't strike a second time."

He then held his cell phone in front of me. "Would you like to call your parents or fiancée and let them know you're alive?"

"No. I want to surprise them at home."

Chapter 56

At 10:45 at night, the walk from the arrival gate to the terminal at Louis Armstrong International Airport was quiet. With hands in pockets, the tequila out of my system, and my gaze directed at the ground, I replayed the interview with the F.B.I. agents from earlier in the day in my head, just as I had done several times on the airplane. I felt confident about my answers to their questions. Even though I acted like an ass at times, I was thoroughly pleased with the end results. Exhausted and longing to see my family, I walked through a set of doors marked 'no return' on my way to the parking lot, where my vehicle had been since last Tuesday. A woman's scream startled me. I looked to my right. In front of a small crowd numbering in the teens, a light mounted atop a camera flashed onto my face. Alongside the camera, and with her hands covering her nose and mouth, stood the woman who raised me. My dad and brother were right behind her. As I approached them, applause erupted from the crowd.

"My baby," cried my mom, the first to hug me. She looked frail, yet happy. "How did you…I can't believe you're alive!" She pushed me back to get a look at my face before hugging me again. "Thank you, God!"

My dad embraced the both of us. "Jax," was all he could get out before starting to get choked up.

Marcus placed his hand on my shoulder. "The things you do to get attention." He was misty-eyed as well. Tears from all three of my family members still wasn't enough to make my eyes water, yet I was teetering on the edge.

"Jackson, how does it feel to be home?" a local news reporter asked once I took a step back from my family.

Before giving an answer, I looked to the crowd. Delain was nowhere in sight. "Relieved. I couldn't wait to see my family again."

"Jackson, you were believed to have been on the flight that crashed near Salt Lake City five days ago. How is it that you're alive?"

"I didn't get on the plane."

"How did the airline not realize that?"

Agent Parker claimed what I did may have been illegal, so I didn't want to admit to it on camera. With a shrug of my shoulders, I told her, "You'll have to ask the airline about that."

"Why didn't you get on the airplane last Friday?"

Announcing to two federal agents that I didn't trust my fiancée was one thing; letting thousands, if not more, know about it felt like I was making Delain out to be a dishonest person. "I wanted to spend some time reflecting on a big decision."

"Can you elaborate on that?"

"Not right now."

"Does it have to do with your upcoming wedding this weekend?"

"No comment."

"Is the wedding still taking place this Saturday?"

With another shrug of my shoulders, I told her, "I'm not sure. I just want to get home and be with loved ones right now." I looked to my family, ready to end the interview.

"Does that include your fiancée?"

"Of course."

"What did you do for the last five days, Jackson?"

"I'm exhausted. Thank you for the interview." I turned my back to the reporter, and began directing my family towards the parking lot. Thankfully, the reporter was done with her pestering.

The other dozen or so people standing around were faces I didn't recognize. They smiled as we walked past them. Four police officers stood near the exit, as did an older, sophisticated-looking gentleman in a dark suit with salt and peppered hair and thick, black-framed glasses resting upon his tanned face. I watched from the corner of my eye as his gaze followed my family and me as we made our way outside. While continuing to the parking garage, I glanced over my shoulder to see the man tucking what looked to be a camera into his jacket. My paranoia was steadily increasing.

Two of the police officers followed us outside, while the remaining two looked to be holding back members of the press.

Outside of the parking garage elevator, my dad asked, "Does Delain know you're alive?"

A man with a large camera atop his shoulder jumped out of a news van parked nearby. His presence prompted one of the officers to push him backwards.

"You have no right pushing me back!" the cameraman shouted.

The policeman said nothing, continuing to stand between us and him.

I waited until we were on the elevator with the remaining officer before answering my dad. "I'm not sure that she does. I haven't talked to her yet."

My brother handed me his cell phone. "Call her."

I handed it back to him. "I want to surprise her at her house. Can y'all drop me off there? My car is here, but I'd rather ride with y'all."

"Sure," my dad answered.

My dad thanked the officer by name while we stood outside his sedan. After we drove off, my family asked many of the same questions I had answered hours earlier in Phoenix. Where did I go? Why didn't I call anyone? Why didn't I get on the airplane? When did I find out about the crash? What did I do while I was gone? I gave the same answers to them as I gave the federal agents. Even though I didn't want them to think Delain was untrustworthy or a bad fiancée, I had to mention Delain's fictitious male friend I was envious towards, as he was the catalyst for me not boarding the plane. No way was I ready to divulge the truth to them; at least not yet.

"Did you hear about Davis?" Marcus asked as we drove towards New Orleans on I-10.

"Yes. What's the mood been like regarding that?"

"In the Fabacher house, it's been joyful," he gleefully replied.

"Marcus, be respectful."

"Mom, he threatened Jackson, got in y'all's faces, and then tried to hit Mikey. "I'm not too upset that son of a…bad person is dead."

"He's a human being, and he has a daughter that was almost a part of this family. Show some kindness," she spoke from the seat in front of me.

"Does urinating on his grave count as kindness?" Marcus asked. "Theoretically, I'm watering his death flowers."

My dad chuckled.

"Honey, don't encourage him."

"Yes, dear. Jax, the mood around town has been somewhat somber. Several hundreds showed up for his wake yesterday. They're predicting over a thousand at his funeral tomorrow."

"You had quite a bit of mourners at your funeral as well," my brother informed me.

When attending funerals over the years, I sometimes wondered what the crowd would look like at my own funeral. I wondered who from grade school and college, as well as how many of my ex-girlfriends, football teammates, former co-workers, patients, and acquaintances I made over the years would pay their final respects at my funeral. There was one person in particular whom I was curious to know if their presence was made. "Was Tiffany there?"

"Nope. I did see her on the news Monday, though," my brother informed me.

"How did she look?"

"Different. She has brown hair now."

Tiffany had blonde hair all her life. She loved it blonde, and never once talked about coloring it something different. "I mean, emotionally how did she look?"

"Devastated. She was crying next to her mom."

"I feel sorry for her. Maybe you should call her tomorrow and offer your condolences." My mom was one to forgive and forget very easily. If Davis would have died of a heart attack that wasn't incited by me, perhaps it would have been the right time to end the twenty months of silence between the two of us and offer my condolences for her loss. I imagine she would have accepted my sympathetic apology and been okay with me attending the funeral. Since I was responsible for his death, I found no need to insert myself back into her life.

"Maybe I will."

My brother placed both of his hands on my left shoulder before rocking me side to side several times. "I can't believe you're alive! You realize that you're probably on every news channel throughout America. When anyone logs onto Yahoo, there your face will be." He couldn't stop grinning. "And what about the wedding? Is it going to happen? Can you imagine the attention that it would get now?"

Extra attention was the last thing Delain and I needed. "I need to speak with Delain first."

"Don't get me wrong. I'm glad you had doubts about marrying her, because you'd be dead if you didn't, but is this male friend of hers really a threat? She doesn't seem like the cheating type."

"She hasn't shown any signs of cheating. I guess I'm just a little paranoid because of Tiffany."

"Are you sure there's nothing else? Five days is a long time to go without checking in with someone you love."

"Marcus, stop pestering him. He's had a long day."

"Yes, sir."

While stopped at a traffic light, I watched as my dad leaned towards my mom. He whispered something to her. I didn't know what was said, but I did find it peculiar that my mom was unusually quiet and sat about as motionless as a statue for the next few miles.

As we exited the interstate, Marcus gave a lengthy stare out of the back window. "I think we're being followed."

My initial thought as I turned around was that the F.B.I. was behind us. I imagined that Agents Parker and Williams flew to New Orleans on a private plane and were following me. Relief momentarily set in as a nearby street lamp revealed a news van behind us instead. As we grew closer to Delain's house, I told my dad to drive a few blocks away so the reporters wouldn't know where she lived.

My dad stopped the car five blocks away from the street where Delain resided.

"I hate to leave y'all, but I need to smooth things over with Delain."

"We understand. Do what you gotta do." While Marcus hugged me, the news van came into view behind us.

"Bye, sweetie," my mom spoke without making eye contact.

I placed my hand on her shoulders. She grabbed it as I told everyone, "I love y'all."

All three repeated the words back to me.

I stepped onto the street. My dad pulled forwards before turning the car, stopping sideways in the street and blocking the news van. I hurried to Delain's house. No one was following me.

As I approached her townhouse, I could see that the living room light was turned on. A tinted black sedan sat in the street two houses down from hers. It looked to be a Chrysler. I had never seen it by her house before. I again thought F.B.I. After knocking, I glanced back at the car until Delain's front door opened.

Chapter 57

Before I could turn my head to make certain my fiancée was standing at the door, someone kissed me as if I were the last man she would ever kiss—and for the last time. I didn't have to gaze into those shimmering emerald eyes to know it was Delain. "You have no idea how much I missed you," she confessed, her lips still pressed against mine. It had only been two and a half days since we last stood face-to-face, but given the events that took place and how intensely Delain kissed me, it felt as if it had been months since last saw one another.

As I stepped back to tell her I missed her, she looked to be on the verge of tears. "Are you okay?"

She gazed longingly into my eyes. "I didn't know if I would see you again. I love you so much, baby."

The words I had so desperately needed to hear had finally been spoken. "I love you too. I don't want to leave you again."

She pulled me inside, locking the door behind us. "You are not to leave my side again." Delain then kissed me with such passion and intensity that I had no reason to doubt her love for me. The last time I could recall her kissing me in such a way was the night she broke down and confessed to having a son, thus leading to our first love-making experience. "I know you've had a long day, but…" Delain unbuttoned my pants while kissing my neck, "I want you right now."

Our body temperatures were too elevated to lie beneath the sheets. We rested on top of them as the ceiling fan circulated above us in the darkened bedroom. Sex was the last thing on my mind, but rejecting her advances would have been futile. She wanted it, and wasn't stopping until I gave it to her. "We should probably talk about the past few days," I told her, still trying to catch my breath. "Did anything happen around here while I was gone?"

"Not a thing. I only left the house once, and that was to go to the grocery store. How was the ride with Caroline?"

"Uncomfortable."

"How so?"

"I never left the backseat, and most of the time she made me lay down. I had to pee in water bottles. You know how hard it is to pee in a bottle, while lying on your side, in a moving car, with someone two feet away? I gotta hand it to her—she's thorough."

"What did y'all talk about during the ride?"

"The plan the three of us discussed. She went over it several times. She kept quizzing me. It felt like I was in school again."

"What else did y'all talk about?"

"Not much. Mostly that…and how she and Brock aren't engaged any longer."

"What?" Delain sounded quite surprised.

"You didn't know?"

"No. When did it happen?"

"She didn't tell you while I was…dead?"

"No. When did they break up?"

"Sometime recently. She told him she needed some time to think about things."

"Like what kind of things?"

Not telling her that Caroline broke up with Brock because she had confessed to loving me wasn't a lie; I just withheld information from her that would complicate things and create more uncertainty in our already chaotic life. "She thinks she may be too young right now to get married."

"I don't agree with that at all. She's very mature for twenty-three. Plus, she and Brock are perfect for one another."

I wasn't oblivious to the fact that Delain was slightly uncomfortable with the relationship Caroline and I shared. She let it be known days earlier that she noticed how my spirits lifted once Caroline started working in the clinic with me. I had a feeling she didn't want Caroline to remain off the market. "You're right. They make a good couple. I hope they get back together."

Delain placed her hand on my chest, rubbing it as she asked, "What were the sleeping arrangements like?"

"How do you mean?"

"Did y'all sleep in different beds, or…?"

"Caroline thought that if she got a room with two beds it could jeopardize our plan."

Several uncomfortable seconds passed before her hand came to a stop. "Y'all slept in the same bed?"

"Yes. The bed was king-sized on both nights."

Delain's heavy breathing, I suspected, was no longer a lingering effect of our recent love-making. "What did y'all talk about before going to sleep?"

There was no reason to further upset her. "Not much. We were exhausted by the time we got to the motel. I fell asleep as soon as my head hit the pillow."

"Tell me everything that happened once she dropped you off."

I told her about my encounter with T.J. and Harold at the gas station, the F.B.I. agents' interrogation, and the greeting I received at the airport along with the reporter's questions.

"What did you tell the reporter when she asked about the wedding?"

"That I wasn't sure."

"What should we…" She leaned towards the nightstand. The lamp flickered on. I covered my eyes as she asked, "What should we do?"

It wasn't a topic I wanted to discuss at the end of such a mentally-exhausting day. "I love you, Lainey, I really do." I slowly opened my eyes, adjusting to the 60 watts of light emanating from behind her. While leaning on my side, I grabbed her hand closest to me. "But I think it may be too soon given the recent events."

I no longer became the object upon which Delain's emerald eyes gazed. She lay on her back, staring at the ceiling.

"Maybe we can postpone it…just a little bit."

She subtly nodded while saying, "Perhaps you're right." There was a hint of dejection in her tone.

"You sound disappointed."

A lengthy pause ensued before she asked, "What went through your head when you were under this bed while Davis interrogated me?"

I lay on my back as well, staring at the ceiling as I told her, "Not to sound overly corny or dramatic, but it felt as if my world came to an end. I was so shocked that I didn't move for about an hour after you left. It was probably the worst day of my life— even more than my wedding. Why do you ask?"

"When I found out this past Sunday that you were under my bed when Davis was here, I felt like the most horrible person in the world. And then I felt even worse when I realized you were going to stay with me and get dumped at the wedding, just so I could get Caleb back. Am I right?"

Even though it was over, it still wasn't easy to talk about. "Yes." She turned to me. I continued to stare at the chain hanging from the ceiling fan as it whipped around in a clockwise direction.

She scooted closer, resting her head on my chest while draping her right arm across my abdomen. "You're so…perfect."

"Nobody's perfect, Lainey."

"If that's true, then you're as close to perfect as possible. I can't believe you stuck around. Most men would have probably salvaged what was left of their pride and left. You were going to let yourself be embarrassed in front of your family and friends for me."

"I didn't feel like I had a choice."

She lifted her head. We locked eyes with one another. Not a word was spoken. I began to stroke her hair a few times. She then moved her head closer, shutting her eyes while placing her lips to mine. "I love you so much, baby," she whispered. "I love you more than I thought I could ever love someone. I just want you to know that."

"I love you just as much."

"I feel like when I'm with you, nothing bad will happen to me. I don't want you to leave."

"I'm not leaving."

"Eventually you'll have to go back home. I don't even want that to happen. I want to see you every morning when I wake up and every night before I shut my eyes."

"What are you saying?"

"I'm saying I don't want you to leave me—ever." She sat up in the bed. "I think we should go through with the wedding this Saturday."

A stolen car in Denver, my fingerprints inside a truck belonging to a man I had shot less than four days earlier, my presence next to a man that died of a heart attack that I caused and could have also prevented, my deceitful interrogation with two F.B.I. agents, Caroline's feelings towards me, Bradley Boudreaux's death, and, lastly, the dilemma of finding a way to bring Caleb back into Delain's life were anxiety-inducing issues that were constantly on my mind. I didn't think a wedding should be added to my weekly agenda, considering that the possibility of being arrested crossed my mind about every five minutes. "I love you and I don't want to leave you either, but shouldn't we wait until we know for sure that we're in the clear of Davis' death? It would probably look bad if you have a husband that's in jail."

"You're not going to jail, baby. We're not going to get caught. I know for a fact that we're not going to get caught. We're the good guys. We're supposed to win."

It wasn't much of one, but I managed to muster a smile. "I love your optimism."

"Well, if you love it so much, then why don't you marry it," she said, her smile more pronounced than mine.

"You're really serious about getting married this weekend; aren't you?"

Straight-faced, she told me, "I've never been more certain about anything in my life, Mr. Fabacher."

It was nearly midnight. If we were to follow through with our wedding plans, we would be husband and wife in about sixty-seven hours. Just before that thought was to lift my cheeks, I was reminded that Delain was forced to date me, forced to make me fall in love with her, forced to make me think she was the last woman I wanted to be with, and forced to leave me at the altar. My law-breaking actions were one reason I wasn't ready just yet to tie the knot, while doubts about Delain's love for me again creeped into my conscious. Only adding to my uncertainty was a blonde-haired girl in San Diego that seemed crazy about me too. "Can we talk more about this tomorrow? It's been a very long day."

She nodded, kissing my neck, cheek, and then lips before resting her head on my chest. "Uno."

"Uno."

I wanted to believe everything Delain had just revealed, yet a part of me wondered if she was using me just to get her son back. I could only hope that wasn't the case.

Chapter 58

Money laundering, bribery, extortion, aggravated assault, impersonation of a federal officer, tax evasion, and embezzlement were crimes allegedly committed by Vincent Dichario and his business partner, Ralph Dantoni, over the course of two decades. Only two of the crimes—tax evasion and one count of aggravated assault— were ever brought to court, with only the charge of tax evasion earning a 'guilty' verdict. Vincent was sentenced to three years in prison, whereas Ralph spent one less year behind bars. Even though they had been out of prison for some time, both were on probation while an ongoing investigation was being conducted into other allegations. Marty Goldstein, arguably the best defense lawyer in all of Nevada, was the reason Vincent and Ralph were free to walk the streets.

The nineteen-month disappearance of Vincent's wife, Krista, had several eyes and fingers aimed in the direction of her husband. Two interrogations were conducted between the Las Vegas Police Department and, separately, Vincent and Ralph. Marty was by his clients' sides for every question. Vincent claimed that Krista was schizophrenic and often talked about running away and starting a new life somewhere in Europe. Ralph also claimed the same about Krista. Since her body had yet to be found, no charges could be brought forward in her death. Her disappearance was as much a mystery as Bigfoot or Jimmy Hoffa's final resting place.

The escort service Vincent began five years before the millennium provided the bulk of his income. Fifty-seven women were employed by Feel Good, Inc. Krista was one of the first employees of the company. After two years of escorting for Vincent, she became his fifth wife. Following the marriage, she continued to work for the company in more of a managerial role. Besides instructing new employees about the ins and outs of escorting, she also kept morale high for everyone involved in the company. Because of her sweet-natured personality and willingness to lend an ear to any one of her girls, she was often called 'Mama'. Unable to bear children herself, she loved the moniker. When she went missing, the mood in Feel Good, Inc. dropped considerably.

Vincent sat behind his desk in a warehouse, recently renovated into the Dicahrio Enterprises Complex—a 12,000 square foot facility located directly behind one of his two gentlemen clubs. Twenty feet in front of his desk, ten 55" rectangular television screens (five at eye level and the other five above those) hung on a wall. The televisions were turned on continuously all day and throughout the night. Sporting events occupied most of the screens. Being that it was early July, baseball games aired on six of the televisions, while horse racing occupied two. The stock report played on the ninth screen, and the national news was broadcast on the tenth. Nearly $2,000 of Vincent's money was riding on a Yankees home victory over the Minnesota Twins airing on television screen number two. With a one run lead at the top of the ninth for the home team, Vincent's attention was diverted from the first screen all the way to number ten at the right bottom corner. The young man on the television screen had a familiar look about him. Unable to place him, Vincent picked up the phone on his desk.

"What?" the gentleman on the other end of the phone asked.

"Get back here."

"I was just back there."

"And you need the exercise, fat ass, so get back here." Vincent slammed the phone before directing his attention towards two of his employees, lying on the plush leather couch to his right. It wasn't uncommon for his girls to relax in the office while on break. "Do you recognize him, Ginger?" Vincent asked, pointing to the tenth screen.

A red-headed young woman, not quite twenty-one years old and with a tattoo of the Empire State Building on her left arm, glanced upward from the issue of *People* magazine before her. While staring at the last screen, she told Vincent, "Nope. Should I?"

"What about you?"

The other girl was fast asleep. Her head rested in Ginger's lap. "She's sleeping."

"Wake her up and ask if she recognizes that man. Now, please."

Ginger nudged her co-worker as Ralph entered the room. "What you need?"

"Who is that on the last television screen?"

Ralph reached into his jacket pocket for a pair of bifocals. He held them up to his eyes, but didn't put them on as he read the bottom of the screen. "'Man believed to be dead resurfaces days before wedding.'"

"He looks familiar, does he not?"

Ralph slipped the bifocals onto his face. His eyes were glued to the screen. "He does. Give me a minute."

"Come on, Ralph. You usually get these things figured out in a second."

"I'm seeing…an elevator ride with the three of us in it…the Bellagio…the month you were staying there."

"That was when Krista was..." Vincent paused, glancing at the girls sitting on the couch. Ginger was once again reading her magazine, while the other stared at the last television screen, "still around."

Ralph removed his glasses. "I remember now. He was just coming from a guy's room. He was that faggot. Remember?"

"Are you sure?"

"Of course I'm fucking sure. I remember everyone."

"But according to the news, his name is Jackson."

"Then he either has a twin, he lied to us, or he's lying to the news."

Vincent stood from his desk chair, slowly approaching the tenth screen. "It does look like the man from the elevator ride. He had lipstick all over his face."

"I'm telling you, Vincent, it's him. He was missing a shoe. He then dropped his tie and you—"

"Holy shit!" Vincent turned towards Ralph. "Do you believe in miracles?"

"I'm Catholic. Of course I fucking do. What kind of miracle are we talking here?"

None of the marriages to his ex-wives, the births of his nieces and nephews, or the opening of his first gentlemen's club and the escort service could deliver the excitement Vincent experienced as he walked back towards his desk. The safe located behind a painting of the Rat Pack contained nothing but cash. He continued past the first safe on his way to the second one, containing more personal items. He pushed his desk chair back before lifting a 6'×4' rug, along with a thick piece of hard plastic the same size as the rug. After dropping to one knee, he eagerly opened the safe. He then handed a black dress shoe to Ralph. "A big fucking miracle," he spoke with a grin. "How much you wanna bet this shoe belongs to him?"

"Who? That faggot on television?"

"He's not a faggot. He lied about that as well. Why would he have lipstick on his face if he was gay?"

"True." Ralph grabbed the shoe, closely examining it. "You think that's the guy that was in the room with," he lowered his voice before whispering, "Krista?"

Vincent nodded. "The kid in the elevator had no shoe on his left foot. A couple days later, I find this left shoe behind the nightstand..." He held up a monogrammed handkerchief, "and this under the foyer table."

Ralph read the initials from the handkerchief. "A.J.F."

"Now look at the name on the screen."

Ralph held his glasses in front of his eyes once more while reading the bottom of the screen. "Jackson Fabacher of New Orleans was found in an Arizona gas station earlier today."

"His name matches two of the three letters on this handkerchief. I think that," Vincent again lowered his voice, "son of a bitch on the television is the same son of a bitch that screwed my wife in my own fucking hotel room."

"I guess there's only one way to find out, isn't there?" Ralph asked. Vincent nodded. "You want me to send Anthony down to New Orleans?"

"No. I'd rather you go. You've never let me down before."

Ralph slipped the shoe and handkerchief into a nearby bag. "And I ain't going to let you down this time either."

Chapter 59

Tiffany Melancon sat at her parents' lengthy kitchen table, alongside her mom, her Uncle Scott, her Aunt Bridgett, her dad's lawyer and good friend of the family Charlie Guichet, and in her lap sat her two-year-old cousin Thomas. Tiffany didn't get to see her cousin often, so when she did, she usually held him for hours. She couldn't wait to be a mother. Since her freshman year of high school, she most certainly thought she would be one by the age of twenty-eight. With five months to go until her twenty-ninth birthday, it was safe to say she wouldn't be a mother by the expected age. The names were already picked out and had been for years—Madison for a girl and Taylor for a boy. There would be no discussing of names with her husband when their children would be born because Madison would be the first girl's name and Taylor the first boy's name—period.

"Does anyone need a coffee refresher?" Tiffany's mother, Victoria, asked the others as light flickered outside from nearby fireworks.

"Mrs. Victoria, I'd love another cup of your delicious roasted coffee," Charlie told her.

Scott handed his sister-in-law his and Bridgett's empty mugs as well. "Can you make that two more please, Victoria?"

"Tiffy, more coffee?"

"No, thank you," she replied, handing Thomas' empty glass to her mom. "But Thomas could use some more milk."

Scott placed his hand on his niece's shoulder. "How you doing, Tif?"

Tiffany shrugged her shoulders. "I don't know. It's a lot to take in right now. I don't want to go to the funeral tomorrow."

"I know how you feel. That's when it hits you that he's really gone. If it'll make you feel better, you can carry Thomas around tomorrow. I know how much you like being with him."

Tiffany glanced at her cousin's face while asking, "Do you want me to hold you tomorrow, Thomas?" His smile prompted her to hug and then rock him back and forth. "You're the most handsome boy in the whole world, you know that?"

Victoria set a tray containing four coffee mugs and a glass of cold milk onto the kitchen table. She looked every bit her daughter, especially since Tiffany had returned to her blonde locks just a few hours earlier. Besides having similar hair color again, their eyes were the same baby-blue hue, their bronze complexion was identical, light freckling adorned both of their noses, and both shared the same affinity for exercising. It wasn't uncommon for men to suggest that the two were sisters whenever they were out together.

"Tiffany, when are we going to meet this boyfriend of yours that your mom has been talking so much about?" Bridgett asked.

"Brett's flying in tomorrow. I'm picking him up at the airport, then we're heading to the cathedral." Tiffany had been dating Brett for nearly nine months. He made well over six-figures, carried no debt except for a house note, was about eight inches taller then she, had a physique that was well on its way to her liking, seemed stable in life, and, she was convinced, would pass down favorable genes to her children one day.

"Brett is adorable," Victoria added. "I can't wait to have him as a son-in-law. Your father would have approved."

"Are wedding bells in the future?" Bridgett asked before sipping her coffee.

On paper, Brett represented everything Tiffany wanted in a spouse. Even though she wasn't in love with him yet, she planned on dating him for another five months before accepting his proposal. A date for the wedding would be set one year after the December proposal, and then either Madison or Taylor would be born before she turned thirty-one. In hopes of conceiving twins to get both with one try, she was already planning on taking fertility pills. Stretch marks and loose skin around the abdomen, she had been told, was more prevalent in new moms in their thirties, and those were two imperfections she was hoping to avoid. "Probably," she answered. "I think it's a safe bet to say I'll be engaged by Christmas. Hopefully the wedding will be a little less traumatic than the last one."

"Speaking of the last one, Ms. Tiffany," Charlie spoke, "can you believe the news surrounding your former fiancé?"

Everything in Tiffany's life had been going in the exact path she planned—until Jackson Fabacher derailed her right off the tracks in dramatic fashion. She still held a vicious grudge, unable to forgive him for what he had done in front of her family and friends. Although she was well aware some of the blame lay on her shoulder, she couldn't comprehend his actions in St. Louis Cathedral. If Jackson talked to her before the ceremony, she knew she would have convinced him to go through with the wedding. They would currently be together, raising Madison and/or Taylor while living a normal, happy life. Despite the anger towards him, she was still upset about his tragic death. "Yeah, it was a little hard to take. Between his and Dad's passing, this week has been brutal."

"His passing? Did you not see the news this evening, my dear?"

"Charlie, what are you talking about?" Victoria asked.

"Jackson Fabacher. He's alive."

"What?" Tiffany calmly asked, at first thinking it was some sort of joke.

Charlie stood from the table. "Mrs. Victoria, do you mind if we turn on your television set?"

Victoria walked into the adjacent living room and turned on the television. "What channel?"

"Any of the news channels," Charlie answered.

Victoria set the channel to CNN. Clips from a Fourth of July parade were being shown.

"I'm sure it will be on shortly," Charlie told them.

Tiffany was not only shocked to hear Jackson may not have perished in the airplane, but also relieved. "Charlie, why didn't you say anything when you first got here?"

"I apologize, my dear. I wasn't sure if that name was allowed to be spoken. Last time his name was mentioned at this table…"

Tiffany vividly remembered the incident. It happened the Thanksgiving immediately following the wedding. Another of her aunts mentioned Jackson's name during dinner. Tiffany's outburst included the pounding of her fists against the table preceded by a scolding of her aunt for mentioning her former fiancé. Davis sided with his daughter, reminding his sister that Jackson's name was never to be spoken unless someone was reading his obituary.

"It's okay, Charlie. I'm over it. Now, how did he not die in the crash?"

"He never stepped foot on the airplane. He said something about wanting to think about a big decis—"

"There it is!" Victoria shouted, pointing at the television.

Tiffany, with Thomas still clutched in her arms, stood from the table and hurried into the living room. "Mom, turn it up!"

"It's a very special Independence Day for one individual who was believed to have died five days ago. In fact, a funeral service was held three days ago for the young man from New Orleans, who was thought to have perished in the airplane crash outside of Salt Lake City last Friday." The story switched to another reporter interviewing Jackson in what looked to be a gas station.

"Jackson, how does it feel to be alive when everyone thought you were dead?"

"Like I've been given a second chance at life."

"Can you tell us why you didn't get on the airplane? Was it a premonition?"

"No, ma'am. I needed to clear my head."

"In regards to what?"

"I'm supposed to get married this Saturday. I was having some doubts."

"Of course you were!" Victoria shouted to the television.

"Mom, shhhh."

"Can you elaborate on those doubts?"

"I wish I could, but that's something personal between my fiancée and me at the moment."

When her father informed her that Jackson was getting married, Tiffany was naturally upset. Jackson beating her to the altar, she felt, was a slap in the face.

"Do you have anything to say to loved ones back home in New Orleans?" the reporter asked.

Jackson leaned closer to the microphone. *"I'll be home real soon."*

"What about the wedding this Saturday? Will it happen?"

Tiffany held her breath as Jackson hesitated before answering, *"I can't answer that at this time."*

"It won't happen. I bet he runs out on her as well," Victoria smugly spoke before putting the coffee mug to her lips.

Thomas' squirming prompted Tiffany to set him on the ground next to the couch. She continued to watch her ex-fiancé answer the reporter's questions. Feelings she thought she would never experience again towards Jackson were beginning to resurface. The hatred she held towards him for nearly twenty months seemed to vanish in a heartbeat. Tiffany missed the handwritten notes Jackson often left for her in her purse or car, and how he held

61

her hand beneath the bedsheets, even after he had fallen asleep. It was the small things she didn't appreciate, until they were no longer in her life. Her current boyfriend didn't leave sweet notes for her, nor did he hold her hand before shutting his eyes. She also realized, while watching the newscast, that her ex-fiancé's smile was much more contagious than her current beau's. Once the newscast was over, she muted the television before standing in front of it. "I need to ask y'all something, and I want you to please give me the God's honest truth. Am I to blame for what Jackson did to me at the wedding?"

"Absolutely not! Do you realize how much money your father and I spent for that wedding? Almost $200,000."

"I'm not interested in the financial side of what happened, Mom. I want to know if I deserved what Jackson did."

"Hell no!" she shouted with a look of detestation about her face. "No one deserves that on their wedding day, and I'm not just saying that because you're my daughter. He's 100% to blame for what happened."

Her mom's answer came as no surprise. Tiffany was more interested in a response from a less-biased individual. She glanced at her aunt and uncle. They, in turn, looked to one another. Before they could speak, someone else divulged their opinion.

"Ms. Tiffany, I have had the pleasure of knowing you since you were able to sit on your daddy's lap. You were just as sweet and caring then as you are now. I was appalled by Jackson Fabacher's actions on the evening of your blessed wedding. It was a classless act and highly inappropriate. That is my two cents on the issue."

"Thank you, Charlie." Ever since Tiffany had known him, Charlie Guichet always seemed to agree with whatever anyone was saying, almost as if he was trying to avoid conflict. She found it peculiar since he was a defense lawyer.

The two people whose answer she was more interested in receiving had yet to speak. Tiffany again glanced at her aunt and uncle. "You want our opinion?" Scott asked, looking every bit uncomfortable.

"Please."

"How honest?"

"Completely."

"Okay." Scott looked at his wife, back at Tiffany, opened his mouth, but was unable to speak. His wife took over.

"Tif, you cheated on him. Marriage isn't about being with someone just to be with someone. It's about trust and being honest with the person you love. You gave him no reason to ever trust you again. If Scott were to ever cheat on me, I can guarantee he would never be able to have sex again because he wouldn't have anything down there to use."

Scott grinned. "One reason I would never cheat is because I'm afraid she's telling the truth. The other, and more importantly, is because I love her with all my heart and I would never want to do something to hurt her. Honesty and loyalty doesn't start when two people say 'I do' to one another. It starts on the first date."

"So, you're saying my little girl deserved to be humiliated in front of everyone she knows on the most important day of her life?" Victoria was visibly upset by her sister-in-law's remarks. "She had to move away from home because of the embarrassment he caused her. How can you say he's not to blame, Bridgett?"

Bridgett calmly addressed her sister-in-law. "I'm saying that she made a bad—"

"She's right, Mom. I screwed up. I hurt him and he hurt me. It's completely my fault."

"What are you saying?"

"I'm saying I'm the one to blame, not Jackson. I've been holding a grudge towards him for almost two years. It's time I forgive him, and I think you should too."

"$200,000 down the drain."

"It's just money." Tiffany approached and reached out to her mom.

With crossed arms, Victoria shook her head side to side. "I'm never going to forget what he did."

"You don't have to. Just understand that I wasn't an innocent victim in what happened. Okay?"

"He should have talked to you before the ceremony, like an adult."

"I agree, but he didn't. I think it's time we all forgive him for what he did. It's taken me almost two years to admit that. We've all learned this week that life is too short." Tiffany couldn't believe the words coming out of her own mouth. It was as if a switch had been flipped inside her upon learning that Jackson was alive. In addition to being able to forgive him, she found him to look the sexiest he ever had while talking to the reporter. "Let's forgive him and move on, Mom."

"I'll think about it," Victoria spoke before finally embracing her daughter.

"And go hug Aunt Bridgett and tell her you're sorry for snipping at her."

Victoria smiled. "Yes, ma'am."

As Victoria hugged and apologized to Bridgett, Charlie pointed at Thomas from the kitchen. "Scott, your son is grabbing something shiny from beneath the couch."

Scott pulled his son's arm from beneath the couch. In his hand, he held the blade of a kitchen knife. "Jesus!" He quickly grabbed the knife from his son's grasp. A thorough examination revealed no cuts on Thomas' hand. "That was close."

"Why's there a knife under the couch?" Tiffany asked her mom.

"I don't know. I haven't been in the house in weeks." Victoria had been staying with Tiffany in Dallas for the last three weeks while she and Davis were in the process of separating from one another. She grabbed the knife from her brother-in-law's hand before examining it. "It's definitely one of mine." She then made her way to the kitchen and inserted the eight-inch chef's knife back into the wood block. Every other knife in the J.A. Henckels knife set was accounted for and in its correct slot.

"Why would Dad have a knife under the couch? That's bizarre."

"I imagine only your father would know the answer to that. Who knows what he was doing since I left." Victoria took a seat at the kitchen table next to Charlie. "I understand you have some business to conduct here tonight."

"Yes, Mrs. Victoria." From the leather satchel at his feet, Charlie removed a small stack of papers. "Since Davis' first heart attack a few years back, he had been updating and revising his will once a month. The last update was made in my office two weeks ago."

Victoria shook her head. "Two weeks ago? I would imagine he didn't leave much in my name then. I had a horrible feeling he was up to no good when he placed the house in his name a while back. He claimed the taxes would be cheaper that way. I can't believe I let him trick me into that."

"On the contrary, my darling." Charlie slipped a pair of bifocals onto his nose before reading from Davis' last written will. "'To my lovely and devoted wife Victoria: I bequeath the house and everything in which it holds, along with the sailboat and the remains of my savings account, which currently stands at around $275,000.'"

Victoria grew teary-eyed. Tiffany knew her mom still loved her father, even though the last few years were considered less than romantic. Fights often erupted, most of which preceded a phone call to Tiffany asking if she could stay with her for a little while. With the exception of the last request, Victoria never followed through with the invitation to stay with her daughter in Dallas.

"'To my one and only offspring Tiffany: I bequeath to you my condominium in the French Quarter. My loyal friend, Mr. Charlie Guichet, will direct you to the condo and offer you the key at which time you see fit. Also, I would like to pass on to you my Ferrari. Please take good care of her and use only premium gasoline.'"

"Condo?" Victoria asked.

"Yes, ma'am. Davis purchased it as a surprise gift for Ms. Tiffany. It was to be presented to her in the near future in hopes of luring her back to New Orleans," Charlie confessed. "Davis hated that she was so far away from the two of you."

Since the grudge towards Jackson seemed to vanish in just minutes, the thought of moving back to New Orleans excited Tiffany. The cherry on top was having a condo in the French Quarter.

"'To my brother Scott: I bequeath to you my restaurant, the Fleur-de-Leans. I have faith that you will continue my legacy and make it one of the most exciting and popular restaurants in all of New Orleans.'"

Tiffany, along with her mom, glanced curiously at Scott. He handed Thomas to his wife before addressing them with clasped hands. "Ladies, when Charlie and I talked about this earlier in the day, my first thought was how the two of you would feel about me taking over the restaurant. I wouldn't feel comfortable doing so if you weren't—"

"I love the idea!" Victoria exclaimed. "I think you'd do a great job, Scott. It would be nice to have the three of you back here as well. Y'all have been gone way too long."

"I'm all for it. Plus…" Tiffany approached Thomas, making a sour face while poking his stomach, "I'd get to see this handsome little man more often."

Scott hugged his sister-in-law while saying, "I'm glad to hear that. I promise I won't let anything happen to the restaurant."

"You'll do an incredible job, Uncle Scott."

"So, Ms. Tiffany, now that Scott, Bridgett, and Thomas are returning to New Orleans, does that mean you'll grace the Crescent City with your presence once again?"

The television briefly stole her attention. She watched as Jackson stood next to his parents and brother in what looked to be the Louis Armstrong airport. "It's starting to look that way, Mr. Charlie."

Chapter 60

Every night before laying her head onto her pillow, Cecile Fabacher would retrieve a bottle of perfumed lotion from the nightstand and pour an amount equal to the size of a dime into her palm. After returning the bottle to the drawer, she would rub her hands together several times before massaging the remainder of the lotion onto her feet. It was a practice she learned from her mom at the age of ten. Around the same time she was moisturizing her hands and feet, Andrew Fabacher's hands were clung to a hard-bound book. The subject matter was either politics, religion, or history. Cecile would kiss her husband goodnight and, like clockwork, be asleep several minutes before him. It was extremely rare for her to fall asleep in complete darkness. For the five nights she assumed her youngest son to be dead, Cecile didn't rub lotion onto her hands and feet, her husband didn't read while in bed, and she didn't fall asleep with a light on in the room. Like her husband, the guilt surrounding the truth of her son's existence consumed her. Cecile hated lying, but she and her husband kept a secret that neither knew how or when to reveal. Now that her son's story was national news, she was afraid the secret may come to light.

"Are you sleeping?" she whispered to her husband in the darkened room.

"No."

"Why not?"

"Too much on my mind."

"What are you thinking about?"

"I'm sure the same thing you are."

Cecile glanced at the clock. It had been many years since she last saw 2:30 in the morning. "What if they show the story overseas? What if he finds out?"

"Let's hope he doesn't."

"That doesn't comfort me." Cecile sat up. "We have to tell him before he finds out."

Andrew turned on the reading lamp above his head. With squinted eyes, he told his wife, "Then we do it tomorrow—first thing. I'll tell him."

"No. I have to do it."

Thursday

Chapter 61

An early morning call from my dad asking if he and my mom could meet to talk to me incited a visit to my parents' house. Fear of being caught by a news reporter prevented Delain from accompanying me, however she did drive me to the airport so I could pick up my SUV. Her reasoning for not wanting to be caught on camera was justified. Anyone who watched the newscast was led to believe I was having doubts about marrying my fiancée, which could be a great embarrassment for her.

My heart felt like it was in my throat as I approached my parents' house. The nearly-paralyzing sensation slowly diminished upon realizing that the red and blue flashing lights weren't in their driveway, but instead a few houses down. Parked in front of the police car on St. Charles Avenue was what appeared to be a news van. Next to the driver's window stood an officer. Both the driver and officer were looking in my direction as I pulled into the driveway. Their eyes remained fixed on me as I walked to the front door.

"I'm here," I spoke after stepping into the hallway.

"We're in here," my dad spoke from the portrait room to my immediate left. My parents were sitting on the couch. Both stood to offer me a long embrace.

"There's a cop car a few houses down," I informed them.

"We called it in," my dad said. "That news van has been sitting outside all morning. A reporter was knocking on the neighbors' doors trying to get information about you. They should be moving any minute."

"It feels like I'm dreaming right now," my mom told me. The morning sun rested upon her face. The area beneath her eyes was puffy and her skin much paler than I could remember. She looked exhausted.

"I hope I didn't cause y'all too much stress over the last couple of days."

They returned to the couch in front of the window. I took to the matching one across from them. A rectangular cypress coffee table separated us. My dad's right and my mom's left hand were clasped together as they sat so close to one another that not even a sheet of paper could be wedged between them. Nearly forty years of marriage and they still acted like they had just met and fallen in love.

My dad rolled his eyes. "Stress is a vast understatement, Jax. It was," he looked at my mom then back at me, "the worst few days of our lives. But, you're alive and that's all that matters."

"How much longer do you think the media is going to be involved? They're already starting to piss me off. Delain's afraid to leave her house right now."

"I wouldn't imagine too much longer," he answered. "I don't know what else they would want to know."

The kitchen phone rang. "Family and friends have been calling all morning," my mom informed me as she stood from the couch. "Let me turn off the ringer so we can have some quiet time to talk."

Once she left the room, I whispered to my dad, "Is mom okay? She doesn't look like herself."

"She's tired. The last few days have been a roller coaster ride. She's doing well considering. How's Delain?"

"She's…doing."

"Poor thing. She was so out of it at your funeral. She thought I had cancer."

"I'm not sure why she would say that." I never lied to my parents growing up. I hated it. Over the last two years, though, a few untruths crossed my lips in their presence.

"The phone is silent. Now the three of us can talk." My mom returned to the velvet couch built by my dad's grandfather. When he wasn't brewing beer, my great-grandfather was building furniture. The two velvet couches in the portrait room, one in the living room, the dining table and twelve adjoining chairs, my dad's office desk, the grandiose bar in the parlour, and the book shelves in the study were all built by the man that died before I was born. Every piece looked like it was painstakingly crafted. He passed away while in the process of building a gazebo in the backyard. The roof was never completed, and the unfinished project still remained. My dad didn't want someone else's hands on my ancestor's work, so the structure became a pergola instead.

"I'm glad y'all asked me to come over this morning. I wanted to discuss something with just the two of you." I leaned forward. My forearms rested on my thighs as I gazed at the ground. "First off, I'm truly sorry for what happened over the last few days. I can't imagine what those days were like."

"You don't need to apologize, Jax."

"No, I do," I said, glancing into both of their eyes. "No parent should have to experience what I put the two of you through. I felt horrible knowing that you thought I was dead."

A streetcar passed by outside the window behind them as my mom asked, "You didn't know for very long though, right?"

If my mom wasn't in the room, there was a chance I might have confessed to my dad everything. I would have told him that Delain accidentally killed a man with her car, that Davis blackmailed her into dating him, and then impregnated her and blackmailed her into dating me. I would then tell him everything that happened from the moment I gave Brad my airline ticket to what transpired in Davis' garage. With his background in law and connections throughout the city, he may have been able to help us. I imagined that just before I would tell him, though, paranoia might set in for me. I would worry that something bad might happen to him if he tried to talk to the wrong person. Just before Davis died, he said he was part of something. I didn't know what he meant by 'something', but it had crossed my mind a few times since his death as to what that 'something' was. "No, sir."

"Stop apologizing and stop feeling bad. You're alive. Your mother and I couldn't be happier."

I flashed a forced, closed-lip smile. "I also wanted to ask if you think Father Peter would still be available to preside over the wedding this Saturday if—"

"You're going through with the wedding?" my mom asked. There was no joyous expression on her or my dad's face, but instead the same 'you can't be serious' reaction as when I first informed them of my intentions to marry Delain.

My dad adjusted his posture before speaking, "You said last night you were having doubts about marrying her. Did you have a change of heart in the last few hours?"

"As of right now, I don't think we should get married this Saturday. I was just curious to know if Father Peter would be available in case our plans were to change."

"I'm not sure," my dad stated. "I can call him and find out. Are you expecting a change of plans?"

"Delain wants to go through with it, but I'm being cautious I guess."

"Cautious about…?" my dad inquired.

"Tiffany cheated on me. I never even considered she might do such a thing. Cheating is the worst thing you could do to someone you love. I don't see how two people can stay together after someone is unfaithful. Not that I think Delain would do it, but it crossed my mind while I was at the Denver airport. It scared me. I then wondered if I was moving things along too quickly with her. That's when I turned off my phone and hiked around for a few days." Judging by the look on my parents' faces, one might think I had just told them I had months to live. "Is everything okay?"

After clearing his throat, my dad said, "We're just glad you're sitting right here. It's scary when you think about what could have happened to you out there."

"I know, but I'm alive and well. Now, what is it that y'all wanted to talk to me about?"

"Well," my dad again adjusted himself on the couch, as if it were impossible to get comfortable, "we wanted—"

"To let you know we're behind you if you want to marry Delain," my mom spoke, cutting him off. "You weren't sure when we last talked to you, so that's what we wanted to tell you. You mentioned she has a male friend that you're concerned about, but I don't see her as the lying or cheating type. She seems like a good girl."

"Are you sure? Y'all appeared concerned just a minute ago when I asked if Father Peter was available for the wedding."

My mom looked to my dad as he said, "We, too, were worried it might be too soon, given the fact that sixteen hours ago you were legally dead. But, now that," he looked to my mom, "we've given it some thought, it might be a good thing for the two of you to tie the knot after all. Since you're going to be with her, we can smile again. Right, honey?"

"Right," she spoke, preceded by a subtle grin. I had trouble deciphering if their smiles were forced or genuine. "I guess we better find out if we can still use the cathedral Saturday night."

"And I'll call the relatives to let them know it's back on."

"Hold on a second. I said I wasn't sure about the wedding yet. I was asking just in case. Let's not call any relatives yet, but it wouldn't hurt to see if the cathedral is still available—just in case."

"When do you think you'll know?" my mom asked. "We would need to inform the guests as soon as possible if it's going to happen."

"By this evening. I'll discuss it some more with Delain after the funeral."

"What funeral?"

Chapter 62

Before I could shut my front door, Logan jumped into my arms. With his legs wrapped around my torso like a koala bear clung to a tree, he kissed my cheeks. "Don't ever fake your death again without letting me in on it."

"I didn't fake my death."

He hugged even tighter as he exclaimed, "Dude, I can't believe you're alive! Can we just stay like this for hours?"

I managed to pry him loose. "How have you been?"

"How have I been? An effing wreck. Do you know what you put me through with your shenanigans?"

It had been nine days since I last stood in my living room. Clothes were scattered about the couch, dust was easily visible on the wood coffee table and matching end table, and empty pizza boxes were piled high in the kitchen trash can. "It's a mess in here."

"It's part of my grieving process. We need to talk right now." He pushed me in the direction of the couch. "You can lie to America, but not to me. Sit down." I stumbled backwards onto the couch. He sat next to me.

"What are you talking about?"

"I don't buy that excuse you told the reporter. When you told me you wanted to marry Delain, I saw how happy you were. It was the happiest I had ever seen you. You couldn't wait to be with her. I don't think you were wandering around the country while contemplating marrying her. Something else is going on."

After my dad, and possibly Marcus, Logan was the last person I would reveal my secrets to. I trusted him completely, yet I wasn't ready to reveal anything and drag him into my situation. "I don't tell you everything, Logan."

"No shit, Sherlock," he spoke, shaking his head side to side. "And I thought we were best friends."

"We are best friends."

"Then tell me what you really did over the last few days."

It was awfully tempting, but for his safety, I couldn't. "The truth is I really wasn't sure if I was ready to marry Delain."

Staring curiously at me, Logan remained quiet for several seconds before saying, "Okay. Let's say for a second I believe you. About when did you start to feel this way?"

I told him the truth. "Around Valentine's Day."

With his bare feet resting on the coffee table, he leaned back onto the couch cushions and directed his gaze towards the ceiling. "If memory serves me correctly, that's about the time you started moping around."

He couldn't have been more right. "Maybe so. I don't remember exactly when it started."

With squinted eyes and his head cocked to the right, he again looked at me while stating, "That was also about the time you told me your dad had cancer."

"Was it?"

"You started to have doubts about Delain around the same exact time your dad was diagnosed with cancer."

"Not the exact same time, but close to it."

"Huh." Logan jumped to his feet. "So," he began walking towards the kitchen counter, "if I call your dad right now and ask him how he's doing with his cancer, he'll let me know; correct?" He grabbed his cell phone.

"Yep." I had no choice but to call his bluff.

"Let's see." After scrolling through his phone, he pressed a button and placed the phone to his ear.

"Who are you calling?"

"Your dad. After the funeral he told me to call him whenever I wanted to talk."

That was absolutely something my dad would have told Logan. I sprung to my feet and hastily approached my roommate. He slowly walked backwards into the kitchen, deviously smiling. "Logan, he's got a lot of stuff going on right now. He doesn't want to be reminded about the cancer."

"I just want him to know that I'm praying for him, that's all."

I extended my arm. "Give me the phone, please."

"Mr. F, it's Logan," he spoke into the phone. "What's happening?"

"Logan!" I was seconds away from tackling him and wrestling the phone from his grasp.

"I was just calling to let you know that your son is a horrible liar." He then threw his phone towards me. I glanced down at the screen. Logan never dialed my dad's number. "Start talking, bitch. And this better be damn good." His bluff worked better than mine. He plopped back onto the sofa, hands resting behind his head and his feet atop the coffee table. "Do I have time to make some popcorn?"

"Shut up." I had to give him a reason that was not only believable, but also had some shock value attached with it so it would be more credible. "I didn't want anyone to know what was going on."

"Which was…?"

"You know the girl Caroline that interned with me for a while?"

"How could I forget her?" The two met when Logan picked me up from work one day for lunch. "She was smoking hot. Even at the funeral she looked sexy."

"Well…"

"You banged her?!" he asked, way too enthusiastically.

"No, but…"

Wide-eyed and grinning, he asked, "But what? A Joe Blob?"

"What is that?"

"Rearrange some of the letters, Dr. Ruth."

"No, dummy. She recently confessed to having feelings for me."

"Sweet!"

"No, it's not sweet. That's why I was having doubts about marrying Delain, and that's why I was a little down over the last few months. I didn't know what to do. I should have talked to you instead of lying about my dad having cancer."

"Yes, you were a dumbass, but hopefully you've learned from your stupidity. As for Caroline, I thought she was engaged."

"Not anymore."

"Why not?"

"She's not ready to get married."

"Because of you?"

I shrugged my shoulders. "Maybe."

"You old dog you! Do you have feelings for her? If so, I don't blame you."

"Perhaps."

Logan's feet danced in unison on the coffee table as he smiled. "Uh-oh. Sounds like you got yourself a little love triangle thing going on."

"Something like that."

"What are you going to do?"

"I don't know."

He jumped to his feet. "I got it!"

"You got what?"

"A solution to your problem. Convert to that religion where you can have more than one wife, and marry both girls. Then you can have your own reality show. People would love to watch two hot girls married to a somewhat attractive guy. Do either of the two show even the slightest signs of lesbianism? That should increase ratings of the show. I can be the wacky best friend that's always popping in—shirtless, of course."

"I'm trying to be serious, Logan."

"You know I'm never serious, but I'll try for a brief moment. Here's my two cents on the matter: don't marry Delain."

I wasn't really looking for advice from him, but grew curious by his suggestion. "Why do you say that?"

"If you're having doubts, don't do it. It's as simple as that. If you have a crush on Caroline, hang out with her some more and see if it's more than a crush. Don't rush into anything, and don't ever lie to me again."

"Yes, sir."

"Since we're on the subject matter, and because we're being honest, can I share something about Delain?"

"Is this coming from serious Logan or normal Logan?"

"Serious."

"Let's hear it then." I took to the loveseat next to the couch.

"I like her, I really do, but I feel like she's hiding something or running away from something or someone."

I tried my best to look at him like I wasn't surprised by his remark. "What do you mean?"

"First of all, she doesn't have a Facebook account. Everyone has a Facebook account. My mom has one and she doesn't even know how to use it. She keeps poking me.

I had to tell her to stop doing that. Secondly, Delain didn't tell me goodbye at your parents' house after the funeral. She just rushed out of there. Marcus told me that she didn't say goodbye to him or his wife either. We both found that a bit odd. Thirdly—and this might be a big one so listen up—when I asked her one weekend when she was over here what the two of you were doing, she told me y'all's plans, but called you someone else's name."

"What name?"

"Tyler. I waited for her to correct herself, but she never did. She didn't even realize that she called you the wrong name. You were in the shower while we were talking. I thought about telling you when you got out, but you were feeling down because of your dad's cancer—or so I thought. Do you know if there's a Tyler in her life? Maybe she has a crush on someone else too."

I knew that her ex's name was Tyler, and on our first date I sensed that she still wasn't over his death. It seemed, well over a year later, she still may not have been over his death. The dilemma of whether or not to tell Logan crossed my mind several times in the split-second that it took for me to open my mouth and tell him, "She dated someone named Tyler for about two years."

Logan rolled his eyes. "Mystery solved. Was she in love with him?"

"I'm pretty certain she was."

"You might want to find out if she's still in love with him. Judging by the fact she said his name instead of yours, I would think that answer is a yes."

"It doesn't matter."

"The shit it does."

"He's dead, Logan. He died in a car wreck before she and I met."

"Oh. Well, do you think she's over him?"

"I don't know."

"Good thing he's not around to come back and sweep her off her feet."

Chapter 63

Tiffany glanced at the recent text from her boyfriend as she lay on her parents' bed. *'Taking off now. See you soon. Love you.'* The words 'I love you' crossed Brett's lips first. He proclaimed them at dinner while celebrating their half-anniversary, three months earlier. Tiffany repeated the three words. It was the first time she had declared her love to a significant other since the night before her wedding. She wasn't ready to say the 'L' word, but felt obligated to say it back. If Brett spoke the words occasionally, she wouldn't have an issue with it. Brett, however, seemed to utter the three-word phrase at least ten times a day. The constant proclamation of his love was starting to annoy her.

Victoria stuck her head out of the master bathroom. "You want to grab a bite to eat before you pick Brett up from the airport?" Purple curlers occupied the lower half of her hair.

Tiffany subtly smiled. "When's the last time you wore rollers in your hair?"

"Your father used to love it when I curled my hair. It's been a few years now."

Tiffany's smile faded upon hearing a reference to her dad. "I'm not that hungry." She had barely eaten in the last few days. "But I should probably eat something." She rolled onto her stomach and proceeded to reply to Brett's text.

"I'm not sure why, but I'm craving beignets. I haven't had them in years. How's Café Du Monde sound?"

'See you at the airport'. Tiffany thought about adding 'love you too' at the end of the text, but decided to put her foot down. After the funeral, she was going to tell Brett that he says 'I love you' too much. She imagined he might be taken aback by it, but it's how she felt and he needed to know. "I don't know if beignets are the best thing to eat while wearing black."

"Good point. How about a sandwich at Maspero's?"

"That's fine." Tiffany set the phone down. While facing the headboard, she noticed markings along one of the eight vertical columns. The marks looked like something had been attached to the column, and then rubbed against it several times. "Mom, how long has this been here?" Her father was meticulous when it came to the condition of his house and car. If something marked up a wall anywhere in the house, Davis had fresh paint over it by the end of the day. If one of the foot-long wood columns were scratched on his headboard, he would have applied the proper wood stain to it immediately.

Victoria emerged from the bathroom in a robe. While leaning over the bed to get a closer look at the scraped column, she told her daughter, "I have no idea. I've never seen it before. It couldn't have been there for long. Your father wouldn't allow it to stay flawed like that. To be honest, I don't want to know how the scratches got there."

If the markings on the headboard were the only thing she found uncharacteristic in the house, Tiffany wouldn't have thought much about it. But the combination of the headboard markings, along with the even more bizarre discovery of a kitchen knife under the couch had Tiffany curious and slightly paranoid. She stood from the bed, glancing around the bedroom before approaching and inspecting the French doors leading to the fenced-in backyard. The locks didn't look like they had been tampered with. She then walked around the bedroom. Nothing else caught her eye. She meticulously inspected every window and door throughout the house. After noticing nothing out of the ordinary, she returned to the bed and placed her nose against the comforter. She detected the faint aroma of a perfume she had never smelled before.

"Mom, do you have any perfume with you I can borrow?"

"Of course. It's in here in my bag," she spoke from the bathroom.

"What kind?"

"Just the same brand I've been wearing since you were born."

"Is Chanel the only perfume you have with you?"

"Yes. You know that's the only kind I ever wear."

Tiffany knew exactly what Chanel smelled like. The scent on her parents' comforter was not Chanel. There was never direct evidence of him doing so, but Tiffany would not have been shocked to discover that her dad had cheated on her mom at some point during their marriage. If it did happen, however, she didn't want to find out about it, especially on the day of his burial. She turned over on the bed, trying to get the notion out of her head. What couldn't escape her thoughts over the next few minutes was the knife. Curiosity got the better of her.

In the living room, she dropped to her knees and placed her left cheek to the floor. A thorough examination below the couch revealed no other foreign objects beneath it. *Was the knife placed underneath here? Maybe it was thrown under here? Or perhaps kicked?* Tiffany proceeded to crawl on all fours while closely inspecting the hardwood flooring. She soon made a discovery. Next to the windows by the backdoor was a centimeter-long incision in the floor. It looked like something sharp created the mark. Tiffany grabbed the knife from the counter block and placed it— with the handle straight up and the tip of the blade due south—carefully into the incision. She let go. The knife stood perfectly straight.

The knife fell here, stuck into the floor, and then was kicked about twenty feet across the floor, stopping under the couch. Why? Dad, what were you up to?

While her mom continued to ready herself for the funeral, Tiffany scoured the house with a microscopic eye. The guest bedrooms appeared untouched, as did her dad's office and the guest bathroom. The police had already searched the game room. Nothing seemed out of the ordinary. Still, she scrutinized the room, before stepping into the garage.

Tiffany found difficulty standing only a few feet away from where her father was believed to have taken his last breath. Since being told the Ferrari was legally hers less than twelve hours earlier, Tiffany imagined she would sell her father's prized possession since it doubled as his casket for several hours. As she sat on the hood of the car, a thought popped in her head. *Dad won't be there to walk me down the aisle when I marry Brett.* Before tears could begin to trickle down her cheeks, she noticed something else peculiar. On the beige frame surrounding the door leading into the house, a marking red in color and about an inch in length stood out. Tiffany knelt next to the door. A closer inspection led her to believe that the darkened spot was not paint, but most likely blood. Further inspection of the garage turned up no more splotch sightings, but she did notice a roll of gray duct tape not neatly stacked atop the three other rolls of tape. An uncharacteristically misplaced roll of tape, a blemish that closely resembled blood, markings on the headboard and the living room floor, and—the most prevalent item to cause concern—the severely misplaced kitchen knife, all combined to create a moderate level of uneasiness for Tiffany. She went back inside to grab her cell phone from the bed.

"I'm almost ready," Victoria spoke from the bathroom.

Tiffany scrolled through her phone on her way out of the bedroom. "Okay." After locating the contact, she dialed the number and stepped into the kitchen.

"Tiff?" a male's voice asked.

"Hey, Mitch."

"How you holding up, sweetie?"

"I've been better. I need a favor."

"Anything for my former partner's daughter."

Mitch was one of three men who were partners with her father while he was on the police force. He was the only one of the three she liked, and the only one who was still active in law enforcement, as an agent for the F.B.I. "Do you mind stopping by the house? I need to show you something."

"Of course. Is everything okay?"

"I think so."

"When do you want me to come by?"

"Um…." She walked back into the bedroom, covering the phone with her left hand. "Mom, how much longer until you're ready to go?"

"Give me ten minutes."

Tiffany removed her hand from the phone on her way out of the bedroom. "In about twenty minutes, Mitch."

"Okay. I'll see you in a bit."

Chapter 64

I had yet to step on a scale, but in the last six days I would guess a good eight to ten pounds had escaped me. My weight loss was incited by guilt. Guilt over Davis, Cliff, and even Hank's death; guilt over whether or not I was ready to marry someone when I had strong feelings for someone else too; and guilt from lying to loved ones as well as federal agents. Another source of my guilt was the death of a young man who would never get to propose to his girlfriend. According to the obituary in *The Times Picayune*, Bradley Boudreaux's funeral was to start at 3:00 in the afternoon, an hour before Davis' was to begin. I wasn't sure how Brad's girlfriend (whose name I couldn't recall) would greet me. For all I knew, she might tell me how horrible of a person I was for allowing Brad to board the plane in my place, and then have me escorted out of the funeral home. It didn't matter what would happen. I felt I had to go, and was grateful Delain offered to accompany me.

While grabbing the black suit I purchased during my stay in Las Vegas, memories of the six-week stay came to mind. Over the past twenty months, it wasn't uncommon for me to occasionally think about my irrational behavior during my brief time away from home. Yet for some reason, as I slipped my arms through the jacket sleeves, I felt tightness in my chest, followed by an abnormally quick beating of my heart. Shortness of breath soon followed, prompting me to sit on the bed. I shut my eyes and was soon able to return my breathing to normal. Within about a minute, what I assumed to be a mild panic attack passed. I finished getting dressed then knocked on Logan's bedroom door. "Logan, I'm leaving. I'll see you later." There was no response. I assumed he was taking a shower or napping, so I didn't bother to knock louder. After opening the front door and stepping outside, Logan's whereabouts were no longer a mystery. My roommate, wearing nothing but his royal blue Speedo, stood on the front lawn with a whiskey drink in one hand and the garden hose in the other. A short, stout man with a video camera stood drenched at the end of the driveway. Another man, who appeared to be out of reach from being squirted with the hose, filmed the incident from behind the hood of a news van across the street.

"You ruined my camera!" shouted the stout man.

"I was watering the grass and you got in the way, Chubbs." Logan sipped his cocktail while squirting the man once more. My best friend then chuckled like a seven-year-old would upon hearing someone pass gas in public.

"I'm gonna sue you!"

"Get in line, Chubby Checker!"

"What's going on, Logan?"

"These leaches are invading our privacy," he yelled loud enough for both men to hear, "so I'm retaliating! This is kind of fun." He then attempted unsuccessfully to squirt the other man across the street. "Get a real job! I'm sure your mail order brides are so proud of y'all!"

There were times when Logan embarrassed the hell out of me, and there were instances when I was proud to have him on my side. The incident on my lawn was somewhere in the middle, but leaning towards the proud side. "I'm off to the funeral. I should be back tonight," I whispered to him.

"Wait. Watch this. That one over there thinks he's a safe distance away. I've been toying with him." He handed me his drink before subtly turning the nozzle. With a quick aim, Logan successfully squirted the second camera man, who then ducked for cover behind the van. "Leave Jackson alone! The story's over, assholes!" Logan continued spraying the water towards the van's doors as I hurried to my SUV. "Go home and whack off while watching your anime porn, you sick bastards!"

Since camera crews had yet to park their vans outside of Delain's townhouse, we imagined they didn't know where she lived. Because she was renting the house and getting her mail delivered to the post office, it was more challenging for them to find her. I made sure to make several wrong turns, to be on the safe side, as I drove through her neighborhood to pick her up.

Once we pulled onto the interstate en route to the funeral home, I told Delain about the news van outside my house.

"How much longer are they going to keep following you?" she asked.

"I don't know."

"They're making me even more nervous."

"Me too." Talking about it wasn't helping my anxiety. "Thank you for coming to the funeral with me."

"I know it's a difficult thing to do, but I want to be here for you." She then squeezed my right thigh before rubbing it. "What did your parents want to talk to you about this morning?"

"To be honest, I'm not quite sure. They seemed…off this morning."

"What do you mean?"

"I get a feeling as if they want to tell me something, but are holding back."

"Maybe it's because they thought you were dead for several days."

"Possibly. I didn't pry since my stress levels are already high enough right now. If it was really important, though, they would have told me. Speaking of parents, I know nothing about yours. Is what you told me in the past true?"

The gentle thigh rubbing came to a stop. "I guess it's about time we talk about that." With both hands resting in her lap, she cleared her throat. "I told you my parents live in Portland. In actuality, they live in Arizona, and they know nothing about you."

Hearing that the woman I was considering marrying had yet to tell her parents about me didn't invoke feelings of pleasantry. "No wonder I couldn't find your dad's phone number when I tried calling him to ask for your hand in marriage."

"I'm so sorry about that. I felt horrible when you said you tried to call him. But to be honest, they don't know much about my life over the last three years. My dad was active in the Marine Corps for nearly three decades. He was very protective over me growing up. If he would have known what Davis was doing to me, he would have driven down to New Orleans and beat Davis to within an inch of his life. I couldn't let that happen."

"They never knew you were getting married in two days, huh?"

She shook her head. "No, and they had no idea I was ever pregnant either. Living several states away made it easier to hide the truth."

"When were you going to tell them?"

"About the baby?"

"The marriage and the baby."

"I don't know," she replied with a shrug, "maybe whenever this whole thing was over. I couldn't get them involved or let you know the truth about who they were. I imagined after I left you at the altar, you might try to contact them. Who knows what would have happened then. Once I got Caleb back, I would have told them I met someone, got knocked up, and that the father is no longer in the picture. And if you and I would have ended up together, I would have told them how you came into my life and made everything wonderful."

"If you didn't tell them about me or the wedding, who was going to walk you down the aisle?"

"Davis hired two people to pretend to be my parents." Delain again placed her left hand on my thigh. "I'm so sorry I didn't tell you sooner. I wanted to tell you, but I haven't gotten to see much of you since Davis' death. I know it's difficult to hear."

Even though I understood why she had to lie to me to protect herself and her son, it was still a hard blow to the gut. I turned to her. There was a look of great sadness in her eyes, making it impossible for me to be angry with her. "It's…okay."

"It's not okay, Jackson. I feel horrible for how I treated you."

"You had no choice."

"I wished I could have told you the truth once I started to develop feelings for you. I should have confessed, and then the two of us could have come up with a plan to take down Davis." She was starting to once again sound like the woman I wanted to be with. "I know you would have come up with something because you haven't let me down since the first day I met you."

"Speaking of the first day we met—that guy that was yelling at you outside the bank. He was…?"

"I don't know who he was, but Davis knew him. When I first saw you outside the funeral home, I had no idea how I was going to meet you. After you drove off, I followed you. When you left your parents' house and went to the bank, I called Davis. Within minutes, the guy showed up. What you saw was rehearsed just seconds before you came out of the bank. Davis probably had that guy follow me while I was following you; that's why he showed up so quickly."

"I had a feeling our first encounter was staged."

"I'm so sorry, baby."

I found myself becoming increasingly upset as I learned the truth. Still, I didn't feel the need to let her know, as it wouldn't have helped the situation. "You did what you had to do. It's just a lot to take in. I imagine that dating Davis was—"

"Horrendous, frightening, and sickening are a few words that come to mind. We dated for a month, but it felt like a year. I was so depressed. Luckily, I found out he was married and saw it as my way out. When I told him we were breaking up, he grabbed my arm and said I wasn't leaving him. I threatened to tell his wife if he didn't let me leave. He threatened to go to the police and tell them I killed the man behind his restaurant. I took my chances. Turns out he was bluffing."

"And when did you find out you were pregnant with his child?"

"The same night I broke up with him. I told him the next day."

"And that's when he hit you?"

She nodded. "In the living room of his condo."

"What condo?"

"He has one in the French Quarter, on the corner of Royal and Orleans. It's directly behind the cathedral."

"That's where y'all…had sex." The words made my stomach turn.

She again nodded. "Thank God I was drugged and can't remember having sex with him."

As we pulled into the funeral home parking lot I asked, "Then how do you know you did it?"

"When I awoke the next morning, my clothes were on the floor and I was sore. I asked him if we had sex and he said yes. The pregnancy test confirmed everything."

Hearing the story again convinced me that I made the right choice by not retrieving Davis' nitroglycerin pills during his fatal heart attack. "I'm just thankful he can no longer hurt you."

She affectionately squeezed my hand. "Me too."

Delain and I sat in the back of the funeral home as a minister presided over the indoor funeral. Upon spotting Brad's girlfriend at the front of the room, her name came to me. Brittany looked just as she did in the picture Brad showed me six days earlier—pearl earrings and a matching necklace, along with a thick black band that held her hair back. Judging by the half-dozen tearful, blank stares she gave me throughout the service, I got the impression she didn't care for me very much. Still, I had to offer my condolences.

Once the ceremony was complete, Brittany wasted no time in making her way towards us. I braced myself as she grew closer, anticipating a slap or verbal assault for sending her boyfriend to his death.

"Jackson Fabacher?" She clutched a handkerchief in her left hand and a black purse in her right.

I nodded. "Brittany?" Neither of us extended a hand to shake.

"I imagine you spoke with Bradley before he boarded the plane."

"Yes."

"You're the last living person to speak with him before he…died."

I again nodded.

Brittany turned her head as someone placed their hand on her shoulder. I could see her jaw tighten as she held back tears. Upon facing us once again, she asked Delain, "Are you the mysterious fiancée the news has been talking about?"

"Yes. I'm Delain."

"I'm Brittany Sinclaire."

"It's a pleasure to meet you, Brittany. I'm so sorry for your loss."

"Thank you."

Delain, I could see, was on the verge of crying as well. Despite the fact there was still some uncertainty about my fiancée, I knew one thing about her—she was a sucker for love.

"Jackson, I would like to talk to you in a little while, if you don't mind. Someplace quieter."

There was only one answer I could have given Brittany. "Of course."

"There's a coffee shop in the Quarter called the Chick-ory. It was Bradley's favorite place to get coffee. Have you heard of it?"

"I have."

"Can you meet me there in an hour?"

"Yes."

"Can you come too, Delain?"

Delain was slow to answer. "Of course."

Chapter 65

Tiffany opened the front door before the doorbell could finish its lengthy chime. Mitch's right hand hovered just above his holstered gun as he asked, "Are you okay?"

"I think so."

Tiffany always felt safe in Mitch's presence. It was hard not to. At 6'2" and 225 pounds of ripped muscle, Mitch Hennessey filled his spare time by teaching a mixed martial arts class two nights a week. When not working or teaching, the never-married, forty-one-year-old federal agent spent his evenings in some of the swankier bars in New Orleans, mingling with women of all ages. When asked why he had never married, his answer to Tiffany was that he had more fun being single, and doubted that he would ever meet a woman that would make him want to settle down. She appreciated his honesty, even if she didn't agree with his lifestyle.

"Please come in. I need your opinion about something."

"We need to make it quick, or we're going to miss the funeral."

Tiffany shut the door behind him. "This won't take long." She led him in the direction of her parents' bedroom.

"Where's your mom?"

"She left a little while ago to grab a bite to eat before for the funeral. I told her to go on without me."

"And what about your boyfriend?"

"I have to pick him up at the airport. In fact," she glanced at her watch, "I think he's about to land." After walking into the bedroom, Tiffany turned to face Mitch. Her back was to the bed. "Did y'all do any type of investigating around the house after Dad's body was found?"

"They did a brief search inside and around the house for anything suspicious."

"Was it thorough?"

"About as thorough as a search can be when it's suspected that the victim died from either a heart attack or accidental carbon monoxide poisoning. Why?"

"Ever since I can remember, Dad was very meticulous about keeping everything tidy and perfectly clean. It felt like I lived in a museum in this house."

Mitch nodded. "I think it's safe to say he had a little O.C.D. His desk at work was always perfect. If someone moved something out of place, he noticed immediately and got a little ticked."

"That's my father." She pointed towards the bed. "Look at the headboard."

Mitch slid his hands through his shoulder-length, dirty-blonde hair several times, tying it back into a ponytail as he approached the bed. Without touching the headboard, he leaned forward. "It's a little scratched. What are you suggesting?"

"I don't know. Follow me." She next led him to the garage, presenting her findings in increasingly suspicious order. She pointed to the duct tape, several feet away from the neatly stacked column of three rolls. "Dad always put stuff back in the exact place."

"Okay," he said with a shrug of his shoulders.

"I'm not finished." She next pointed to the bottom of the door frame leading inside the house. "What does that spot look like?"

Mitch knelt in front of the door. "Like something red in color was hit against the frame."

"Doesn't it look like blood?"

"Possibly."

"I still don't have you convinced, huh?"

"I'm not quite sure what you're trying to convince me of," he answered upon standing.

"Let me show you one more thing." She walked him into the kitchen. "Last night, my aunt, uncle, Mom, Charlie, and myself were discussing Dad's will. All of a sudden, my nephew pulled," she retrieved the large kitchen knife from the wood block, "this knife from beneath the couch. Do you think Dad would let a knife just sit under the couch?"

Mitch's dirty-blonde eyebrows grew closer to one another. Puzzled, he told her, "No, he would not."

"And check this out." She walked into the living room where she knelt next to the tiny slit on the floor. After placing the knife blade into it, she let go. The knife stood perpendicular to the floorboards. "I think this knife was right here before being kicked or thrown across the floor, stopping beneath the couch."

Mitch's hazel eyes stared inquisitively at the knife, and then along a path leading to the couch several times. He pretended to kick the knife with his foot. Nothing stood in the way of the knife's projected trajectory to the couch. "It is possible that the knife was kicked from this spot towards the couch."

"Very possible." As Tiffany bent over to grab the knife, Mitch swatted her hand before she could touch it.

"Don't touch it." He removed a handkerchief from his pocket. "I need a plastic bag."

"But I already touched it."

"It's okay."

Tiffany retrieved a Ziploc bag from the pantry. With the handkerchief in his left hand, Mitch grabbed then placed the knife inside the plastic bag.

"What do you think happened here, Mitch?"

"I don't know. Do you have any latex gloves?"

Tiffany opened the cabinets beneath the sink. She held up a pair of yellow rubber gloves. "What about these?"

"I have some in the car. I'll be right back."

Tiffany anxiously looked at the mark on the floor, starting to wonder if perhaps her dad's heart attack was linked to the knife, the marked-up headboard, the misplaced roll of duct tape, and the mysterious spot on the door frame. Before she could begin to contemplate what happened in the house, her cell phone rang. It was her boyfriend.

"Baby, we just landed. Where are you?"

"Stuck in traffic. I'm on my way."

"Okay. I'll grab a drink at the bar. I can't wait to see you."

"Me too."

"I love you."

Tiffany hesitated before replying, "I'll see you soon." She hung up, not ready to leave.

Mitch entered the house, a pair of latex gloves already covering his hands, and walked straight into the bedroom. Without touching the bed, he leaned close to the markings on the vertical column of the headboard. Delicately, he traced his pointer finger along the scratches.

"Rope marks," Tiffany asked.

"No. Something harder. Maybe…hold on." He hurried to his car, returning with a pair of handcuffs. Eight columns were carved into the king-sized headboard. The markings were on the second column from the left. He placed the cuffs against the first column. "I need to test something. Is it okay?"

"Go for it," Tiffany replied with crossed arms.

After examining the column once more, he placed one of the cuffs around it. While grabbing the other end of the handcuffs, he jerked it up and down several times. "Look."

Tiffany leaned forward. "The marks are pretty much identical."

"Yep."

"So, someone was handcuffed to the bed?"

"It appears so."

"What do you think Dad was up to?"

Mitch didn't make eye contact with Tiffany as he answered, "I don't know."

She felt he was withholding information from her. "You sure about that?"

After redirecting his gaze towards the headboard, he answered, "Yep."

"Mitch, you're holding back. What are you not telling me?"

"Nothing," he replied, continuing to look away from Tiffany.

She placed her hand on his shoulder. "I'm freaking out a little bit right now because I think maybe Dad was possibly involved in some sort of conflict the night he died. You better tell me if you know something."

Mitch finally locked eyes with her. "Why were your mom and dad separated before he passed away?"

"She said he was never around anymore. She got tired of being by herself. She thought if she left him, he'd beg her to come back home."

While removing the latex gloves, he asked, "What did your dad tell you?"

"Nothing. He wouldn't give me a straight answer. What did he tell you?"

Mitch was slow to answer. "Nothing."

"He didn't tell you—his closest friend—why he was separated from my mom?"

"No."

Tiffany hated being lied to. "Bullshit. We both know you're lying. I want to know what you know right now, Mitch."

"I don't—"

"Tell me now!" yelled a red-faced Tiffany. "I want to know the truth!"

Mitch's face was void of expression as he told her, "Your dad…" His voice trailed off.

"Say it, Goddamnit!"

"Your dad…liked women."

What Tiffany suspected for years was finally being brought to light. "Liked?"

"He…may have had a…girlfriend on the side."

Tiffany wanted to doubt Mitch's claim, but knew it was true. "I had a feeling."

"I'm sorry you had to find out."

"Me too."

"I think these markings are from him and—"

"Enough said. Dad was into the kinky stuff, and not with my mom. I get it."

"Do you want me to see if the mark on the garage door is blood?"

Tiffany grew worrisome that the blood belonged to some skanky slut her dad was sleeping with. She didn't want news getting out about his adulterous ways. "Don't worry about it." When Tiffany awoke hours earlier, she experienced great sadness in knowing she had to bury her father in the afternoon. Mitch's disclosure that he was unfaithful to her mother for what was probably more than one occasion created an even greater feeling of sorrow. "I need to use the restroom. I'll see you at the cathedral."

"I'm sorry, Tiffany."

"Don't be. You didn't do anything wrong. Thanks for coming over, Mitch."

While staring into the bathroom mirror, Tiffany pictured her dad handcuffed to his headboard, while a twenty-something year old sat on top of him, perhaps taunting him with a knife in some sort of sick and twisted sex act. Her only hope was that her mom and the public would never discover the truth. After reapplying mascara, she remembered that Brett was waiting for her at the airport. She needed to be in his arms.

With her purse in one hand and keys in the other, she opened the front door. Mitch's car was still in the driveway. He wasn't in it. "Mitch!" she yelled from the living room.

"In the garage!" he yelled back.

She walked into the garage to find Mitch leaning over the driver's seat of her dad's Ferrari. Latex gloves, once again, covered his hands. "What are you doing?"

"This is interesting."

She walked towards him. "What?"

"The knife under the couch did seem odd to me. I came to see if I could find anything suspicious in here. Put this on." He removed then handed her one of his gloves. "Now, slowly and very lightly trace your fingers around the entire steering wheel."

The touch was very smooth, with the exception of two spots that were slightly rough, almost sticky. "What is that?"

Mitch grabbed the duct tape. "Well, since the two non-smooth spots are the exact width of this duct tape, and since you pointed out that the roll of duct tape was misplaced, it leads me to believe that someone was bound to the steering wheel with this tape." Mitch retrieved then scrolled through his phone before placing it to his ear. "And knowing how much your father loved this car, I don't know if he would allow anyone to be duct taped to the steering wheel."

"Who do you think was duct taped to it?"

"Your dad was found dead right in front of it."

"You think someone bound him to it?"

"Pete," Mitch spoke into the phone. "I need you to come to Davis' house….I know it's starting soon, but I need your forensics expertise pronto…At the base of the garage door—possible blood sample. I need it sent to the lab and I need the results quickly…The side door will be open. And, Pete, keep this on the hush." He hung up. "Is it an open casket?"

"Yes."

"I need to see your dad before they bury him."

"Why?"

"Possible evidence of his murder."

Chapter 66

Cool air blew from an overhead vent onto Delain and me as we sat across the table from Brittany. In the thirty minutes since we last saw her, she showed further signs of someone suffering an agonizing heartbreak—cheeks smeared with mascara, a nose rubbed raw from numerous tissue wipes, and a look suggesting her smile wouldn't surface for months, perhaps years. The reasoning behind her desire to talk to both Delain and me still remained a mystery.

"Thank you for meeting with me, Jackson," Brittany spoke. Her forearms rested on the table, her fingers interwoven with one another, "and you as well, Delain. I know it might be a strange request, considering we have never met."

Delain, sitting to my left, made the conscious effort to hold my hand beneath the table, rather than on top. I imagine she did so out of respect for Brittany's recent loss.

"You're very welcome," I told her. "And I don't think it's strange."

A woman with Auburn hair tied back into a ponytail approached our table. "Welcome to Chick-ory, ladies and gentleman." Her nametag read 'Georgia'.

"Hello," I spoke.

"Y'all must be coming from Davis' funeral too. I just got back myself a little while ago," she spoke with downturned lips and a subtle shaking of her head. "A good man was buried today."

It seemed everyone was deceived into thinking Davis was a saint. "No," I sternly told her, "we're coming from another funeral."

"I'm so sorry for your loss. What can I get y'all to drink?"

"Coffee please," Brittany said.

"Same for me," Delain, her gaze aimed towards the table, told her.

"Hot tea please."

"You got…wait a minute." Georgia's stare intensified as she pointed her pen towards me. "You're the guy from T.V. You were on the news last night."

There was no sense in trying to lie. "Yes."

"No kidding." She grinned. "Aren't you glad you gave up that ticket on the plane?"

I'm not sure how, but Brittany managed to keep from breaking down into tears as a stranger reminded her of her loss. Georgia didn't realize it, but her comments were not well-received by anyone at the table. She was quickly becoming someone I didn't care to speak with. "We're in a bit of a rush, Georgia. Can we get the drink order in please?"

"Of course. Sorry about that."

Brittany's eyes followed Georgia as she walked away. "No one close to me has died before. That was the first funeral I have ever been to." Once Georgia stood behind the counter, Brittany's gaze returned to us. The look on her face was one of the saddest I had seen. Since I was part of the reason her boyfriend was deceased, my anxiety levels continued to creep upward. "Jackson, I was hoping you would be at the funeral this afternoon."

I wanted to ask why, but instead replied with, "It was a beautiful service." It was the most cliché comment I could have given.

"When I heard he exchanged tickets with you, I imagined the two of you conversed with one another. This may sound peculiar, but I would love to know what the two of you talked about."

A dilemma presented itself. I had mere seconds to decide whether to tell her the whole truth, which, more than likely, would produce several tears, or tell her the partial truth and perhaps save her some heartache. "Brad asked if I was from New Orleans. He noticed a fleur-de-lis tag hanging from my carry-on. I told him that I was. He said he had lived here all his life, and then he talked about how good the food was." I stopped, not wanting to say much more.

"He does, I mean, did, love the food here. If he hadn't become a dentist, he was going to attend culinary school. He was such an amazing cook. What else did the two of you talk about?"

I turned to Delain. We had yet to discuss the reason behind Brad's wanting to take an earlier flight home. If we had talked about it, I would have looked for a subtle nod instructing me to tell Brittany everything, or a slight shake of the head suggesting I shouldn't mention the engagement. I needed her opinion. "This may be rude, Brittany, but do you mind if I take Delain outside for about fifteen seconds?"

"Not at all."

I let go of Delain's hand as we made our way outside. The Chick-ory had six floor-to-ceiling glassless 'windows' encompassing the corner-lot establishment. I made sure we were in between two of the windows, out of Brittany's sight.

Delain curiously looked on as she asked, "Is everything okay?"

"I don't know what to tell her?"

"What do you mean?"

"Brad was going to propose to her."

Delain sighed. "Oh crap."

"Do I tell the truth?"

She glanced upward while in thought. The descending sun had cast hues of red, orange, and purple into the sky. It was one of the most beautiful sunsets I had ever seen. "I think you need to."

"I figured you'd say that."

"She needs to know the truth."

"You're right. I don't want to upset her any more, though."

"I'd want to know the truth. Wouldn't you?"

Judging by the repetitive bouncing of Brittany's knees (a trait shared with her late-boyfriend), she was anxiously awaiting our return. As I grew closer to the table, she looked to be shaking.

"I'm sorry about that, Brittany. Are you cold?" I asked.

"A little. The air is blowing right on me." Without asking permission, I placed my jacket around her shoulders before sitting down. "Thank you. Is everything okay? I hope I'm not putting you on the spot, Jackson."

"You're not. As for my conversation with Brad in the airport, there is more."

"I had a feeling there might be. Please tell me everything," she begged. "I have to know."

Delain again grabbed my hand beneath the table as I began. "Brad talked about you. He even showed me a picture of you that he carried in his wallet."

"What did he say about me?"

"How much he loved you."

Her bottom lip began to quiver. "Anything else?"

Delain firmly squeezed my hand as an already depressed young woman was about to receive information that was likely to further sadden her. I hated that I had to tell her. "Brittany, the reason Brad and I switched flights is because he was in a rush to get home."

"Why?"

It was time to rip off the band-aid. "He was going to…propose to you this past weekend."

Brittany's lips ceased quivering, the look of sadness in her eyes turned to a blank stare, and her jaw became relaxed. "I knew it," she mumbled.

"I'm sorry you had to find out this way."

Her blank stare continued as she calmly asked, "Did he tell you how he was going to propose?"

"Yes."

"Please tell me."

"Here we are." Georgia placed two coffees and a tea on the table. "I don't mean to be nosy, but do you have a sister?"

I glanced upward to see Georgia staring curiously at Delain.

"No."

"I had a customer yesterday that looked just like you, but with blonde hair."

"I'm an only child."

"You must have a twin out there. Y'all enjoy. Let me know if I can get you anything else." As Georgia walked off, Delain shrugged her shoulders.

Brittany's trance-like stare vanished, giving way to a look of despair. "How was he going to do it, Jackson? I need to know."

I uncomfortably began. "Dinner was first. He was going to bring you to—"

"The Fleur-de-Leans?"

I nodded. "How did you know?"

"That was where we went on our first date. It was our favorite restaurant. Have you two eaten there?"

"No," Delain blurted out.

"We met Davis a few times," Brittany said. "He was so nice to us."

Delain gave me a look as if to say 'what is wrong with everyone?' "I've heard other things about him, but that's for another conversation," she told Brittany.

"So, Brad was going to propose to me at the Fleur-de-Leans?"

"No. That was just the beginning of the evening. Next, he was bringing you to Rock n' Bowl. Some band was playing there that he wanted you to hear, but I can't remember their name."

"Five Finger Discount?"

"That's the one."

A grin, ever-so-slightly, appeared on her face. "On our second date, we shared our first kiss. It was on the dance floor of Rock n' Bowl. That was the band playing that night."

"He said you made a comment that night how they would make a great wedding band."

"I did." She looked to be on the verge of crying. It was obvious she was using great restraint to keep from breaking down in the crowded coffee shop. "He was such a good listener. Is that where he was proposing?"

I shook my head. "Afterwards he was bringing you, and I apologize because I don't remember the location, but a house somewhere in the city, I think on Oak Street."

Brittany covered her mouth with both hands. "Oh my God."

"You know the house?"

The battle to subdue her crying raged on. While nodding, her hands began to tremble and her jaw again tightened. Upon lowering her hands, she told us, "My dad died from ALS when I was ten. He was only thirty-seven years old. His insurance didn't pay very much for his treatments, so he and my mom had to use all of their savings." She paused, inhaling deeply before continuing. "Because he was young, and the disease snuck up on him, he didn't have time to establish a life insurance policy. My mom went back to work, but after a year, she could no longer afford the mortgage. The house was my parents' dream home. The first three years they lived there were spent meticulously restoring it." Brittany grabbed the cup of coffee before her with both hands. Instead of taking a sip, she gazed into it. "It looked like a plantation home, but on a smaller scale. There was a wrap-around porch in front with a swing that I used to sit in with my dad and watch the sun set. He loved sunsets." Brittany looked out one of the windows. With a slight turn of her lips, she said, "He would have loved this evening's sunset." She took a sip of her coffee before continuing. "The house was old. The floors creaked, roaches were a common sight, and it wasn't well insulated. Even though it was chilly in the winters and warmer in the summer months, I loved that house. I cried for days when my mom sold it. I used to drive past it every so often to see how it was holding up. Last time I saw it, Katrina ravaged it. I told Brad I wanted to buy it one day and fix it up, just as my parents had done. Is that where he was…?"

I nodded. The house was where Brad's story ended, but there was one last piece of information he confessed to me. "There's something else Brad told me."

"What?"

"He bought the house for y'all to restore and live in. It was going to be a surprise for your birthday."

Every set of eyes in the Chick-ory were cast upon a blonde-haired young woman as she wept into a paper napkin. Delain walked over and placed her arms around Brittany. "I'm so sorry. Bradley sounded like a remarkable man."

"I loved him so much," she cried. "I don't know what I'm going to do without him."

It was difficult not to blame myself for his death. If I hadn't switched flights with him, Brittany wouldn't have been crying as if her world was over. I was then reminded of the events leading up to his death. I wouldn't have switched flights with him if he didn't ask if I knew anyone who had adopted a child. I wouldn't have even talked to him if I didn't go on the Denver trip. I wouldn't have gone on the trip if I hadn't worked at Al's clinic. I wouldn't have worked at the clinic if I had not gotten fired from my previous job. I would still be at my other job if I hadn't left town for seven weeks. I wouldn't have left town for seven weeks if I would have married Tiffany. I would have married Tiffany if I didn't tell Mikey about the video. I wouldn't have told him about the video if I had never seen it. And I never would have seen the video if about ten other occurrences didn't align themselves perfectly. Never did I think showing the video would not only affect my life, but a complete stranger's as well. When Georgia handed Delain a clean hand towel to give to Brittany, I couldn't get the notion out of my head that the repercussions of the video were far from over.

Once Delain returned to her seat, Brittany grabbed both of our hands. Still trembling beneath my jacket, she told me, "Thank you for telling me the truth. I needed to hear it."

"I'm so sorry you had to find out this way."

"Do you mind if I ask y'all something personal?"

"Anything," Delain told her.

"I watched the news story about you, Jackson, while I was getting ready today. It seemed as if you were having cold feet about getting married." I looked to my left. Delain's eyes were aimed deep into my soul. "I don't want Brad's death to be irrelevant. He died because of love. I hope the love he had can live on with the two of you."

The subtle closed-lip smile Delain flashed caused me to do the same.

"I've known the two of you for only a few minutes, but I can see how in love y'all are with each other. Jackson, don't you want to marry her?"

I wasn't thinking about Davis interrogating Delain as I looked into her eyes, or about how our first meeting outside the bank was staged, or that she lied to me about her parents. I instead recalled her reaction when I lifted my mask at Davis' house three days earlier. The way Delain kissed me after jumping into my arms was all the proof I needed. "Yes."

"When?"

I glanced at Brittany, and then back to Delain. Both looked like they needed some uplifting news. "This Saturday."

Chapter 67

Tyler grabbed the cardboard box hidden deep within his bedroom closet. Behind several articles of winter clothing, and beneath a tin of old baseball cards and a plastic storage container possessing his G.I. Joe collection from childhood, lay the first item he would grab if his house were to catch on fire. The box had been hidden for over two years, out of sight for anyone to see. The only way to locate it would have been by snooping—and Tyler's last girlfriend, Sophia, did just that. When he returned from the gym one recent evening, the cardboard box was sitting atop his kitchen table. He recalled the last conversation he had with Sophia while setting the box on his bedroom floor.

"Why do you still have this stuff?" she inquired.

"Why were you digging through my closet?" he asked back.

"Do you still have a thing for your ex-girlfriend, Christina?"

"Why would you ask that?"

"If you and I are going to move forward, you have to throw this crap away."

"And if I don't throw it away?"

"Then I'm leaving."

"I'm going to need my key back."

Tyler opened the box. Everything that reminded him of Christina was inside it: pictures, handwritten notes, copies of e-mails, movie and concert stubs, souvenirs from trips together, mix CDs with his name on them, and a framed poem she had written for him. Of all the gifts Tyler had received from Christina, the poem was by far his favorite. He had read it so many times he could recite it by memory.

Thirty-four hours had passed since he last heard anything from John about Christina's whereabouts. Thirty-four hours spent imagining how complete his life would be with his ex-girlfriend in it. Thirty-four hours spent wondering what his first words would be once he saw her again.

Tyler placed one of the mix CD's into his stereo before spreading the entire contents of the box about his carpeted bedroom floor. As U2's 'All I Want Is You' played, Tyler grabbed the last note Christina had written for him. It was dated eight days before she returned from her friend's bachelorette party in New Orleans.

To my beloved Tyler, I can't believe it's been two years since our first date, and a little over two years since we first met beneath the arch. I've been so incredibly happy with you in my life. I can't put into words how much I love you. The way I feel is like something out of a fairy tale. I've waited many years for my Prince Charming, and the wait has been worth it. I can't wait to spend the rest of our lives together. I love you forever! Uno!

As Tyler reached for another letter, his phone rang. Just as he felt every other time his phone had rung since his first meeting with John, Tyler grew excited while grabbing the phone from his pocket. His excitement lessened as 'private number' flashed on the screen. Sophia had been calling him repeatedly over the last couple of weeks. When he stopped answering her calls, she learned how to program her phone number to come up as a private number. He placed the phone on the ground before beginning another letter from Christina. The phone again rang. 'Private number' came up once more. He reluctantly answered. "Hello."

"Are you ready?" The voice did not belong to his ex-girlfriend, but to the only person Tyler had been desperately wanting to talk to, besides Christina.

"For what?"

"To see her."

Tyler jumped to his feet. With great enthusiasm he asked, "Now?!"

"Pack a suitcase. Make sure to bring a nice suit. Be at the airport at 7:45 tomorrow morning. Your flight leaves for 8:50. Don't check your suitcase. Scan the credit card my secretary gave you yesterday morning at the Delta kiosk. I'll see you curbside at 9:30."

"Where am I flying to?"

"You'll find out when checking in. How do you feel, Tyler?"

"Nervous…but more so excited. Is she married?"

"Not yet."

"What do you mean 'not yet'?"

"Currently she is not married."

"How did she look?" There was no reply. "John?" Tyler glanced at the screen. The call had ended. He wasn't upset John didn't answer him, as he was too elated to become upset. Tyler grabbed the picture closest to him. He and Christina sat in a canoe. She leaned backwards, her head resting on his chest as he draped his arms around her. Her effervescent smile, paired with the overly optimistic sensation coursing emphatically through his veins, incited goosebumps on nearly every inch of his body. "Babe," he spoke to the picture, "we're about to be reunited."

Chapter 68

Scott Melancon approached his wife as she held their sleeping son in her arms. She sat in a circular booth in the dining room of the dimly lit Fleur-de-Leans. An already long day that concluded with the mentally fatiguing funeral of Davis had exhausted both Bridgett and Thomas.

"Honey, can we come back tomorrow?" Bridgett asked. "The restaurant will still be here."

Scott leaned over, kissing first his wife on the lips and then Thomas's forehead before taking another glimpse across the dining room. "I forgot how much I loved this place." The four walls surrounding the lavish dining room contained grandiose murals depicting various traditions of New Orleans past: parading at the Rex Carnival, an afternoon ride on a steamboat, workers harvesting sugarcane on a plantation, and patrons buying fresh fish and other delectable goods at the French Market. Even though the restaurant had been established for only a decade and a half, the building itself was much older. The gas lit chandeliers, thick hardwood floors, antique chairs and tables, and vintage mirrors instilled a turn-of-the-century dining experience.

"Your brother did a good thing here."

Ten years had passed since Scott last ran a restaurant. He nearly forgot how much he missed mingling with the customers, the non-stop chaos in the kitchen, haggling with the food and liquor vendors, and the overall enjoyment that came with running a successful restaurant and bar. The last establishment he ran was smaller than the Fleur-de-Leans, and not nearly as popular or upscale. While looking into the bar area, inspiration struck Scott. "I think there's enough room that we can probably fit the Steinway in there, and we can hire someone to play. I'm thinking half-price martinis on Tuesday nights. Maybe you can tickle the ivories again." Scott grinned as he envisioned his wife sitting behind their piano in the bar.

"I haven't practiced in years."

"I love it when you play. It reminds me of the first time we met. I have never seen something or someone so stunning as you, sitting behind the piano playing Cole Porter. I was smitten before we ever said a word to each other."

Gently rocking Thomas, Bridgett smiled. "Me too."

Scott's hands rested on his hips as he silently counted the chairs in the dining room. "Eighty-four."

Bridgett stood from the booth. "It seems like you're ready to run a restaurant again."

"I'm ready for the challenge. I feel like this is where we belong. It's going to be a lot of work. I just want to make sure you're on board with this before I sign the papers."

She glanced at her watch. "I'm happy that you're back in your hometown. I think the three of us belong here. Right now, however, we belong in our hotel room. It's eleven o'clock, and way past Thomas's bedtime."

"Do you mind taking the car back? I want to check out the kitchen. There's been a few changes in there since the last time we visited."

"How are you getting back to the hotel?"

"I'll take a taxi. I won't be too far behind you." Scott grabbed Thomas from his wife's arms, carrying him to the SUV through the rear entrance of the building. After securing his son in the car seat, he stood outside the driver's door. Through the open window, he kissed his wife. Eight years later, he still found it impossible not to smile after kissing the woman who seemed to grow more beautiful with each passing day.

"You're excited about this, aren't you?" she asked.

"I didn't think I would be, but after looking around just now, I'm feeling the butterflies again. I just hope I don't ruin everything my brother worked so hard for."

"You're not going to ruin the restaurant. If anything, you're going to make it even better." She leaned forward. Scott planted another kiss on her lips.

"I hope so. I'll see you in a little bit."

"Don't be too late. By the way…" She grinned while telling him, "I think our piano would be perfect in the bar area…and maybe I'll play a song or two on half-price martini nights."

"I love you so much, Mrs. Melancon."

"I love you too, Mr. Melancon. See you in a bit."

Scott opted to re-enter the restaurant through the more lively entrance on Bourbon Street. The walk brought a reminiscent smile to his face as he weaved through the rambunctious crowd. The unflattering smell of 'Bourbon brew' (a combination of urine and beer) collecting in the street gutters, along with the roars of drunkards of all ages conjured memories of his many years spent partying in the Big Easy.

While inserting the key into the front door, he felt a tap on his shoulder. Scott turned around to see a couple just older than him. "Are y'all reopening soon?" the woman asked him.

"Yes, ma'am."

"Can I ask how much longer? We've been eating here every Friday night for the last couple of years. It's our favorite restaurant."

A date had yet to be determined. "Next Friday night."

"We'll be here for the reopening," the grinning gentleman stated.

"I look forward to seeing y'all. I'm Scott Melancon, by the way. Davis' brother."

Both offered looks of condolences. "We're so sorry to hear of your brother's passing," the woman spoke. "He was a good man."

"Yes, he was. Thank you." Scott shook both of their hands. "I'll see the two of you in here next Friday night."

Scott closed the front door behind him. "I guess I got a week to get this place up and running again." There was no turning back and no time to waste. The excitement had already begun. He walked into the office. A list of the current employees and their phone numbers was pinned to a board. He planned on calling everyone on the list in the morning to see who was interested in returning to work. A meeting would then be held on Sunday to get to know his staff. While looking through the drawers of his late brother's desk, Scott heard the front door open. *I thought I locked it.*

Scott grew startled by the sight of six individuals standing in the darkened entrance. "I'm sorry but we're…" A heavy-set gentleman stepped forward into the dim light. Scott let out a sigh of relief, "Oh, hey there, Charlie."

"Scottie, it seems you're eager to get the restaurant re-opened. The front door wasn't even locked."

"I must have forgotten to lock it. What brings you by, Charlie?"

"We had a feeling you might be here. I want to introduce you to some gentlemen that were good friends with your dear brother." The other five men stepped forward. All were dressed in dark suits, and were recognized by Scott as attendees at his brother's funeral. "I hope we're not intruding, Scottie."

"Not at all."

"Good to know," Charlie told him with a pat on his shoulder. "Let's start with the handsome devil on the far right." Charlie stood to Scott's left as he began. "Scott Melancon, meet Mr. Mitch Hennessey. The blonde-haired gentleman with arms bigger than my thighs was partners with your brother many moons ago in the New Orleans Police Department. He now works for the Federal Bureau of Investigation. Not only can he bench press a small car, but he is one of the finest investigators I have ever had the pleasure of knowing. And as a lawyer for the better part of four decades, I have met quite a few investigators."

"Nice to finally meet you, Scott," Mitch spoke with an extended right hand. "Your brother spoke highly of you over the years."

Scott wasn't certain, but he thought that he noticed a peculiar act performed by Mitch during the funeral. He was the only person in the cathedral that appeared to have touched Davis' body as it lay in the coffin. "A pleasure to finally meet you as well, Mitch."

"The slim gentleman next to Mitch is Mr. Alfonso Broussard. Mr. Broussard was one of the most honorable judges in the history of our great state. He has since retired."

"I'm sorry for your loss," the judge said with a wave of his hand. In addition to his slenderness, the judge was quite tall, despite having a slouch in his posture. What stood out even more than his frailness was the cheap looking toupee atop his head. The curly, dark gray rug wasn't even close to matching the patches of straight, silver locks above his ears. Scott guessed his age to be closer to seventy.

"Good to meet you, Your Honor."

"The red-headed gentleman in the middle is the judge's nephew, Mr. Redmond Broussard. I'll bet you five dollars, Scottie, that you cannot guess as to what his nickname may be."

"Um…Red?"

Charlie reached in his wallet, retrieving then handing Scott a five-dollar bill. "Good guess."

Unlike his uncle, Redmond stepped forward to shake hands. He looked to be around the same age as Scott, and while on the skinny side, not nearly as frail or as tall as his uncle. "I wouldn't be where I am today if it wasn't for your brother. I felt like my own brother died when I heard of his passing."

Scott nodded while shaking his hand.

"Redmond is the CEO of the most successful waste management company in all of New Orleans. There is nothing that he can't get rid of. The dapper gentleman to his right is none other than world-renowned, Doctor Percy Weller."

Of all the men before him, Percy Weller was the only face that was somewhat recognizable. "You look familiar," Scott told the older man with crow's feet, a tight jaw, and combed-back dirty blonde hair, accented with a slight touch of gray.

Percy extended his right hand. "I went to grade school with your brother. I first met you at one of your parents' famous luaus." Scott and Davis' parents hosted a luau every summer, even going so far one year as to purchase a live pig, which was killed by Davis and his friends before being roasted. Scott hated the pig-slaughtering and was very vocal about it to his parents. The remaining luaus featured a pig that was already deceased upon arrival at the Melancon residence.

"Percy, good to meet you again."

"If I'm not mistaken, you cried one year when we killed a pig in your parents' backyard."

Scott smiled while shrugging his shoulders. "At eight years old, I guess I was a little upset by what was going on."

"I hope we didn't turn you into a vegetarian with our crazy antics back then."

"Nope. I'm very much a meat-eater."

"And last but certainly not least is the second nephew of the group—my nephew, Mr. Roger Ainsworth. He is my sister's son, so our last names are not the same. Roger is the most thorough accountant you will ever meet. Be sure to keep your receipts for every purchase made for the Fleur-de-Leans. He will see to it that you receive every dollar in which you are entitled." Even though Roger had a receding hairline, a hint of a beer-belly, and wore a thick pair of unflattering glasses, Scott believed that Roger was once a handsome man, but seemed to have let himself go.

"Mr. Melancon, I took care of your late brother's finances, and I look forward to working with you as well. I have some papers I need you to look over and sign."

"I have an accountant back home. He's been with me for several years."

"Roger is the best around," Judge Broussard stated.

"I'd switch to Roger," Percy suggested. "He's extremely knowledgeable. He found an additional $11,000 owed to me by the government last year."

Scott felt he had no choice in the matter. "Sounds like I have a new accountant."

"I look forward to working with you." Roger's tone was very drab, almost depressing.

"Scottie, you have now met 'the krewe', as your late brother called our little ensemble."

Scott, slightly uncomfortable and somewhat apprehensive by the late night visit, turned to his left. "What do you mean by 'the krewe'?"

Charlie casually walked towards the wall separating the bar and dining room, placing his hand over the dimming switch. The gas chandeliers flickered brighter in the dining room. "Your brother started something special a few years back." Charlie took a seat in one of the four circular booths lining the wall beneath the Rex Carnival mural, the same booth Bridgett and Thomas occupied minutes earlier. "The five gentlemen behind you, your brother, and yours truly would meet for lunch nearly every Friday right here in this very booth. We talked about everything from business to politics to sports."

"Kind of like a networking group?"

"Some might call it networking. Others might see it as an excuse for seven middle-aged men to get together and share some laughs over cocktails and your brother's delicious New Orleans cuisine."

"Middle-aged?" the judge asked, approaching the booth at an even slower pace than Charlie.

"Judge Broussard, you are only as old as you feel."

"And I feel about a hundred years old."

"And you look every bit of it, old friend. So does that dead squirrel sitting atop of your head."

"Kiss my ass, Charlie."

Charlie chuckled while patting the judge on his shoulder. "We enjoy the occasional jab at one another as well, Scottie. It keeps us youthful."

"A networking/social group sounds like something I could use."

"Yes indeed, Scottie. We want you to join us—mostly so we have a place to eat and drink on Fridays. That is, if you want to continue the tradition your brother started."

"I don't see why not."

Mitch next approached the booth. "If someone ever gives you trouble, you just let Charlie know. We'll handle the rest."

Scott grew even more apprehensive by Mitch's comment. "What do you mean by 'trouble'?"

Redmond followed Mitch into the booth, sitting next to his uncle. "We watch each other's back, in both personal and business matters. For instance, last year Roger suspected that his wife may have been cheating on him. Mitch followed her one night and saw her leaving a hotel with another man. I confronted her the next day and told her that I happened to see her leaving the hotel, and if she didn't stop cheating, I was going to tell her husband."

Roger sat next to Mitch. "From that moment on, our relationship became stronger than ever. These guys saved my marriage."

Percy was the next to speak. "Your brother bought two buildings side by side in hopes of tearing down the dividing wall to make this large dining room that we're currently sitting in. The French Quarter Historical Association said he couldn't tear the wall down. The judge right here made some calls. The next day the F.Q.H.A. informed your brother that the wall could come down."

"We could go on for hours about how we've helped one another over the years," Charlie stated.

Scott looked around the table. "I guess it wouldn't hurt to have a lawyer, retired judge, renowned doctor, federal agent, accountant, and waste company CEO on my side."

"Glad to have you aboard," a smiling Redmond said. "This calls for a celebration."

"Anyone care for a drink?" Scott asked.

"Hey!" the six men shouted in unison.

Redmond stood from the booth. "You have a seat, Scott. I'll get everyone's drinks."

Mitch was the first to shake Scott's hand. "I think you're going to be a fine addition to the krewe."

Friday

Chapter 69

I awoke in a cold sweat. Pain radiated from my chest, extending down my left arm. Breathing proved to be quite difficult. In an attempt to not wake Delain, I crawled out of bed and into the bathroom, quietly shutting the door behind me. My heart was beating with such force that I was certain she could hear it even in the deepest of sleep. I crawled into her closet. On hands and knees, I attempted to take a deep breath. Getting oxygen into my lungs seemed impossible. The notion that I was having a heart attack stayed with me for some time, until realizing I was too young to have one, and it was more than likely another panic attack. I tried to imagine something calming. I pictured Delain's head resting on my chest as we lay on a desolate beach. The sand was as white as refined sugar, the water clear and smooth as a sheet of glass, and a brush of cool air blew upon us. My imagination did nothing to calm me. Once dizziness set in, I realized the attack was lasting longer than the previous one—which incited even further panic. I lay on the floor, gasping for air like a goldfish laying outside of its bowl. The claustrophobic closet wasn't helping. I crawled back into the bathroom and lay on the cool, tiled floor. Sweat protruded from every pore of my skin. I removed my shirt while continuing in my attempt to breathe normally. I was certain I wasn't going to make it through. Death seemed evident. Light soon flickered beneath the door leading to the bedroom, preceding the opening of the door.

"Are you okay?"

I couldn't answer her. The muscles needed to talk felt like they were paralyzed.

Delain knelt beside me. "You're sweating profusely and you're white as a ghost." She then felt my wrist. "Jesus! Your heart's pounding! Baby, what's wrong?" She grabbed both sides of my face.

I tried to focus on her eyes. Her face was blurry.

"I'm going to call 911." She tried to stand. I grabbed her arm. I didn't want her to leave my side or call the paramedics. She curled up next to me, intertwining her leg with mine as her head lay softly on my chest. "It's okay," she calmly spoke. "You're going to be fine, baby. I'm not going to let anything happen to you. I love you."

Not long after Delain held me, the effects of the attack started to diminish. The dizziness went away, my breathing returned to a near-normal level, the sweating ceased, and I no longer felt paralyzed. "I'm okay," I mumbled, out of breath.

She lifted her head from my chest. "Are you sure?" A mournful look appeared on her face.

"Yes."

"We need to cool you down." She retrieved a washcloth from beneath the sink. While holding it under running water, she asked "Was that a panic attack?"

"I…think so."

"Was it your first one?"

I took a few breaths before answering, "Second."

"When was the first one?"

"Yesterday."

"Was it like this one?"

I shook my head. "This was worse."

She placed the cold washcloth around my neck while kneeling next to me. "Are you worried about Davis' death?"

There was no sense in continuing to act as if I believed everything would be okay. "A little bit."

"Is it the wedding too? Do we need to postpone it?"

I did feel as though we were rushing into it without first making sure we were in the clear about everything that had transpired in the last week. I wanted to tell Delain about the actual events that took place with my getting back to New Orleans, but that would most likely add stress to her already chaotic life as well. "No. We're doing the right thing."

She kissed my forehead. "I know life may seem a little crazy right now, but things are going to start getting back to normal real soon."

Two panic attacks in less than twenty-four hours were a pretty good indicator that I couldn't have agreed with her any less. "I hope you're right."

"I just wish those stupid reporters would go away. I saw a van outside last night after you fell sleep. They must have found and followed us after Bradley's funeral or the coffee shop. They're stressing me out as well. I don't know why they can't leave us alone. What are they hoping to catch?"

So far, Delain had done a phenomenal job of avoiding being caught on camera—and I was starting to think that was the problem. "You."

"What?"

"It's human nature to be curious. I'm assuming people want to see what you look like."

"You think so?"

A question I had been asked by each reporter had yet to be answered, and I was sure that was another cause for their pestering. "Your face, along with a wedding date, would probably get them to go away."

"Or show up at the ceremony."

An idea so simple then hit me. "You're right. They probably would show up at the ceremony. Can you see if the van is still outside?"

She peered out of her bedroom window. "Yep. It's two houses down."

"Perfect. We're going to tell them we're getting married."

"Are you crazy, baby? And what do you mean 'we'?"

"The sooner they know the date, and the sooner they see you, the sooner they will leave us alone." With the assistance of the counter, I made it to my feet.

"But you know I don't want to be on camera," she reminded me, her tone unsettled.

"They don't know what you look like, Lainey. You see what I'm getting at?"

The concerned look on her face soon gave way to a more understanding expression. "Oh, I think I see what you're saying."

"Good. Now go get dressed so we can get these leeches out of here."

Delain and I held hands while gingerly walking down her driveway. She laughed as I pretended to whisper something in her ear. Just as we had hoped for, a female reporter approached us before we could open the doors to my vehicle. A cameraman was several feet behind her. "Jackson, is this your fiancée?"

I smiled at the young woman holding my hand. A platinum blonde wig the length of her chin hid her flowing brunette locks, while a magnetic nose ring, a temporary tattoo of a red rose on her right shoulder, and a plethora of make-up helped to alter her typical appearance. An oversized pair of sunglasses covered her eyes. "Yes, it is."

The reporter ran her fingers through her hair as her cameraman lifted the camera onto his shoulder. Once he nodded, she held a microphone to her mouth. "This is Natalie Meyers with Channel Four news. I'm standing here with the runaway groom, Jackson Fabacher, and his fiancée, whom is no longer a mystery." She held the microphone to Delain's mouth. "What's your name?"

"Delain."

"Delain, how did you learn that Jackson was still alive?"

"I saw it on the news." Not only was her appearance altered, but her voice as well. Her spontaneous Texas twang nearly caused me to chuckle.

"What were you thinking once you heard the news?"

"How lucky I was to still have him."

"Were you concerned that he was having doubts about marrying you?"

"Yes, but," she looked at me, "things are incredible now." We both smiled at one another.

"What about the wedding? Is it tomorrow as originally planned?"

"No," I answered. "We pushed it back to next month. August 18th, same time and same location. Any more questions?"

"Are you in love with her, Jackson?"

"Of course. Any more questions?"

"Do you regret letting someone else take your place on the ill-fated flight?"

"Yes. Any more?"

"Do you feel like you've been given a second chance at life?"

"Yes. Any more?"

"Jackson, Davis Melancon was nearly your father-in-law before you played a video of his daughter's indiscretion at your first wedding. Were you upset to hear about his passing this week?"

The reporter's comment, although truthful, angered me. I had to subdue the anger as I answered, "Yes. Any more?"

The reporter's lips moved, but no words were spoken.

"We'd like to get back to a normal life without being harassed and stalked by reporters. Are you sure you don't have any more questions that will require further stalking, Ms. Meyers?"

Speechless, she shook her head side to side.

"Thank you. Have a blessed day." We got into my SUV, drove for a good fifteen minutes, and then returned to Delain's townhouse. Not only did the van not follow us, but it was no longer parked down the street. Our plan just might have worked.

Following breakfast, Delain and I placed phone calls to most of the guests that had already RSVP'd to inform them the wedding was still going to take place. I called my parents first. Father Peter was able to preside over the ceremony, they told me, and the cathedral was still available. I asked them to call the relatives, while I called my friends. To keep the wedding as secretive as possible, we decided to not have the rehearsal dinner at the original location. My parents offered to host an intimate, quiet dinner at their house. The attendees would be my immediate family, plus most of the extended family. Delain didn't want to invite her bridesmaids, mostly because she wasn't close to the two of them. I didn't get into a discussion of why she didn't have many close friends, since I was certain the answer had to do with her necessity to start a new life after killing a man.

"I'm glad the wedding is happening, but I feel bad the rehearsal dinner is just my friends and family," I told her as we sat at her kitchen table.

"It's okay. I feel like your family is mine now."

"Speaking of family, what about your parents?"

She crossed her arms, leaning back in the chair. "I was thinking about that."

"And...?"

"I want them here, but I know how they are. They're going to be upset I'm only giving them a day's notice before the wedding, and that I didn't tell them sooner about my engagement. I can picture my mom complaining the whole time and wondering why I didn't let her and my dad know. I love them, but I'm afraid it will make things a whole lot more stressful. God knows we don't need any added stress right now."

It was upsetting to me that her parents wouldn't be attending the wedding. "Then when are you going to tell them you're married?"

"As soon as this...ordeal is over."

"And right after we get Caleb back."

Delain grabbed my right hand. "That's why I love you and can't wait to marry you."

I still didn't know how we would accomplish such a feat, but she needed to hear it. "There's no one else you want to invite tonight or tomorrow?"

As she glanced at the list in her hand, I imagined how lop-sided the pews would look like at the cathedral. "There is one person I didn't call yet."

"Who's that?"

"Caroline. Should I call her?"

Despite the circumstances, I felt that Delain and I were growing closer to one another; so much so that Caroline hadn't crossed my mind in nearly a day. "No harm in trying, but I don't know if she'll be able to find a flight that will get here in time."

"There's one way to find out."

She dialed her number while I recalled the last conversation shared with my former co-worker. I imagined it might be awkward seeing her on my wedding day, considering the last time we were together we both confessed to having feelings for one another. As Delain spoke to Caroline, I couldn't decide if I wanted her there or not.

Delain covered the phone with her hand. "She's looking at flights online right now."

I grinned, nervously awaiting an answer.

"I'm starting to get hungry. How about you?"

Over the last week, my appetite had diminished greatly. I needed to eat, even though I didn't have the urge to. "I could eat some—"

"Are you sure?!... Well, I can pick you up...Don't be silly...Okay. I'll see you at 5:00. You better pack quickly...See you soon." A grinning Delain hung up. "Caroline found a flight. She's coming this evening."

I found Delain's excitement perplexing. "Great."

Chapter 70

Mitch placed the last bite of his homemade egg, bacon, and cheddar cheese burrito into his mouth on his way into the forensics lab. A healthy and very strict eater, Mitch allowed himself three cheat meals a week. He found it kept him from going off the deep end. As a vastly overweight teenager, who was ridiculed often by his peers, Mitch vowed to never return to his former state of obesity.

Pete motioned Mitch over to his desk. Many of the faces in the lab were unfamiliar to Mitch, as his time with the New Orleans Police Department ended a decade earlier. Pete was the only forensics expert who was working at the time Mitch and Davis were police officers.

"Boy, have I got something for you," Pete stated while waving a piece of paper in the air. Pete was much shorter than Mitch. He was also thinner, paler, less athletic, older, and much balder than his friend. Patches of light brown hair above his ears and across the back of his head was all that remained.

"And I for you." Mitch held up a plastic bag.

"What's with the knife?"

"I'll tell you after you tell me what you found."

"Okay. So, I took a sample of the dried substance on…" He paused until the co-worker walking past his desk was several steps away, "Davis' door. It was in fact blood, but not Davis'."

"Whose was it?"

"Slow down, handsome." Pete was gay and didn't attempt to hide his attraction towards Mitch. Mitch knew it, using it to his advantage whenever expedited results in evidence testing were needed. "So, I put the DNA from the blood into the CODIS system to see if I could get a match with it."

"And did you?"

He placed his arms into the air as a referee would once a football player crossed the goal line with football in hand. "Touchdown! The DNA matched this man." Pete handed him the piece of paper.

Mitch glanced at the picture before reading the man's name and hometown listed below it. "Hank Bowery. Mobile, Alabama."

"Does he look familiar?"

"No. Should he?"

"Did you hear about the man that held two young women in his makeshift dungeon while men paid to have sex with them?"

Mitch nodded. "It was in Mobi—this is the guy?!"

"Sure is," an overly excited Pete answered.

Mitch shook his head in disbelief. "That's not possible. You're saying this piece of shit was in Davis' house recently?"

"I seriously doubt it. I read the police report. The victims said Hank never left his house. Hank was shot and killed sometime around five in the morning this past Sunday. We deduced that Davis died of a heart attack somewhere between 1:30-2:30 on Monday morning."

"Are you sure the blood was Hank's?"

"I performed the DNA test three times, and then ran it through CODIS just as many times. It is without a doubt Hank Bowery's blood. Now, his body wasn't the only one found shot to death in Mobile. Another man by the name of Cliff Robertson was also found at the scene. The victims claimed they heard the two men quarreling upstairs before shots were fired. If both men were shot to death, then I can think of only one way that the blood made it to Davis' house."

Mitch sat in Pete's chair. He rested his hands behind his head as he rocked back and forth with the plastic bag in his lap. "Since the blood sample was at the bottom of the doorway, it had to have been on a shoe. It must have been kicked against the frame, and probably not intentionally."

"That's what I was thinking, Mitchy."

"And whoever kicked the doorway was possibly at Hank's house during the shootout."

"Not possibly—definitely. There's no other explanation."

"Does Davis have a connection with Hank? Was he in his house in Mobile early Sunday morning?" Before Pete could answer, Mitch answered himself. "Not a chance."

"I agree."

"This is getting a little bizarre, Pete. Question."

"Go."

"The shirt Davis was wearing the night he died—where is it?"

"It's still here. I told Victoria I was going to drop it off—along with the rest of the clothing he was wearing that night—at her house when she was ready for it. It's in my locker in a bag."

"Perfect. Check the cuffs to see if there is any duct tape residue."

"Why?"

"Did you happen to notice Davis' wrists during the autopsy?"

Pete shook his head. "There was no bruising or anything else that stood out of the ordinary about them. Why do you ask?"

"I checked Davis' wrist at the funeral, but they didn't appear to have been missing hair, nor did I feel any type of stickiness to them. I'm wondering if his sleeves were rolled down before being duct taped."

"Duct taped? What are you talking about?"

Mitch glanced to his right and left before lowering his voice. "There is evidence, Pete, to suggest Davis might have been duct taped to his steering wheel the night he died, and there may have been a struggle inside his house."

"What are you suggesting?"

"I think Davis Melancon was killed."

"But he had a heart attack. I saw his heart myself. All the signs were there: scar tissue, clogged artery."

"And I think someone may have brought him to have a heart attack."

"Second-degree murder."

Mitch nodded. "And our suspect may have been in Hank's house when he and the other fellow were killed, hence the blood on Davis' doorframe. We may have a serial killer on our hands, Pete."

Pete's eyes lit up. "You think so, Mitchy?"

"Stop calling me that. I need you to go to Davis' and look for more evidence." He handed the plastic bag to Pete. "This knife was found beneath Davis' couch. See if you can get a print from it. While you're at it, sweep the master bed for hair or any other DNA sample. I'm going to be out of town for a day or two."

"Where are you going?"

Mitch stood. "Mobile, Alabama."

Chapter 71

Beads of sweat gathered on Tyler's forehead as he stood curbside at Louis Armstrong International Airport. The humidity in Atlanta was often high, but the air in New Orleans seemed much thicker and damper than in his hometown. While awaiting the arrival of the man with no last name, Tyler began to wonder if 'John' was in fact a made-up name. He glanced at his watch. It was 10:28.

"You need to wind that back an hour," a man's voice spoke into Tyler's right ear. Tyler didn't bother to turn around. The voice was recognizable. "You're going to be in town for a few days."

"You sure are good at sneaking up on people."

"It's a gift."

Tyler removed his watch, adjusting it to Central Standard Time. "I can't wait to hear what you have to tell me."

John stepped forward. "I can't wait to tell you. My car is in the parking garage across the street."

"How did you find her?"

"I'll answer all questions once we're in the car. Follow me."

John drove a Chrysler sedan, jet black with tinted windows. Tyler buckled his seatbelt then positioned the air conditioner vents towards him, allowing cold air to blow directly on his face. "How did you find her?"

John looked over his shoulder while backing out of the parking spot. "You thought that Christina changed her name. You were right."

"What is it?"

"Delain Schexnaydre."

"Delain is her middle name, and…I could be wrong, but I think Schexnaydre is her mom's maiden name. How did you find that out?"

John began to drive towards the garage exit. "I don't want to tell you too much about my previous employers, Tyler, but I used to work for the government. My job was to find people. Thankfully, I still have…let's call it 'access' to some of the programs I used over the years. I searched anyone who changed their name in the last three years, then cross-referenced those names with Christina's age, race, and gender. Four matches came up. I started with the one that had a P.O. Box in New Orleans. I came down here, scoped out the post office, and saw her picking up her mail the next day."

Tyler couldn't stop smiling as John approached a toll booth. "I can't believe you found her. What else do you know about her? You said she isn't married, but is she dating anyone?"

John waited until after paying the parking lot attendant to tell him, "I said she isn't married yet. Her wedding is tomorrow."

Tyler's smiling quickly waned. "What? Are you kidding me?"

John smirked. "Nope."

Tyler's head fell back onto the headrest. "Great," he dejectedly spoke. "I guess that's the end of that."

"Tyler, if you're giving up already, I might as well turn around and let you go back to Atlanta." Instead of following the signs to merge onto I-10, John remained in the airport lane, approaching the ramp leading to the departure gates. "Quitters make me sick."

"But she's engaged and the wedding's tomorrow."

"So? You think this is the first engagement I've had to dissolve?" The car came to a stop in front of the curbside check-in. "If you're giving up on Christina, then you might as well get back on the airplane." John unlocked the doors.

"You've had to break up an engagement so close to the wedding before?"

"Tyler, Christina is supposed to get married tomorrow. She's not going to get married tomorrow. Do you believe me?"

"I guess."

John reached across Tyler, opening the passenger door. "Do…you…believe…me?"

"Yes."

"Thank you. Now, shut the door and listen." Tyler did as told. John locked the doors before pressing on the accelerator. "Have you watched the news this week?"

"A little. Why?"

"Did you see the story about the man who was believed to have died in the Salt Lake City airplane crash, but instead secretly gave up his seat to someone else because he got cold feet about marrying his fiancée—the 'runaway groom' as they have been calling him?"

"I caught a little bit of it. Why?"

"Did you see where the man was from?"

"I think from here, if I'm not mistaken."

"You're not mistaken. Guess who his fiancée is."

"I don't have a clue. Who?"

John stopped at the traffic light, turned to Tyler, and then smugly grinned.

"No! It can't be!"

"Oh, but it is."

"Are you fucking kidding me?! Christina?! My Christina is his fiancée?!"

"Yes, sir." John patted Tyler's knee. "I want to thank you for getting me involved with the most exhilarating case I have ever come across."

"You've got to be shitting me!"

John continued towards the interstate as he told Tyler, "This thing is so complex. You and the rest of the world have no idea. I've seen and heard things you would not believe."

Tyler believed his chances of being with Christina again were greatly diminishing with each piece of information that passed John's lips. "Did they show her on television?"

"Yes and no. Just a little while ago a reporter interviewed her and her fiancé outside of her house."

"Great," he sarcastically replied. "That means her face will be everywhere."

"Not necessarily. Christina, wisely, altered her appearance. She wore a wig this morning, along with a fake tattoo on her arm, lots of make-up and big sunglasses, and the clever girl even changed the way she talked. I don't even think her parents could recognize her."

"Why would she alter her appearance?"

John looked to Tyler and then back at the road. "You, my friend. I don't think she wanted you to come find her."

"That's good to know. Now I feel much better about being reunited with her."

"I don't think she wanted you to find her, Tyler, because I suspect she still has feelings for you."

Tyler desperately wanted to believe him. He needed proof. "Why would you think that after telling me she didn't want me to find her?"

"Your ex-girlfriend didn't leave you to go find herself in California. She left because something happened that was beyond her control."

Tyler waited several seconds for John to give him an answer. "And that was…?"

"I can't tell you yet, but you will discover the answer to that real soon."

"Of course you can't tell me." His tone was again sarcastic. "The answer I have been dying to know for almost three years can't be told to me by the man I'm paying the big bucks to. Perfect."

"Do you want Christina back or not, Tyler?"

"Yes, and I'd like to know what the hell is going on."

"You will soon find out. I'm telling you only what you need to know right now. I assure you it's for your benefit. I'm tired of sounding like a broken record, so this is the last time I will ask. Do you trust me?"

Tyler nodded.

"Good."

As John merged onto the interstate, Tyler asked, "Christina has to realize that since her fiancé ran away, he's not ready to get married; right?"

John again smirked. "Here's the thing— he didn't really run away. It's one big lie. The runaway groom, whose name is Jackson, told the reporter this morning that they're getting married next month, but that back there told me otherwise."

Tyler looked in the backseat. A device that looked similar to a satellite dish, yet smaller, and a set of large headphones stood out among the equipment. "You've been eavesdropping on her?"

"I've been following her for nearly a week. I know a lot about her now. How do you feel about brunettes?"

"She's not a blonde anymore?"

"Nope."

"I loved her long blonde hair." A long, exasperated exhale ensued as Tyler sunk deeper into his seat. "I'll be honest with you, John. In the last few minutes, I've heard a lot of evidence that would make it seem impossible for Christina and me to be together again."

"It does seem that way. I promise we have the upper hand in this situation, though. We're holding a royal flush, while they're all hanging onto a pair of aces."

"Who's they?"

"Everyone else."

"What's the next move then?"

John handed Tyler a small, flesh-colored hearing aid. "See if this fits." Tyler placed it into his right ear.

"It fits."

"Perfect. Christina is picking up a friend of hers at the airport before the rehearsal dinner. Five o'clock this evening at the airport we just left is where you will see your true love for the first time in almost three years. How do you feel?"

Tyler turned to John. The thought of seeing Christina in only a few hours aroused the kind of smile he hadn't flashed in almost three years. "Nervous…but extremely optimistic," he truthfully answered.

"That's the kind of attitude I need out of you, Tyler. It's about time."

With a sudden influx of confidence flowing through his veins, Tyler repeatedly slapped both hands on the dashboard while saying, "Christina will be mine again."

"Yes she will."

Chapter 72

"First time flying, dear?"

Caroline turned to her right, positioning her left ear closer to the elderly woman seated next to the aisle. "I'm sorry?"

"Is this your first time flying?"

"No, ma'am. Why do you ask?"

"You've been staring at the back of the seat for about an hour now." The woman's accent hinted at a Northeast dialect, perhaps the New York/New Jersey area. "I figured it could only be one of two things: you're either nervous because it's your first time flying or you're trying to use your psychic powers to move the row in front of us forward. I was hoping it was the latter because the leg room on this plane was obviously intended for midgets."

Caroline smiled at the woman tightly clutching to her purse. "It seems my powers are useless on upholstery."

"Does it work on little alcohol bottles? I'd love another gin and tonic, but I'm not paying five dollars for a thimble of alcohol. I bet the Jews run this airline."

Caroline wasn't quite sure if she heard the woman's comment correctly. She spoke as if she didn't. "The bottles are a little small."

"You're telling me. When the stewardess put the bottle in my hand, for a moment I thought I was grabbing my late husband's member."

Caroline, certain she heard the last comment correctly, let out an 'I can't believe you just said that' laugh. "I'm not sure how to follow that, ma'am."

"It's okay, dear. I didn't know what to say the first time I saw it either. I asked him if he needed a minute. He said, 'what do you mean?'" Caroline again laughed. "Please don't think I'm one of those fast women. That was the night of my honeymoon fifty-two years ago, and it was only the second man I had relations with."

"I wasn't thinking that."

"Good." The elderly woman then nudged Caroline's shoulder while whispering to her, "You see that man up there with the towel on his head?"

Caroline partially stood, noticing a man with a turban two rows in front of them, before returning to her seat. He looked to be of Indian descent. "Yes."

"Do you think he's going to blow the plane up?"

"I think we're safe."

"I've been watching him. If he makes any sudden moves," she patted her purse, "I got mace in here."

"I didn't think you could bring mace on an airplane."

"I placed it in my brassiere before going through security. I may be up there in age," she said, tapping her pointer finger to her forehead, "but this old broad still has a few tricks up her sleeve."

"I'm sure you do." Caroline reached into her purse for two drink vouchers. "I'm going to order a cocktail. Is it okay if I get another one for you too? I don't like to drink alone."

"That's awfully sweet of you, dear. I've never turned down a free drink, and I'm not starting now." She extended her right hand. "I'm Dorothy."

"I'm Caroline. Nice to meet you, Dorothy." After shaking her hand, she pressed the 'attendant' button above her head.

"Such a pretty name."

"Thank you. My parents met at a Neil Diamond concert."

Dorothy placed her hand over her chest. "Oh, that man's voice. I hope he still has my undergarments."

"Come again?"

Dorothy smiled. "At a concert long ago, I threw my undergarments on stage while he sang about a girl becoming a woman. He looked right at them and chuckled."

"That's definitely a story right there. They wavered between naming me Caroline, Rosie, Cherry, or Holly."

"I like Caroline. My niece is named Caroline too. She has an earring in her tongue. Do you have one?"

"No, ma'am."

"She also has a tattoo on her arm of some Japanese symbol. God only knows what it means. Do you have a Jap symbol tattooed somewhere?"

"No." Caroline laughed. It was hard to get mad at the racial slurs coming from a woman aged somewhere in her seventies. "You're not very politically correct, are you?"

Dorothy rolled her eyes. "I'm too old to be politically correct, dear. Besides, everyone is so sensitive and easily offended these days. If you call a black person 'black', you're apparently a racist. And you can't say a person is 'Chinese'. If their eyes are slanted, it's got to be Asian-American. I'm no longer white, but Caucasian. I grew up in another time when things were much simpler." With a sour look, Dorothy added, "People are such pansies these days." Caroline again laughed. Older people, especially women, didn't typically speak the way Dorothy did. "I could go on all day about how screwed up the world is. I'm just glad I won't be around in a couple of years to see the worst of it." With her hands held up, she said, "I'll get off my soapbox now."

"Did you need assistance?" asked the flight attendant.

Dorothy spoke before Caroline could. "Could you be a dear and have the colored stewardess come back around with the alcohol tray again?"

Caroline, slightly embarrassed, could only smile at the flight attendant.

"I'll have the flight attendant, Diandra, come back around," the straight-faced attendant spoke back.

"Thank you, my angel." As she walked off, Dorothy turned to Caroline. "Since this isn't your first time flying, something must be on your mind. A penny for your thoughts?"

Caroline's closest friends back home didn't know how she was feeling. No one knew what she was going through. "It's complicated."

"My entire life has been complicated, dear. Try me."

Caroline adjusted her legs to get more comfortable before beginning. "I was engaged until recently, but I'm not any longer. He loves me with all his heart, but I don't feel the same way right now. Four months ago, I met a man that I've fallen in love with. I'm certain he's the one I'm supposed to be with. He's engaged as well, and is getting married tomorrow. His fiancée is wonderful, and she's been through a lot. It's a tough situation."

"Did you need a cocktail, ma'am?" asked the bubbly, African-American flight attendant.

Before Dorothy could say something inappropriate, Caroline spoke first. "One gin and tonic for her, and I'll take a rum and coke."

"Are you Diandra?" Dorothy asked the attendant.

"Yes, I am."

"Are you married?" Dorothy next asked. Caroline grew uneasy as she anticipated something embarrassing to cross Dorothy's lips.

With a smile, Diandra poured tonic water into a plastic cup. "Yes, ma'am."

Dorothy reached for the cup and bottle of gin. "Good for you." Caroline held her breath as Diandra poured coke into a cup. "You're very pretty."

"Why, thank you."

"Are you married to a white man?"

Caroline sunk lower into her seat as the attendant answered, "Actually, yes, ma'am, I am."

"My late husband was white too." Caroline hurriedly grabbed the cup and bottle of rum from the attendant. "He was Jewish, so he was stingy in two areas: his wallet and his—"

"Here's the vouchers!" Caroline exclaimed. "Thank you."

As Diandra rolled the cart forward, Dorothy replied, "She was nice. I bet she married a wop. Those Italians love everyone."

Caroline poured most of the rum into her coke before ingesting nearly half of the cup's contents in one sip. She finished the rest with another lengthy sip.

"Thirsty?"

"You could say that." Caroline poured the remainder of the rum over the ice.

Dorothy had trouble in twisting the cap from the bottle of gin. She handed the bottle to Caroline. "Would you mind, dear?"

Caroline contemplated not helping for fear that even more inappropriate comments would spew from her intoxicated mouth. She soon caved in, opening the bottle and pouring a small amount of gin into the tonic.

"What are you, a nun? Pour the whole bottle in there, dear. I'm not flying the plane. And while you're at it, tell me more about your tough situation."

"I wish I could."

"You can." Dorothy grabbed the drink from Caroline's hand. "It's not like I'm ever going to meet these people."

"Good point." Caroline thought telling someone else might feel therapeutic. "His fiancé and I went through a dramatic time together. I would feel horrible if I came between them. She would probably hate me forever."

"How old are you?"

"I'll be twenty-four in October."

Dorothy shook her head. "So young. So innocent. So naïve."

"How do you mean?"

"I was like you once. I used to care way too much what people thought of me. I wanted everyone to like me. If someone didn't like me, I felt awful. One day, Mother couldn't take my crying anymore. She grabbed me and said, 'Dorothy, there are millions of people out there. Not everyone is going to like you. If you don't stop pouting about people not liking you, I'm not going to like you anymore.'"

"That seems a bit harsh."

"It was, but it worked." Dorothy placed the gin and tonic to her lips. After swallowing, she continued. "I took what she told me and finally got the courage to approach the boy I had a huge crush on since I was thirteen years old. His name was Tony Giovanni. One day he and his girlfriend were sitting by the lake. I walked up to both of them, looked Tony right in the eyes and said, 'Anthony Giovanni, I've had a huge crush on you for four years now.' I then stuck out my hand. 'This is your one and only chance to be with the best thing you'll ever know. I'll treat you right, and you'll die a happy man many years from now.'" Dorothy took another sip while staring at the seat in front of her.

"What happened?"

"His girlfriend said, 'You're my best friend, Dorothy. What are you doing?' I said, 'Stealing your man, Roberta. I love him, and I don't care what you think.'"

"What did Roberta say?"

"Nothing. She was stunned. Tony looked at me, back at Roberta, and then grabbed my hand. Some might say it was true love that brought us together. Others might say it was because I was busty, and Roberta looked like she had two ant bites on her chest." Dorothy smiled as she continued. "Nine months later, we were married. I invited Roberta to the wedding, but she never made it. I didn't lose any sleep over it because I married the man of my dreams. I loved him so much."

"And you were married for fifty years?"

Dorothy turned to Caroline. "He got drafted into the war less than three months after we were married. He died in Normandy."

Caroline covered her chest with her left hand. "I'm so sorry."

Dorothy half-heartedly smiled. "That's life, dear. One day the man of your dreams is finally in your arms. The next he's laying face down on a beach with a rifle in one hand and a picture of you in his other. I like to think I was the last thing he thought about before he went to heaven."

Caroline was on the verge of crying. "That's so sad."

"Harold was my second husband. I loved him so much, and I don't regret marrying him. I just wish I had more time with Tony. I still think about him and wonder what our kids would have looked like or where we would have retired to. If you love this boy as much as I loved Tony or Harold, tell him how you feel."

"I kind of did already."

"What did he say?"

"Well…some things have happened in our lives lately and the timing may be bad for him to leave his fiancée."

"If it's meant to be, it will happen. Don't give up. How would you feel if he were to marry his fiancée and you would never get to spend time alone with him again?"

Caroline took all of three seconds to come up with an answer. "Like I may never recover from it."

"Then go get him. You're a beautiful young woman and," Dorothy put her hand to Caroline's right breast, "you're busty too. That should help."

"When he looks at me, I feel like the only person in the room. He told me he has feelings for me."

"Then he probably does, dear. Tell him how you feel again, but be more assertive about it. Steal him away from his fiancée. You have nothing to lose."

"Maybe you're right."

The gentleman wearing the turban stood from his seat before turning around. Dorothy set her drink down, quickly reaching into her purse. Caroline noticed the bottle of mace in Dorothy's hand. "I'm watching you, Gandhi," she whispered as the man walked past them. Dorothy was old, perhaps senile, but beneath all the bigotry, there was a story that offered Caroline hope.

"I'm going to do it, Dorothy. I'm going to tell him how I feel, and I don't care what his fiancée thinks of me."

"Good for you. Wait…he isn't one of those wetbacks trying to sneak into our country, is he?"

Caroline giggled. "No."

"Good. Go get him, dear."

Chapter 73

"Who are you? What do you want?" an elderly woman asked from behind a screen door. Her voice was deep and coarse. Glasses hung from a metal chain around her neck.

The man on her porch flashed a badge and identification as he asked, "Blanche McGovern?"

"Who wants to know?"

"My name is Mitch Hennessey. I'm with the F.B.I. I need five minutes of your granddaughter's time, Ms. McGovern."

Blanche held her glasses up to Mitch's identification, squinting while peering through them. "She's been talking with the police all week. She's exhausted. Why can't you just leave her alone? She's been through enough already."

"Yes, ma'am. This will be the last time anyone will talk to Rebecca. Five minutes is all I need with her."

Blanche scratched between the numerous pink rollers on her head as she told him, "Let me see if she wants to talk. If not, you have to leave." She then shut the door.

That's not how this works, lady. Mitch scanned the porch beneath his feet. Not only were floorboards missing, but the wood that remained looked as if it had been infested with termites for some time. Aesthetically, the front yard was in no better condition than the dilapidated porch. An old refrigerator sat on the lawn next to a rusted metal drum that appeared to have been used for burning trash. Most of the grass was either dead or missing completely, and what green grass remained grew tall around the tires of a white Pontiac Firebird. The automobile incited pleasant memories for Mitch. His first car was an '84 Firebird. Upon noticing the pop-up headlights, the rear spoiler, the hatchback, and the design of the rear tail-lights, Mitch knew the car was built between 1982 and 1985. Since it looked nearly identical to his old Firebird, he thought it might actually be an '84 model.

Mitch again glanced at the police report while waiting for the door to open. Rebecca's mother was in jail for a second stint. Her charges included identity theft and possession of cocaine with intent to distribute. Rebecca's father abandoned the family years earlier and was nowhere to be found. A high school dropout, Rebecca had been living with her grandmother at the time of her abduction. She seemed to have a long road ahead of her. Mitch looked up upon hearing the door open. Rebecca stood next to her grandmother behind the screen door. She wore sweat pants and a t-shirt several sizes too big.

"Rebecca, my name is Mitch Hennessey. I'm with the F.B.I. I just need to ask you a few questions. May I come in?"

"Okay."

Blanche opened the screen door. Mitch entered, immediately spotting at least four cats in the living room. A white cockatoo with yellow markings above his head sat atop a birdcage in the corner of the room that smelled of cigarettes.

"That's a pretty bird you have, Ms. McGovern."

"Pretty bird," the cockatoo repeated.

"That's Pierre. He's the smartest bird alive," Blanche declared. "You can have a seat on the loveseat, officer."

Mitch didn't feel the need to tell the woman he was an agent, not an officer, as he took to the loveseat. "Thank you."

"Thirsty, officer?" Blanche asked while removing a cigarette from the front pouch of her floral print muumuu.

"Thirsty, officer?" Pierre repeated.

"No, thank you. I won't be here long."

Rebecca and her grandmother sat on the adjacent couch. With the cigarette in her mouth and a lighter in her hand, Blanche asked, "Do you mind if I smoke, officer?"

Mitch detested cigarette smoke. To not appear rude, he grinned while telling her the same lie he tells those that light up near him. "I'm allergic to cigarettes, actually. I can't breathe for days if I inhale the smoke."

Blanche placed the cigarette and lighter back in her pouch. "Guess I can wait five minutes."

Mitch focused his attention on Rebecca. Just as her grandmother had stated moments earlier, Rebecca appeared exhausted. Bags were visible under her eyes, her hair could use a good washing and a combing, and Mitch got the impression she had eaten very little over the last few days. "First of all, Rebecca, I just want to ask how you're doing."

She was slow to answer. "Tired. I haven't been able to sleep the last few nights."

"She has to sleep with the lights on. The darkness makes her feel like she's back in that dungeon."

"Have you been able to eat the last couple of days?"

"I don't have much of an appetite right now."

"I'm sorry to hear that." Mitch looked down at the police report before beginning what he hoped would be a friendly interrogation. "Rebecca, I don't want to ask you any redundant questions, so I'll just get to it." He glanced back at Rebecca. "The police report said that you and another girl, Maria Sanchez, heard two people shouting in Hank Bowery's living room before hearing gunshots. Do you remember how many gunshots you heard?"

"Four." Her answer matched the same on the police report in his hands.

Mitch nodded then asked a question that wasn't on the report. "Were the shots fired one after another, or was there a delay between any of them?"

"It's so hard to remember."

"I know it is. And I'm sorry for having to put you through this again."

"Why are you doing this, officer?"

"I'll get to that in just a second, ma'am. Rebecca, were the shots fired one after another?"

She placed her hands over her eyes for several seconds, seemingly in deep thought, before giving an answer. "Each shot was a few seconds apart."

"How did you and Maria get out of the basement?"

"When Hank chained us up, I managed to steal the keys. We uncuffed ourselves once the shootings were over and made it upstairs."

"How did you steal the keys?"

"The chain was long enough that I could reach into his pocket. Maria distracted him while I grabbed the keys."

"You're a clever girl. That was very brave of you to do that."

"Thank you."

"I'm almost done here, Rebecca." Mitch paid close attention for any of the tell-tale signs of someone telling a lie as he asked the next question. "Was there anyone else in the house? Could there have been a third person upstairs while you and Maria were in the hidden room?"

Her eyes remained focused on Mitch. "No." There was no hesitation or fumbling with her answer. Her hands remained still, and there was no nervous blinking. She was either telling the truth, or had lied enough times that it felt natural to her.

"I only ask because the government believes there was a third person involved in the shootings. When the government believes something, they tend to want to know the truth. I believe you, I just don't know if they will."

Rebecca crossed her legs before running her hand through her dirty blonde hair three times. "It's the truth." Signs of nervousness were beginning to show.

While scanning through the police report on the way to the house, Mitch discovered that Hank's nearest neighbor—a man by the name of Earl Farriday— lived nearly a half-mile away. Earl told the police that he heard nothing during the early morning shootout. Mitch decided to take a gamble. "A neighbor of Hank's named Earl Farriday happened to be on his front porch during the shootout. He saw someone drive past his house on the way to Hank's property just minutes before the shootout occurred." Rebecca began to ever so slightly shift her body. "Was there someone else in the house, Rebecca? I promise that no harm will come to you if you're honest with me. That window is quickly closing though. I need to know the truth right now. I'm going to speak with Maria after this. If she tells me something different, we're unfortunately going to have to take a trip to the F.B.I. office, where a lot more questioning will take place with men that aren't nearly as nice as me."

Rebecca looked at her grandmother then back at Mitch. After closing her eyes, and with great hesitation, she slowly nodded.

Mitch perked up in the loveseat. "There was a third person in the house?"

Rebecca again nodded.

His hunch had been confirmed. "Did you happen to see this person?"

"Yes."

"What did this person look like?"

She opened her eyes. "I don't want to go to jail."

"You're not, Rebecca, as long as you tell the truth. What did this third person look like?"

"I don't know. That's the truth. He had a mask on and said we couldn't see his face."

"Then it was definitely a male?"

Rebecca nodded.

"Was he someone that had visited you or Maria in the hidden room before?"

"No. He had never been down there."

"Are you certain?"

"Yes. He didn't know how to operate the trick wall in the closet, and I didn't recognize his voice."

"Rebecca, I need to know every detail you can remember about him. Let's start with his appearance—skin color, eye color, any visible tattoos?"

"He was white. I could see the skin around his eyes and neck. He was about six feet tall, and I'm pretty certain he had brown hair. I could see it hanging out the back of his mask. I couldn't see if he had any tattoos because he was wearing pants and a long-sleeved t-shirt."

"Eye color?" Mitch asked, writing on the back of the police report.

"Not blue. A light brown—almost green."

"Hazel?"

"What color is hazel?"

Blanche turned to her granddaughter. "Like mine."

"Like mine," Pierre reiterated.

"Be quiet, Pierre," Blanche told him.

Rebecca nodded. "Yes. Hazel."

"What about the way he talked?"

"He wasn't from up north; somewhere in the South. There was nothing peculiar about it."

"Did he have a limp or funny walk or anything else that stood out about his appearance?"

"No."

"Did he say anything about where he was going or where he was from?"

Rebecca still had an uncomfortable look about her, as if she didn't want to say anything else. "Is he in trouble?"

"I'm not at liberty to say."

"He saved our lives. If it wasn't for him, we'd still be chained up in that dungeon—or dead. I don't want anything to happen to him."

Mitch found another flaw in her statement to the police. "So, you didn't steal the keys from Hank and uncuff yourself?"

With her stare aimed at the ground, Rebecca subtly shook her head. "He unchained us. I'm sorry for lying."

"It's okay. As long as you're telling the truth right now nothing will happen to you—I promise."

"What will happen to him?"

"I will do my best to make sure nothing bad happens to him. We just need to know the truth, so we can close this case for good. Did he say where he was going or coming from?"

"No. He just asked us not to tell the police he was still in there or the woman he loved may be in danger."

Mitch stopped writing. "Still in there? He was in the house while the police were there?"

A cat jumped onto Rebecca's lap. While gently petting the light gray feline, she answered, "Yes."

"Where?"

"In the attic."

Mitch grew excited at the new evidence brought to his attention. "The attic, huh?"

"Yes. One of the officers went up there but didn't see him. I guess he was hiding."

Mitch knew where his next stop would be. "Is there anything else you can remember?"

"No."

Mitch stood from the loveseat. He removed a card from his wallet and handed it to Blanche. "If something else comes to mind, please call me at this number. Rebecca, you are a very brave girl and you did the right thing."

"If you ever find the man, please thank him for saving my life."

"I will find him, and I will relay the message. Thank you for your time."

Chapter 74

Paranoia was something Delain had lived with for the better portion of three years. It had become so much a part of her life that she no longer knew how to live without it. She couldn't help but feel an even heightened sense of suspicion while walking through the airport. The feeling that someone was watching her was enough to incite several glances over her shoulder as she made her way towards the arrival gate. Even though Davis' death was ruled a heart attack, she felt as if she, Caroline, and Jackson weren't out of the clear just yet. The expectation that every police officer she saw was about to approach her with gun and handcuffs drawn was still high.

After glancing at the arrival information on the screens in the bustling terminal, Delain looked at her watch from behind the pair of oversized sunglasses that frequently adorned her face over the past week. Caroline would be walking through the gate in less than ten minutes. While waiting for her only friend's arrival, a mural painted above her head grabbed her attention. Of the twenty-seven musicians depicted in the painting, only two were recognizable. The man with protruding cheeks playing the horn was the man whom the airport was named after—Louis Armstrong. Harry Connick Jr. was the other recognizable face. She hadn't been in New Orleans very long to know the faces of the remaining twenty-five musicians. Also depicted in the mural were cherubs playing instruments. Even though Harry Connick Jr. was still alive, Heaven is where the musicians were gathered. Just as she had done several times over the last few years (and even more so over the last week) she again questioned Heaven and God's existence. Raised with a strong religious upbringing, she wanted to accept the beliefs her parents instilled in her, yet with the events that had plagued her over the last three years, there was ample evidence to suggest that God wouldn't allow such things to happen to her if He was real. Still somewhere in the middle, the debate was put on hold as she reached for her vibrating cell phone.

The incoming text message from Caroline read, *'Just landed.'* After placing the phone back in her pocket, she took notice of the police officer a few steps away. His gaze was directed nowhere near Delain, but she was prepared to turn and walk in the opposite direction in a hastily manner if he were to engage in lengthy eye contact with her. While staring at him from behind her glasses, she noticed a well-dressed man several yards behind the officer. He was far enough away that she couldn't see his face, but his gait was a familiar one. As the man grew closer, Delain found difficulty in breathing, blinking, or moving any part of her body. She stood about as motionless as the musicians painted above her head. Once the man walked past the officer and made eye contact with Delain, his mouth hinged open, his eyebrows squinted together, and his rolling suitcase fell to the ground. It was too late to hide from a man she had been eluding for almost three years.

"Christina?" the gentleman asked. She attempted to speak his name, but couldn't move her lips. "Is that you?"

As she swallowed, it felt as if a golf ball was slowly sliding down her throat. "Tyler? What are…what…how…?"

"It is you. Oh my God." Tyler spread his arms as wide as his grin. An embrace ensued. "I almost didn't recognize you behind those glasses. And your hair is different too."

Still very much shocked and in disbelief, she told him, "I decided to go dark. What are you doing here?"

Tyler stepped back. The smile Delain never grew tired of seeing for two years remained on his face as he told her, "I have a job interview tomorrow with a company in downtown New Orleans. What are you doing here?"

"Just picking up a…I'm sorry. I'm a little…"

"You seem flustered, Christina."

Someone calling her by her birth name was a peculiar feeling. "I think I am. I can't believe we ran into each other like this."

"I know. What are the odds of that?"

Upon finally catching her breath, she removed her sunglasses and held out her arms. "Give me another hug, you." Besides being nervous, she also felt comfort while momentarily revisiting her former life. The image of when they first met beneath the arch at the University of Georgia came to mind as she pulled away. "You look good, Tyler."

"Gracias. You look even better than I remember."

"Your hair isn't short anymore," she pointed out.

After picking up his suitcase, he told her, "I decided to let it grow. Speaking of hair, I loved your blonde locks, but I'm digging the brunette thing you got going on."

While running her left hand through her hair she told him, "Thank you."

"I was just about to ask if you're dating anyone, but seeing that," he pointed to her left hand, "I would say that's a big yes."

Delain glanced at her hand. "I am…engaged."

"Well…then I guess a 'congratulations' is in store."

"Thank you."

"When's the big day?"

"Um…tomorrow."

His smile vanished. "Tomorrow? Like in tomorrow tomorrow?"

She nodded, deciding the conversation needed a change of direction. "What's new with you? Are you still in Georgia? How's your mom?"

"She passed away about two months ago."

Delain gasped, placing a hand over her mouth. "Tyler, I'm so sorry. That makes me incredibly sad."

"It's so crazy that I ran into you like this. Right before my mom died she talked about you."

"What did she say?"

Tyler placed his pointer finger to his right ear before saying, "I better not say right now. Maybe the next time we run into one another I can reveal that. But, I can tell you that she said to tell you how much she loved you if I ever saw you again."

"I loved your mom too. She was such a special woman." Delain adored Tyler's mom. She had no doubt she would have made an incredible and loving mother-in-law. News of her recent passing brought about not only feelings of sorrow, but also guilt. Another conversational change was needed "What about your love life? Are you seeing anyone?"

"I just broke up with someone."

"I'm sorry to hear that."

"It's okay. She wasn't the one."

Delain tugged at the cross necklace around her neck, wondering why she found delight in hearing that Tyler wasn't attached to anyone.

"I see you're still wearing the necklace I gave you."

She nodded. "It's one of my favorite pieces of jewelry."

"I would hope it's second to your engagement ring."

Again she nodded. "Of course. It's my favorite piece of jewelry, after the engagement ring."

"How was California?"

"I'm sorry?"

"When you broke up with me, you said you were going to California to start a new life. How did that work out for you?"

"Not too good. I ended up here in New Orleans."

"Is this where you met your fiancé?"

Delain glanced at the group of passengers exiting the terminal gates. "Yes." Caroline was nowhere to be seen. "We met outside a bank."

"What's his name, if you don't mind me asking?"

"Jackson."

"Jackson what?"

She was hoping to avoid the latter question in case he had been watching the news over the last three days. "Fabacher."

Tyler's eyebrows again grew closer to one another. "Wait…he isn't the same Jackson Fabacher that's been on the news the last couple of days, is he?"

At first contemplating a lie, she instead reluctantly answered, "Yes."

Tyler smirked while shaking his head.

"What?"

"Nothing."

"What? You can say it."

With a shrug of his shoulders he told her, "The guy got cold feet about marrying you. I would think if someone loved you and wanted to be with you then they wouldn't have to question whether or not they wanted to marry you."

"I know it looks bad, but it's not what it seems. He loves me with all his heart."

"And how do you feel about him?"

Another group of passengers walking through the arrival gate momentarily stole her attention. Caroline was at the front of the line. *Shit! If she calls me Delain, Tyler will want to know why I changed my name.* "I'm sorry. What was the question?"

"How do you feel about him?"

"Um…the same," she nervously replied.

"Then I'm happy for you."

"That means a lot to me," she told him as a grinning Caroline approached.

"There's the bride-to-be. How are you, sweetie?"

"Good," she answered as the two embraced. "Caroline, this is Tyler. Tyler, this is my friend Caroline."

"Nice to meet you, Caroline," Tyler spoke with extended hand.

Caroline, appearing perplexed, extended her hand as she asked, "You're…Tyler?"

Delain's heart began to palpitate as she suddenly remembered telling Caroline about Tyler days earlier on her couch. She was the only person who knew the truth about her ex-boyfriend. While Tyler glanced at Caroline, Delain subtly shook her head side to side and her eyes grew big as she repeatedly mouthed the word 'no' to her friend.

"You've heard about me?" Tyler then turned to Delain. "You told her about me?"

Before Delain could conjure a lie, Caroline spoke, "You are Tyler…Smith, correct? From Houston, Texas?"

"No. Tyler Bennett from Atlanta, Georgia."

"Oh, I apologize. I thought you were her friend Tyler Smith, the blind date she was setting me up with for the wedding tomorrow night. That's a bummer because you're hot. That would have been a fun blind date." She then asked Delain, "Is Tyler Smith as hot as Tyler Bennett?"

A relieved Delain grinned. "He's a real sweet guy."

"Real sweet guy? That makes it sound like he's not that cute," Caroline spoke. "Don't you agree, Tyler B.?

"When 'sweet' is first used to describe someone, that's usually not a good sign," he added.

"Thanks a lot. Can I bring Tyler B. instead?"

"That might be a little awkward," Tyler said.

Delain breathed a sigh of relief as Caroline did an exceptional job of deterring what could have morphed into a confession of the truth. "Caroline, how was your flight?"

Glancing around the terminal, she answered, "Interesting. I met an elderly woman who would bring down the house at a KKK comedy show. Speaking of…" Caroline crouched behind Tyler. "There she is."

"You're afraid of that sweet old lady?" Tyler asked.

"Don't be fooled by her support hose and wrinkles. She's about as sweet as a saltine cracker. She does give good advice though."

"What did she give you advice on?" Delain asked.

"An important life decision." The woman walked past them. Once she was out of view, Caroline stood upright before asking, "What brings you to New Orleans, Tyler?"

"I have a job interview with a company tomorrow morning."

"Does that mean that you're moving here?"

"Not sure yet."

"And is this the first time you two have seen each other since…the last time you guys saw one another?"

"Yep. The last time we saw each other, Christina had just broken up with me and was moving to California to find herself."

"Who's Christina?"

"Caroline," spoke a frantic Delain, "I don't see any luggage in your hand. I'm assuming you checked your bag."

"I did."

"Can I meet you downstairs at baggage claim in about one minute? I just want to say goodbye to Tyler"

"Sure. I'll see you downstairs. Tyler, it was good to meet you."

"And you as well, Caroline. I hope you have a pleasant time with your date at the wedding tomorrow."

Caroline flashed a closed-lip smile before walking towards the escalator leading to baggage claim.

"If you were in my shoes—"

Delain held up her hand, interrupting Tyler until her lip-reading friend was out of sight. "If I what?"

"If you were in my shoes, what question would be on the tip of your tongue right now?" he asked.

"Why?" she immediately answered.

"Why what?"

"Why did you breakup with me out of the blue?"

He nodded. "I've waited almost three years for an answer. Not a day has gone by I don't ask myself that exact question. Christina, I don't understand. Either I'm the stupidest person in the world for thinking we had something remarkable, or something crazy happened when you came down here for that bachelorette party. Given the fact you're living here, I'm leaning towards the latter. Tell me I'm wrong."

She glanced upwards at the mural then back at Tyler before shaking her head. "You're wrong."

"Bullshit!" he yelled before lowering his voice. "Bullshit, Chrissy. What happened to you? You wrote a note a week before you broke up with me saying how much you loved me and couldn't wait to be with me. I think I have the right to know why you did a 180 on our relationship overnight. I haven't been able to get close to another woman because of what you did to me. I need an answer. Please give me something so I can move on with my life."

Delain had to dig deep mentally to keep from breaking down in front of him. An image of Caleb in his stroller kept her from confessing the truth. She hated that she couldn't tell him, but it was the only way to protect him and those close to her. "I fell out of love with you."

"In just one weekend away from one another?"

Delain nodded. "I didn't mean for it to happen. It just did." She had trouble looking him in the eye.

Tyler stared blankly at her before saying, "I understand. It was good seeing you again, Christina." He began to walk off.

"Wait," she said while tugging at his suit jacket. "That's it?"

"What do you mean 'that's it'? You're getting married tomorrow to the runaway groom, and you said you fell out of love with me. For almost three years I've been trying to find an answer. I guess I just got it."

Delain noticed he was shaking. It was obvious he was visibly upset. The only other time she saw him that way was when she ended their relationship.

"Where are you staying?"

"In a hotel."

"Which one?"

"The Doubletree on Canal. Room 407. Why?"

She shrugged her shoulders. "I'm not sure. I just wanted to know."

"Good luck with Jackson. I'm sure he won't run away from you a second time. He can't be that stupid." Tyler leaned forward, planting a kiss on her forehead before saying, "Uno." As he walked away, she again grew speechless.

Chapter 75

My parents' house was bustling with the same excitement as one of their over-the-top Christmas extravaganzas. Hors d'oeuvres were served by well-attired waitresses, drinks were mixed by two professional bartenders (who took the place of my dad behind the bar), a skilled pianist played classical music on my parents' Estonia grand piano, a photographer snapped photos while quietly roaming around the parlour and surrounding rooms, and a sketch artist captured the night onto canvas. What I thought would be a quiet sit-down dinner with family and close friends was quite the opposite.

In addition to my immediate family, every member of my extended family was at the house, along with Logan, Al and Betty, a handful of my parents' close friends, my previous groomsmen and their wives, the wedding planner, and Father Peter. At fifteen minutes past 7:00, the only two people not in attendance were my fiancée and Caroline. While I anxiously paced in the hallway with hands in pockets, my mom approached me. She held a flute of champagne in one hand and a mint julep in the other.

"I hope you don't think we went overboard," she commented while handing me my first mint julep in weeks.

"You and Dad are always going overboard. I should have expected it."

"Are you upset?"

"Have I ever been upset with the two of you before? I love what y'all did. The only thing that makes me nervous is word leaking out about the wedding tomorrow. I don't want to talk to another reporter or see any more news vans outside the house."

"There's no need to worry about that. Your father and I told everyone here to keep the wedding a secret until after it was over. I think it's safe to say everyone in the house can be trusted. Your wedding is going to go off without a hitch. Now, where's that beautiful fiancée of yours?"

"She should be here any second." After placing the drink to my lips, I continued to pace in the hallway. Delain was never late for anything. Any time we had plans to be somewhere, she made it a point for us to leave early. Punctuality was her strong suit, so I found it odd she was fifteen minutes late for her own rehearsal dinner.

"You're nervous."

"Is it that obvious?"

She nodded. "A little bit."

"I thought I was hiding it pretty well."

"You are, but a mother can tell when something's on her son's mind."

"So much has happened in the last week. I felt like I hadn't had a chance to catch my breath yet."

"Are you ready to marry Delain?"

I stared into my drink while answering, "I'm sure I will be by tomorrow."

My mom placed her flute of champagne on the table next to the grandfather clock before hugging me tightly. "If you're not ready, Jackson, don't be afraid to postpone it. I'm sure she'll understand. Can you promise—"

My mom was interrupted by the opening of the cloakroom door. Caroline, the first to walk into the hallway, flashed a joyous grin. Delain, a few steps behind, showcased a less-than- enthusiastic smile.

"Y'all are here!" my mom exclaimed.

"I'm sorry, Mrs. Cecile. It was my fault. My plane was a few minutes late." Caroline and my mom shared an embrace. I had no recollection of the two ever meeting.

"You two seem to know one another."

"I met your mom at the get-together here after your funeral last Sunday. Now, there's a sentence you don't hear very often." Caroline then hugged me. The last time I saw her, we had professed feelings towards one another. Strangely, it didn't feel awkward as we embraced—at least not to me.

"Caroline, your aunt and uncle are in the parlour. Let's go tell them you're here." My mom placed her hand on Caroline's shoulder. As they walked off, Delain kissed me. Of all the kisses we shared over the previous eighteen months, the one in my parents' hallway on the night before our wedding was nowhere close to one of our unrivaled kisses, and our embrace felt like I was hugging a stranger.

"How are you feeling?" I asked.

"Good."

"Any problems picking up Caroline?"

"Nope," she answered while peering precariously down the hallway. "I thought we were just having a quiet dinner tonight. It sounds like a lot of people are back there."

"I thought that too. My parents went a little over the top." There was no smile upon her face. "You want to go see everyone?"

"Yep." She walked ahead of me. Something was wrong.

After meeting the guests, Delain and I, along with my brother and, to my surprise, Caroline, met with Father Peter and the wedding planner in the study to rehearse the wedding. Delain had, apparently, asked Caroline if she would be her maid-of-honor on the way to my parents' house. She said she felt more comfortable with Caroline next to her instead of the previous choice—a co-worker of hers that she wasn't remotely close with.

The wedding planner, the same one who organized my brother's wedding, had everyone line up as we would in the cathedral. "The sooner we get through this, y'all, the sooner you can get..." she grabbed the drink from Marcus' mouth as she continued, "back to the party. After the maid-of-honor and best man walk down the aisle, then Delain will walk down. Will your father be escorting you, Delain?"

"No. I'll be walking down by myself."

"Okay. Once you walk to the altar, Jackson will stand next to you. Then, Father Peter will take over."

"Jackson, will there be any videos that I need to know about this time?"

"No, Father."

"Are you certain there won't be any surprises this time?"

While glancing at Delain, I told him, "I sure hope not."

Once the rehearsal was over, everyone began to exit the room. I grabbed Delain's arm before sliding the door shut. We stood alone in the study. "What's wrong?"

"Nothing," she answered.

"Are you having doubts about tomorrow?"

She shook her head. "No. Are you?"

I had no doubt she wasn't telling the truth. "You seem different, like you're not even here."

Delain wasted no time in grabbing the back of my head and planting the second kiss of the night on my lips. Unlike the previous, the latter kiss was filled with more fervor.

"Tomorrow's a big day," she said upon stepping back. "I was nervous, but I feel better now." A smile appeared on her face. "Let's go have some fun, baby."

Throughout the evening, I wasn't sure if Delain was enjoying herself or just putting on a front. I wanted to believe she was madly in love with me and wanted to marry me for all the right reasons, but my uncertainty increased by her aloof behavior throughout the night. Earlier in the day when she held me on her bathroom floor following my panic attack, I felt like she never wanted to leave my side. Half-a-day later, she was someone else completely.

Due to the large crowd, there wasn't enough space for a sit-down dinner. Instead, food rested on the dining room table and partygoers could eat as they pleased. I offered to make Delain a plate, yet she said she wasn't hungry. After making myself one, I sat next to my eighty-year-old uncle. We were the only two in the room.

"How are you feeling, Uncle Lawrence," I asked loudly. My uncle's primary orders during the Korean War included reloading ammunition into machine guns for his fellow servicemen. He never wore ear plugs.

"Great, Marcus. You still have your automotive shop?"

Not only was his hearing nearly gone, but he had been showing signs of Alzheimer's for about a year. I found it was best not to correct him. "Yes, sir."

"I'll bring my Chevy by tomorrow, if that's okay."

"Of course."

As he patted my knee, Caroline entered the dining room. "Is this where the handsome men hangout?" She flashed her infectious smile at the both of us from across the table.

"The handsome single men," spoke my windowed uncle of ten years. He stood, removing his fedora. "Have a seat, young lady."

"I don't want to take your chair." Caroline must have already met my uncle because she knew to talk loudly.

"Good idea." He nudged me with his cane. "Take his."

Caroline laughed as Uncle Lawrence's daughter, my aunt, walked into the room. "It's time we get going, Dad. We have a long day tomorrow."

"But I was just about to ask this young lady if she wanted to take a ride in my Chevy."

My Aunt Rose shook her head. "Firstly, you don't have a car anymore. And, secondly, no more flirting, Dad. You're a little too old to be dating Caroline."

"Who said anything about dating? I just want a few minutes alone with her to show her a night she'll never forget," he said with a wink.

"And we're done here." Rose grabbed her dad. "Caroline, it was good to meet you tonight. I apologize for this dirty old man. Jackson, we'll see you tomorrow evening at the cathedral."

"I'll see you tomorrow, Uncle Lawrence," Caroline loudly told him. "Save a dance for me."

"I'll save all the dances for you," he spoke with a grin before addressing my aunt. "Can we stop at K&B and get some ice cream on the way home?"

"They closed down years ago, Dad," Rose told him with a roll of her eyes as they exited the room.

Caroline and I stood alone, separated by the lengthy dining room table built by Lawrence's father. She wore a strapless, plum-colored dress that stopped just above her knees. As always, she looked stunning. After grabbing a plate, she told me, "I haven't got a chance to talk to you all night."

"I know. How have the last couple of days been? Have you talked to Brock?"

"A little," she told me while scanning the food options. "He wants me to reconsider being engaged to him."

"Are you?"

"I'm not sure right now. I'm in no rush to get married. I want to wait to make sure I'm with the right person, and I want that person to have no doubt they want to be with me. Don't you agree that's the right thing to do?" She scooped a serving of jambalaya onto her plate.

"Yes. And speaking of," I lowered my voice, "Did Delain say anything to you at the airport or on the way over here?"

"What do you mean?"

"She seems different tonight. Do you think she's having doubts about the wedding?"

"She didn't say anything about it to me. Why? Are you?"

"No," I dishonestly answered.

"Nothing out of the ordinary happened tonight. She picked me up at the airport, we ran into a friend of hers in the terminal, went back to her place to get changed, and then came here," she told me while scanning the table.

"A friend?"

She placed a finger sandwich onto her plate before again making eye contact with me. "Some guy."

"What guy?"

She was slow to answer. "I shouldn't say anything, Jackson. I promised Delain."

Apprehension overcame me. Caroline, I suspected, knew why Delain wasn't acting herself all night. I also believed she wanted me to know because if not, she would have never mentioned anything at all. "You have to tell me, Caroline."

"I can't."

I then told her the one line that never fails when trying to extract information from someone who secretly wants to share it. "I promise I won't say anything to her."

"I don't know, Jackson. I like Delain, and I don't want her to get mad at me."

Her answers only increased my already stomach-churning curiosity. "She said she'll get mad if you tell me?"

"She didn't say she would, but I suspect she might."

"She won't get mad because I won't tell her anything."

"You promise?"

"I promise."

She switched the plate to her left hand, then leaned across the table and extended her right hand. "Pinky swear."

I wrapped my pinky around hers. "I pinky swear I won't say anything to her."

"And if I do, Caroline will be very upset and may never talk to me again."

"And if I do, which I won't, Caroline and I will never speak again."

She let go of my finger. "His name is Tyler."

"As in her ex-boyfriend, Tyler?"

"Yes."

I shook my head. "That's impossible. He died in a car wreck."

"Maybe it was another Tyler that she dated. Bennett is his last name."

I couldn't recall Tyler's last name, but knew how long they were together. "Did she mention how long she dated this Tyler?"

"Um…" Caroline walked around the table, stopping right next to me, "two years, I think."

"That's how long she dated the one that died in a car wreck."

"Hmmm. You don't think she lied about the car wreck, do you?"

I had a difficult time believing Delain would tell a lie as morbid as someone dying when he was very much alive, which is why I believed it was a coincidence that she dated two Tylers for the same amount of time. I also found it peculiar she so happened to run into a former boyfriend just one day before she was to marry me. It could have been another coincidence, but my gut was saying it was something else, considering her behavior for the night. "What did they talk about?"

"Not much. But then again, there's no telling what was discussed before I got there. I walked out of the arrival gate and saw them already talking." The knots in my stomach grew tighter as she continued. "Then I was asked to leave. I'm not sure what they talked about after I left. It was a couple of minutes until Delain met me at the baggage claim."

"Who asked you to leave?"

"Delain."

The coupling fear of being arrested for anything from car theft to murder, along with the feeling that Delain was again hiding something caused my doubts about her to return. I felt anger, betrayal, confusion, and disappointment. "I need to talk to her to see who this Tyler was at the airport."

Caroline grabbed my arm, calmly saying, "But you pinky swore."

"Then how do I bring this up to her? She's hiding something."

"I'll talk to her tonight when we get back to her house. By the time I'm done with her, she'll be calling you to confess everything."

"Why do you think that?"

"Delain trusts me. I need you to do the same. Everything is going to work out for you. You look handsome tonight, by the way. I didn't get to tell you earlier."

"Thank you. And you look gorgeous as always."

"Can I have a hug?" My response didn't involve words, but instead the action of giving her what she had asked. I made sure my head was on her left side. "It's all going to work out for you," she whispered into my ear.

"I hope you're right."

"I care about you and want what's best for you, Jackson— whatever that may be." Before I could tell her the same, she stepped away from me. "Let's get back to the festivities, shall we?"

"After you." Before I could follow her, something outside the window quickly moved. I walked towards the window, placing my hands up to the glass to get a better view. The only thing moving outside was a tree limb, yet it was moving much slower than the object that initially caught my attention.

"What is it?" Caroline asked.

"Nothing. Let's go mingle."

At eleven o'clock, an announcement by my dad let everyone know that the rehearsal dinner was over. Typically, parties at the Fabacher house ran well past midnight, but my parents insisted everyone get rested up for the following day. I was greatly supportive of their decision to end the party. Even though I had tremendous experience in pretending everything was wonderful in my life, I was mentally exhausted. Delain's coldness throughout the night never grew warm. Several times I caught a glazed look in her eyes as she talked to my friends and family. The goodbye embrace I shared with Caroline was much more magnetic than the one my fiancée and I shared, and the kiss Caroline planted on my cheek was much more affectionate than the one Delain placed upon my lips. As they left, I wasn't so sure a wedding would be taking place in twenty hours.

By eleven-thirty, those remaining in the house were my parents, Marcus, Logan, and myself. Logan was too intoxicated to drive, so I offered to drive him home after dropping Marcus off at his house. While everyone helped in cleaning up the kitchen, the doorbell chimed.

"Someone probably forgot something," my mom stated while placing a hand-washed plate onto the drying rack. "Can you see who it is, Jackson?"

As I opened the door to the cloak room, I could see through the distorted glass that the person at the front door was a male, about the same height as me, hair the same color as mine, and that he was wearing a suit. No one from the party came to mind. I opened the front door.

Various scholars debate on the number of words in the English vernacular, with their answers ranging from 200,000 to well over one million. I couldn't muster a single word to say while staring into the eyes of the person standing before me.

"Jackson, I find you," he spoke in broken English while smiling ear to ear. He appeared the happiest I had ever seen a person.

Footsteps clacked behind me. "Who's here?" Logan asked upon joining me in the cloak room. "Hoooooly ssssshit! How drunk am I?" Logan glanced at me then back at the visitor.

"May I come in?" he asked, his accent hinting an Italian dialect.

I stepped backwards through the cloakroom before turning around and hurrying down the hallway, my gait quick and unsteady. I felt light-headed, confused, but mostly petrified as I walked into the kitchen. Longing to be in the middle of a twisted nightmare, I realized I was very much awake. As I stared at my parents, I came to the realization that my life was never going to be the same again. It was going to be worse—much, much worse.

My mom's gaze was directed into the sink. "Who was at the door, sweetie?" she asked. I couldn't answer her. She glanced upward, her smile waning as soon as she made eye contact with me. We stared at one another. The dish in her hand soon fell into the sink.

"Are you okay, Mom?" Marcus asked.

My dad hurriedly walked past me, on his way to the front door.

"What's going on, Jackson?" Marcus asked. I could only stare at my mom. My brother soon hobbled past me. My mother and I only stood a few feet apart, but it felt like an ocean separated us.

"I'm sorry," she softly spoke, her expression void of any sort of emotion. "I'm so sorry, Jackson." She then began to cry.

An out of breath Marcus returned to the kitchen. Something then snapped inside of me; a feeling of rage, a feeling as if I could lift a car or punch a hole through a brick building. "What the fuck did you two do?!" I yelled with such force and intensity that I not only felt heat radiating from my face, but also grew even more light-headed. I had never yelled at either of my parents in twenty-nine years, nor said the 'f-word' in their presence. "Why is there someone on our porch that looks exactly like me?!"

Marcus stood between us, pointing to the hallway as he said, "Both of y'all out there now."

My mom's eyes remained locked with mine as she walked past me and into the hallway. I followed several feet behind her. Marcus placed his hand on my shoulder as I walked past him.

In the cloakroom next to Logan, my dad stood, his hands resting on his hips while his head shook side to side. Guilt was plastered all about his face. "I think it's time we have a talk."

"You think?!" I was livid. Tiffany cheating on me and discovering that Delain dated me just to get her son back—none of those events could compare to how betrayed I felt as I stood in my parents' hallway.

My dad walked to the front door. "Why don't you come inside," he calmly told my doppelganger at the front door. "Everyone, into the study please."

"No." My favorite room in the house wasn't where I wanted to learn a family secret. "I don't want memories of that room to be tainted with what I'm about to hear." I pointed to the portrait room. "In there."

My dad grabbed my mom's hand, leading her to the velvet couch in front of the window. She looked as if she could barely stand. Marcus stood next to the other couch, where my mystery twin sat.

Logan stood just outside the room in the hallway. "I think I'm gonna go to the parlour and have a drink while y'all talk."

"Why don't you have a seat, Jax?"

"I'm fine standing. Someone better start fucking talking."

Chapter 76

My visibly-shaking mom was unable to speak. My dad took the reigns as I frantically swayed back and forth between the two couches with my arms crossed. The trembling sensation that encompassed my entire body made it nearly difficult to stand.

"In 1977, I was urged by fellow councilmen and friends to run for mayor. 'A young, energetic mayor is what the city needs' they told me. The idea was too enticing to pass up. After talking it over with your mother and your grandparents, I decided to throw my hat into the ring."

I knew my dad was on the city council in the seventies and ran for mayor, but I never knew the details of his campaign. They never talked much about it, and I never asked.

"The first two debates went extremely well. At one point, a poll had me in the lead. The stars were beginning to align for me to become the next mayor. Then…" He and my mom exchanged uncomfortable glances, "something happened." My mom grabbed his hand as he continued. "One night after a debate, while sitting in a hotel lounge with my campaign team, we were bombarded by these campaign groupies. After a few rounds of drinks, they started to become friendly with us. One by one, the women grabbed a member of my staff and took him away. By the end of the night, me and one of the women were all that remained." My dad paused while staring at the ground. My mom's hand was still clutched to his. Upon looking up, I noticed his eyes were red. "She grabbed my hand and said she wanted to talk in a quieter place. I…I…reluctantly went upstairs to her room. I knew it wasn't a good idea, but I couldn't stop myself. Your mother and I were having some problems in our relationship. In a moment of weakness, I caved." He began to tear up. Very rarely did I see my dad cry, yet I had seen him do it twice in the last three days.

"You cheated on mom?" Marcus asked, just as shocked as me.

"I didn't have intercourse with the woman, but I let her do something to me that I shouldn't have."

"Oral sex?"

My dad wiped at his eyes while nodding. "It was a setup. A man hid in the closet with a camera. Two days later, the pictures were sent to my office with a note that read 'drop your candidacy for mayor or the pictures will be seen by everyone in New Orleans.' That evening I resigned from the race. Dropping out wasn't the hard part. Having to face your mother and tell her what horrible thing I had done was the difficult part."

In the blink of an eye, I became furious at my dad for cheating on her. Never did I think either one of them would do such a thing to the other. As long as I could remember, their love for one another seemed like it was indestructible. I was reminded that looks can be terribly deceiving.

"What did you do, Mom?"

"I left."

"Why don't I remember that?" Marcus asked.

"That was when you went to live with your grandparents for a couple weeks."

"That's why I only saw one of you at a time when you came to visit."

"I didn't want to see your father. I missed him dearly, even though I was so angry at him. Even though he didn't have sex with the woman, and it was a setup, I still didn't want to be around him. It was too much for me. I became vengeful and acted foolishly myself."

I had a feeling the 'saintly' picture I painted my mom to be for decades was about to be tarnished.

"At the time, I was a curator at the New Orleans Museum of Art. An Italian artist was in town promoting his work. He took a liking towards me. I felt the best way to get back at your father was to return the favor. However, things went a little too far and we ended up…."

"In bed together," Marcus blurted out. My mom nodded.

"He was my father?" my newly-discovered brother asked.

"Yes," my dad answered.

The trembling sensation I was experiencing intensified upon learning that the man I had called 'Dad' for almost thirty years was not actually my biological father, and my brother was only half of whom I thought he was. I became light-headed, just before nausea took over. The room began to spin. My knees buckled under the enormous weight that had been emotionally bestowed upon me. My dad jumped up from the couch, grabbing me as I fell to the ground. "Breathe, Jax." His face was blurry.

"You're not my dad," I told him from a seated position on the Oriental rug.

"Yes, I am." He nodded, trying to convince me otherwise. "I will always be your dad."

"And Marcus is only my half-brother." I wanted to run out of the door, get in my car, and drive as far away from New Orleans as possible. In my weakened state, though, I wouldn't have made it out of the portrait room. I pushed myself backwards from his grasp until my back touched the wall. Marcus helped me to my feet, offering his cane for assistance.

"Don't say that, Jackson," cried the only person in the room that wasn't a 'half' or 'step' family member. "He is your father, and Marcus is your real brother."

Marcus, on the verge of tears, asked, "How could y'all keep this from us?"

"On several occasions we tried to confess what had happened, but just before we were about to tell the truth, neither one of us could say it. Your mother and I agreed several years back that it was best if we didn't come out with the truth. Over the last few days, however, the guilt started to weigh on us more than it ever had. We were worried that the news story might play internationally, and Angelo would see it."

"Who's Angelo?" Marcus asked.

They both pointed to my twin.

"Sorry I no introduce. Me name is Angelo Giuseppi from Bali, Italy. My father passed few years ago. On deathbed, he told me of a twin brother. Before he speak where he lived, he stopped breathing. He was in sleep for weeks before he died. I saw news story two days ago on American channel. I cried when I saw your face, Jackson. You and she," he pointed to my mom, "are only family left."

It was too much to process, and there were still questions unanswered. "Why were the two of us separated? Who in their right mind would do something like that?"

"When I became pregnant, I knew Angelo's father, Dominick, was the father. It wasn't until I started showing that your father realized what had happened. We debated whether or not to tell Dominick the truth. Once I finally did, he said he wanted the child and would take he or she back to Italy and never return to New Orleans. Naturally, I told him no. He said that he was getting a lawyer and was going to let the courts decide. Once word got out that I had an affair and got pregnant, the Fabacher name would be ruined. Nonetheless, we were prepared to go to court. Then something unexpected happened. I gave birth to two boys." I glanced at Angelo. Even though his English wasn't perfect, he seemed to understand every word my mom spoke. "Dominick then proposed that he and I should each receive a child. I told him we weren't separating the twins. Then, things got scary."

Marcus exhaled loudly. "Define scary."

"Dominick showed up here one night, but he wasn't alone. Six men, all dressed in black and wearing ski masks, threatened us with shotguns. He said if we didn't cooperate, things were going to get violent," spoke the man I could no longer call Dad.

Angelo looked embarrassed as he asked, "My father did that?"

The man who raised me hung his head low. "I'm afraid so."

"What happened next? Did you just let this…bully pick a twin like it was a puppy or something?" Marcus asked them. "I'm pretty sure that's illegal."

"The doctor who delivered Jackson and Angelo was your Uncle Steven, and he did it right here in this house. I went into labor two weeks earlier than expected."

I knew I was born upstairs in my parents' bedroom, but I was not aware that my uncle had delivered me. He, apparently, carried the Fabacher secret with him to the grave five years earlier.

"Steven knew about our predicament immediately after I gave birth. He agreed to help us hide the birth of Angelo. What he did was highly unethical and illegal. He could have gone to jail if the proper authorities ever found out, but he loved me and all of you very much. He didn't want to see any harm done to this family. After three months of nursing, Dominick returned to Italy with Angelo. He agreed that neither he nor his son would never return to New Orleans. Some agreements, I guess, are meant to be broken."

"I sorry for coming to here, but I not aware of the rules. I wanted to know truth."

"You got it, Angelo. We all got the truth tonight," Marcus, seemingly just as upset as me, told him. "So, that's why I went back to live with grandma and grandpa for three months. You weren't sick, mom. You were hiding the other twin."

"Our hands were tied, Marcus. We did what we had to do to protect this family."

"I just can't imagine giving up one of my children. It's unthinkable to me."

"We had no choice," my mom said while weeping into her husband's handkerchief. "I made a horrible mistake and got pregnant by a man I didn't love. The lives of everyone in this family were affected because of my actions. But the crazy part is I wouldn't change anything that happened in the past." There wasn't a dry spot on my mom's face as she clutched her husband's hand. "I love my family. Your father and I went through hell, and it brought us closer to one another. We love each other so much."

"It wasn't your fault, dear. I'm the one who made you do what you did. I'm the one to blame for what happened. Boys, your mother is a saint. I don't want you to think otherwise. She only did what she did because of my stupidity. Now that the truth is out, say what you need to say right now. After tonight, we will never talk about this again."

A tearful Angelo stood from the couch. "Is it okay if I give hug to you?" It was beyond eerie to see my mom hugging someone who looked exactly like me. I was nowhere near ready to share an embrace with her.

"I'm just in complete shock right now," Marcus spoke as I handed him back his cane. "And what about Angelo? We can't just send him back outside. If anyone sees him and thinks he's Jackson, there's going to be some explaining to do."

"Angelo, where are you staying?"

"Not sure. Maybe hotel. I came here from airport in taxi. Found house number in phonebook."

"You're going to stay here tonight. Okay?"

"Si.Yes."

My mom reached her arms out to me. "Jackson, please give me a hug."

I didn't approach her. "I need to get home and attempt to process what I just heard, all while getting ready for my wedding tomorrow."

"I'm going home with Jackson," Marcus declared, "and we will talk about this some more tomorrow." Neither one of us hugged or kissed our parents goodbye as we did every other time when leaving their house, and I didn't give a farewell to my twin either. I followed closely behind Marcus, holding onto his shirt, as we made our way to the hallway. I could barely walk.

Logan emerged from the parlor with a cocktail in hand. "Goodbye Mr. and Mrs. F. I'll see y'all tomorrow. I didn't hear anything that was spoken tonight." He followed us outside and into Marcus' BMW.

Marcus grabbed his cell phone. "I don't know what to say."

"I heard everything," Logan admitted from the backseat as we backed out of the driveway. "I'll take the Fabacher secret with me to the grave."

Marcus placed his phone to his ear while saying, "This is a screwed up, Lifetime movie-of-the-week type of shit. Hey, Mel," he spoke into the phone. "I'm sleeping at Jackson's tonight. I'll be back in the morning...Just want to spend some time with him before the wedding...When I get back, I have something to tell you...No. It can wait until tomorrow...Kiss the boys goodnight for me...I love you too."

"There's no doubt this situation is screwed up. I can see why y'all are upset, but your parents are the two most loving and caring people I have ever known. They would do anything for the both of you."

"No shit," Marcus replied.

"Logan, I just found out that my dad is not really my dad. Do you understand that? My real dad was nothing more than a piece of shit bully who blackmailed and threatened my mom, and then basically stole one of her children away from her. The man I thought was my dad is nothing more than...a stepdad. Technically, I'm not even a Fabacher. I'm a...what's his last name?"

"Giuseppi."

"My name is Jackson Giuseppi, and I have a fucking identical twin brother!" The urge to punch through the windshield stayed with me for several seconds until finally diminishing.

"The reality is that the truth is out. How you decide to deal with it is up to y'all. Personally, I think your parents did what they had to in order to protect the two of you."

"What are we going to do, Jackson?"

"I don't know. But I do know I'm never stepping foot in that house again."

Chapter 77

Marcus and I sat at my kitchen table until nearly three in the morning. We were both shocked and appalled by not only the infidelity of our parents, but their inability to reveal the truth about our brother. The discovery that our dad wasn't my biological dad was still impossible to fathom. The reality of it had yet to sink in. I knew in the morning, on the day I was to wed, the truth would hit me like a ton of bricks. Even though Marcus was downgraded to my half-brother, I had never felt so close to him as we hugged one another before bed. I felt he was the only family I had left. The thought was enough to almost, but not quite, bring a tear to my eye.

The sound of a loud pop incited a jolt as I lay in my bed not yet asleep. I sat up. The nightstand clock read 4:32. My initial thought was that someone had broken into the house. I scanned the bedroom for a weapon. It was too dark to see anything. Not wanting to flip on the light switch for fear that the possible intruder would notice someone had been woken up, I used the light from my cell phone to search for something to provoke fear to a burglar. I could find nothing menacing, so I grabbed a memento from atop my dresser. I quietly opened my door, staring down the darkened hallway into the living room. The sound of something moving on the tiled kitchen floor sent chills down my spine. I entered the hallway, slowly stepping backwards to the guest room where my brother was sleeping. Without knocking, I entered the room to find him already sitting up in the bed.

"What's going on?" he quietly asked. "What was that noise?"

"I don't know," I whispered, "But something or someone is in the kitchen."

"Is it Logan?"

Logan's room was directly across the hallway from the guest room. I snuck into the hallway before prying his door open. A shirtless Logan was laying facedown across the bed with his pants around his ankles and dress shoes still upon his feet. I tried to shake him. He didn't move.

Marcus entered Logan's room with his cane in hand. "I heard someone moaning in the kitchen," he whispered to me.

"Should we call the police?"

"Let's see who it is first. Do you have a gun?"

Given recent events in my life, the thought of owning a gun seemed like it was justified. Unfortunately, I never made the effort, nor had the time, to legally purchase one. "No. Just this." I showed him the souvenir hurricane glass from my first date with Delain.

"Stay behind me."

I held onto Marcus' t-shirt as he hobbled down the hallway. As we grew closer to the living room, we could see light emanating from a flashlight to our left. Whoever was in the kitchen was most likely on the floor, judging by the low trajectory of the light. Marcus continued against the hallway wall until he was less than three feet from the kitchen entrance. The flashlight shut off. I could hear someone moving about the floor. I held the glass tightly in my right hand. Marcus grabbed the handle of his cane with his right hand and the middle of the shaft with his left. I grew uneasy as he slowly peeked around the corner. He then stepped back and placed his hands over my ear as he whispered, "Turn the living room lights on when I tap your foot for a third time." The light switch was behind us on the wall. He squatted towards the ground. I felt his cane tap my foot once. I took a deep breath as he crawled closer to the kitchen. He tapped me again, and again I inhaled deeply. My hand trembled next to the light switch as I tried to imagine who was in the kitchen. Not a single person came to mind. Marcus' cane thrice hit my foot. I flipped on the living room lights. Marcus jumped into the kitchen. I followed directly behind him, cocking my right hand back and ready to heave a Pat O'Brien's hurricane glass at whoever was before us.

"Who are you?" Marcus asked the portly man sitting against the cabinet door beneath the sink. The man's hands covered his face, while blood oozed from a hole about the size of a half-dollar in the man's right leg near his groin. A gun lay next to the man. Marcus knocked it across the floor with his cane before shouting at him, "Move your hands!" Once the man did, his identity was no longer a mystery. I had a good idea as to why he was in my kitchen. It seemed my past had finally caught up to me. "Who are you?"

"Fuck you," the right-hand man of someone whose wife I slept with a year and a half earlier retorted while grimacing.

"His name is Ralph," I told Marcus upon lowering my arm.

Still clutching tightly to his cane, Marcus's attention remained on Ralph. "Who is he?"

"He works for a man named Vincent. Vincent is a Las Vegas mobster."

"But why is he…why are you here, Ralph?"

"I have something I want to return to Jackson." He reached his hand into his black tracksuit jacket. Marcus held his cane closer to Ralph. "What are you gonna do, beat me with that stick?" Ralph smirked while throwing a shoe towards me. "Recognize this, Loverboy?"

The shoe I left in Krista's room lay sideways on my kitchen floor. "Whose shoe is that?" Marcus asked.

Pointing at me, he said, "Jackson left it behind after he fucked my boss's wife. You thought you got away with one, didn't you, asshole?"

"I didn't have sex with your boss's wife? That's not even my shoe."

"Oh yeah?" Ralph then threw a second object onto the floor. The monogrammed letters were easily visible.

"Dad's handkerchief? Why does he have it? What's going on? Are you involved with the mob, Jackson?"

"Brothers, huh? Well, it seems your brother thought he could fuck a mob boss's wife in Las Vegas and get away with it. Unfortunately, he left his shoe and handkerchief behind with his initials— A.J.F. Andrew Jackson Fabacher. You thought you pulled a fast one over on us in the elevator, didn't you, 'Vincent'?"

Marcus was still in attack position as he asked me, "Is he telling the truth?"

There was no sense in lying. All the evidence was on the kitchen floor. "Yes, but I didn't know she was married until we were done."

"Let me see if I got this right— my brother had sex with your boss' wife and you came all the way here to kill him in his sleep?"

"We got fuckin' Albert Einstein in the house. How did you ever figure it out?"

"And we have the hitman of the year on the kitchen floor, bleeding by his own bullet. Your boss must be proud of you." Ralph had become increasingly pale in the short time he had been on the floor. Blood continued to ooze from the bullet hole even as he attempted to slow the loss with both hands. His femoral artery must have been hit. In just a few more minutes, he would most likely bleed to death. "You gonna call an ambulance or let me die on your floor?"

"My phone isn't working," Marcus told him. "Neither is my brother's."

Ralph shrugged his shoulders. "Looks like this is my final resting place then. I guess I have your dog to blame for my death."

"I don't have a dog."

"Fuck you for calling me a liar! I slipped in dog piss." He pointed to a puddle of yellow liquid on the floor that was beginning to mix with the surging blood. "I can smell it."

"You don't have a dog," Marcus said to me.

"No, I don't." It then occurred to me where the mysterious urine came from. "I have a Logan."

Ralph again reached into his jacket. "What are you grabbing?" Marcus asked him.

"My cellphone. I need an ambulance." As he pulled it out, Marcus swatted at it with the cane, sending it across the kitchen floor.

"If you live, who's to say you won't come after my brother again?"

With a nod, Ralph said, "Smart man, but not smart enough."

"What are you talking about?"

"You obviously don't know my profession. You think I would travel here alone?" Ralph cupped his hands around his mouth before yelling, "Tony! Take 'em down!"

Marcus turned to me. "Grab the gun, Jackson." Before I could do so, I noticed Ralph's right hand reaching into the back of his sweatpants. I pointed for Marcus to turn back around. Just as he did, Ralph pointed a gun towards me. Marcus flung his cane forward. It was no longer in one piece. His left hand held the shaft of the cane, which was merely a casing for what was inside. His right hand gripped the handle of a lengthy metal blade as it protruded from Ralph's chest. My brother's cane, it appeared, was more than a cane. The gun fell from Ralph's hand as he gasped for air. I looked on in shock.

"Call the police," Marcus told me, still gripping the blade as it remained embedded in Ralph's chest.

I had witnessed three men die in the last five days. The fourth death was just moments from occurring. It was something I still had not gotten accustomed to. "Holy shit!"

"Jackson, relax. My phone is on the nightstand next to my bed. Go get it and bring it to me so I can call the police." If Marcus appeared any calmer, he would have been asleep.

"What about Tony?"

"There is no Tony. He wouldn't have mentioned someone else if there actually was someone else. He said it to distract us. Plus, if there was a Tony, he would have been in here after hearing the earlier gunshot. Now, go get my phone."

I hurried to the guest bedroom, pounding loudly on Logan's door along the way. "Wake up, Logan!" I returned to the kitchen. Marcus' hand was no longer on the cane/sword as it remained buried in Ralph's chest. I handed him the phone. Ralph didn't appear to be breathing. "Is he dead?"

"Yep." Marcus pressed three numbers before placing the phone to his ear. "I need the police, ma'am," Marcus spoke into the phone. "An intruder broke into my brother's house with a gun. I just killed him."

As he told her the address, I had to take a seat on the ground. The queasiness I was experiencing was only partially due to the dead body on my kitchen floor. Hank and Cliff's dead bodies were much more grotesque and unsightly compared to Ralph's. What had me ready to vomit was the fact that if it wasn't for Logan's urine, I, and most likely my brother and Logan, would all be dead. Two people close to me were nearly killed because of my wrongdoing.

"The police are on their way. How are you feeling?"

"I'm about to throw up."

Marcus squatted next to me. "Don't look at the body then."

"That isn't what's bothering me. If he didn't slip in Logan's piss, all three of us would probably be dead right now. I'd feel horrible if that happened."

"No, you wouldn't," he spoke with a grin, "because you would be dead and wouldn't have any feelings at all."

"How are you so calm right now, and how can you smile after what just happened?" Marcus was a claims adjustor for an insurance company for seven years. I knew he was used to seeing pictures of people killed in automobile crashes, but actually killing someone, at least in my previous experience, had me wanting to vomit, not cracking jokes.

"I just saved my brother's life. Do you know how good that feels? Plus, this guy was a piece of shit. He was going to kill you for sleeping with his boss's wife. There's one less thug in the world now."

"And since when did you start carrying a sword inside of your cane?"

"A couple of years now. A friend said he could design it for me. After our little incident at the mall twenty years ago, I figured it wouldn't hurt to have a little extra protection. I never thought I would get to use it." He then dialed another number before putting the phone to his ear.

"Who are you calling?"

"The person I should have called before the police." He then said into the phone, "Hey, Dad…No, I wouldn't say everything's all right. Someone broke into Jackson's house with intentions on killing him….It's okay. We're fine. I killed him…Yes, sir, I already did. They're on the way…Hold on." Marcus handed me the phone. I didn't want to talk to him. He put the phone back to his ear. "Dad, he's a little shaken up right now. He'll be okay in a while….We'll see you soon."

As Marcus hung up, I had a horrible suspicion that killing Ralph was equivalent to cutting off the tail of a highly venomous snake. I had just avoided a hit on my life, but feared another attempt would be made by Vincent as long as he was alive. I also feared that loved ones, especially Marcus, may get pulled into whatever Vincent had in store for me once he discovered what had happened. Mikey had already been killed because of my actions. The thought of Marcus being killed because of me incited an unwelcomed feeling that was occurring way too often as of late . I dropped to my knees. My chest tightened, I had trouble breathing, and I instantly grew warm.

Marcus squatted next to me. "You look a little pale right now…and you're sweating. You don't look so hot."

I tried to talk, but couldn't get a word out. Vincent held a gun to my brother's head. His face is swollen and bloodied as two men force him onto his knees. Vincent then tells him, 'This is what happens when your brother sleeps with my wife,' before pulling the trigger. The pain in my chest and left arm intensified more than it did during the previous attacks. A chill overcame me, preceded by the all-too-familiar paralyzing sensation of fear.

"Do you want me to call an ambulance?" I couldn't talk, but managed to subtly shake my head a couple of times. "I know you had a rough night, Jackson, but you're going to be okay. I won't let anything happen to you—I promise. Nod if you understand me."

Logan soon appeared before me. While attempting to adjust his eyes to the light, he asked, "What's wrong with him?"

"I think he's having a panic attack."

"I have some Xanax." He turned around. Pointing into the kitchen, he yelled, "What the shit! Who the hell is that?!"

"Logan, relax! Get the Xanax!"

"There's a dead man in the kitchen with a sword in his goddamn chest! How can I relax?!"

"He tried to kill Jackson. Now get the damn Xanax!"

Logan hurried into his bedroom, quickly returning with a prescription bottle and a glass of water. He shoved a pill in my mouth, followed by a sip of water. I knew I needed to swallow, but couldn't. Water spilled down my chin. The pill fell onto the ground. Marcus shoved the pill back into my mouth, and then grabbed the cup from Logan. After pouring another sip into my mouth, he held my lips closed with one hand, while pinching my nose with the other.

"Swallow, Jackson. It will help."

It felt as if I were drowning. While trying to bat my brother's hands away from my face, Logan held my arms to my side. I attempted to squirm out of his grasp. Luckily, I was unsuccessful. The pill slid down my throat. My brother removed his hands from my face.

"He swallowed it, Logan. Let him go."

I remained on the floor. Both looked on with concern while I continued to breathe heavily. "Are you okay?" Logan asked before popping a Xanax in his mouth as well.

"Take deep breaths, Jackson. You're gonna be fine."

I started to breathe loudly while focusing on Marcus' face. "I…I'm…sorry."

Marcus grabbed both sides of my face with his hands. "You don't need to be sorry about anything. You did nothing wrong." His words did nothing to comfort me.

"Who is the dead guy in the kitchen?"

"A mobster. He tried to kill Jackson tonight."

"A mobster? From where?"

"Las Vegas."

"Why did he try to kill Jackson?"

"Jackson slept with a woman in Vegas. Turns out she was married, and not only that, married to a mob boss named Vincent."

"And that's him?" he asked, pointing to the kitchen.

"No. That guy works for Vincent. He slipped in your piss on the kitchen floor."

Logan approached the body, carefully stepping around the blood while getting a closer look at Ralph. "Who stabbed him?"

"Me."

"Isn't that your cane?"

"Yes."

"That's awesome! I want one!"

"The police are going to be here any minute, Logan. Go get dressed."

The chills began to subside, and the frightening sensation of death slowly escaped me. The Xanax seemed to speed up the recovery time quicker than the previous panic attack. Still, I felt exhausted as Marcus helped me to my feet.

"Are you feeling better?" he asked.

I nodded.

"Holy shit!" Logan's grinning, wide-eyed expression as he turned towards us was perplexing to me. "You're saying that my urine saved our lives?"

"It appears that way," Marcus answered.

Logan turned back around. With a pointed finger towards Ralph, he shouted, "You piece of shit! You came into the wrong house!" He proceeded to kick the corpse.

"Stop, Logan! Get out of there!" Marcus yelled.

He returned to the living room. "No need to thank me, Jackson. Your being alive is thanks enough." He then wrapped his arms around Marcus and me.

"Logan, are you going to put some pants on?" Not only was my best friend without pants, but also without any underwear.

"Let's just enjoy this moment for a second, fellas, and ponder what really happened—Marcus' secret ninja skills and my lack of drunken potty training saved your life tonight, Jackson."

I was a bit taken back by how carefree Logan and my brother were of the situation. I backed away from the embrace. "How come you two aren't freaking out about what just happened? Do you realize that a mobster sent his right-hand man here to kill me? Do you know what will transpire as soon as he realizes what happened? I'm sure he's going to retaliate and send someone else after me—and possibly the two of you now."

"We tell the police everything and they go after whoever this mobster guy is," Marcus suggested. "They'll probably run his records, see who he's connected with, and get the F.B.I. or someone to take him down—done."

Perhaps I watched too many gangster films in my days, but the police rarely had luck in bringing down a mob boss. Usually, it was someone from the inside, such as an undercover agent, and it usually took years to pull off. "What will the police do? Put me in a witness protection program until Vincent is brought down?"

"I think you're overreacting," Logan said on his way to the kitchen. "This mob boss is probably scared shitless now that his main man is dead. I don't think he's going to mess with you any longer."

None of their words helped to put me at ease, nor did watching Logan as he grabbed a pair of rubber gloves from the sink and placed them on both hands. He squatted next to Ralph before digging through his pockets. "What are you doing, Logan?"

"Finding out who this guy really is." He patted Ralph's pockets. "Smart hit man. No wallet. We'll have to find out his name another way."

"His name is Ralph, Logan."

He looked at me. "Ralph what?"

"What does it matter?"

"What are you going to tell the police when they get here? The truth? That you slept with a married woman and her husband sent someone to kill you?"

I wasn't very fond of word getting out that I slept with a married woman. In fact, I wasn't looking forward to the continued press coverage that was sure to follow. There was no way I was going to be able to hide the truth. The downward spiral was continuing, and it didn't appear that it was going to stop anytime soon. "I have to tell the truth. I don't see any way around it."

"There's no need to search him, Logan," Marcus said.

"I just want to know who this son of a bitch is in case the police don't find out who he is." After grabbing a clean glass from the cupboard, Logan pressed every finger from Ralph's right hand against it, leaving five visible fingerprints. He next placed the glass in a Ziploc bag.

"What do I do, Marcus? I'm sure this is going to be on the news tomorrow."

"I was thinking that as well. Young man thought to be dead turns up alive, and three days later avoids being killed by angry mobster's right-hand man."

"I know. The authorities are going to start asking more questions. I can't handle any more of that right now. That panic attack I just had wasn't the first one. It wasn't even the first one I had today."

Marcus grew concerned. By the way he was looking around the house, it was obvious he was attempting to hatch a plan. "Tell me exactly what happened in Las Vegas involving the gangster's wife. And by the way, when were you in Vegas?"

"He went there after the wedding disaster."

"We met at a blackjack table. She was flirtatious from the beginning. After a few drinks we went to her room."

"Where?"

"A suite at the Bellagio. We had sex before she confessed that she was not only married, but married to a mobster. I tried to leave the suite, but her husband and," I pointed into the kitchen, "him were coming down the hallway. She managed to get them to turn around before they came into the room. I took the elevator, but they must have gotten off briefly on another floor because the elevator stopped before I could make it to the lobby. I was in the elevator with the two of them. They noticed I wasn't wearing a shoe and joked that the husband of whoever I was sleeping with must have walked in the room. I told them I was gay."

"And then what?"

"One of them called me a faggot and I walked off. I made my way home the next morning."

"Hold on." Logan slowly paced the room with his head down before staring at me with inquisitive eyes. "Are you saying that you slept with a married woman the same night Mikey was killed by a jealous husband?"

"Yes."

"That's a horrible coincidence. Do you realize that you could have been—"

"Yes," I spoke with conviction. "And I've been living with that guilt for a year-and-a-half."

"We've all done things we're not proud of. You're okay, and that's all that matters."

"But why did he just send someone to kill Jackson now and not sooner?" Logan asked my brother.

It didn't take long for Marcus to say, "The newscast. They must have saw the news, and then put the pieces together. He probably found your shoe in the suite and remembered you from the elevator. The handkerchief was the final giveaway. There's no telling what happened to his wife."

"I guarantee he whacked her," Logan blurted out. "Mob men don't turn their heads when their wives cheat. We've all seen Scorsese films. And if he did kill her, which he did, then what if he tries to blame Jackson for her death? After all, he has proof of him being with her."

"And we now have that proof." Marcus grabbed then handed me the handkerchief and shoe. "We need to hide these somewhere safe."

The faint sound of sirens began to grow louder. "Shit! They're almost here!" My anxiety intensified, yet I didn't feel any oncoming symptoms of another panic attack.

"Okay, here's what we're going to say: you two were fast asleep and heard nothing. I heard the gunshot, came out here, saw the man on the ground, and stabbed him before he could fire the second gun. None of us know this person and we have no idea why he came here."

"Got it," Logan said. "I'm going to hide this under my bed." With the plastic bag containing the glass in one hand, he grabbed the shoe and handkerchief with the other before hurrying to his room.

"And put some pants on damnit!" Marcus yelled to him.

My hands were trembling. "I'm scared."

"Don't worry. Nothing's going to happen to you. I won't let it."

When red and blue lights flashed on the living room walls, I knew the longest night of my life was far from over.

Chapter 78

As Marcus opened the front door, I could see a second police car pull into the driveway. My brother immediately held his hands up to show that he was unarmed. Logan, in navy blue sweat pants along with his white dress shirt, stood next to me in the living room. Our hands were both up as well.

"Logan, take the gloves off."

He lowered his hands, removed the gloves and placed them in his pockets just as two Caucasian Sheriff's deputies entered the house with their guns aimed at the three of us.

"Hands where we can see them, gentlemen," one of the deputies demanded. He was on the heavy side, looking every bit of 250 pounds and not quite six feet tall.

"They already are, Captain," a still inebriated Logan said. If anyone was going to screw up what we had discussed, it was going to be him.

"What happened here?" the heavy-set officer asked while peering into the kitchen.

"That man," Marcus pointed, "broke into the house and shot himself after slipping on the floor."

"What is sticking out of his chest?" asked the second deputy. He was younger than his partner, and had a more athletic build.

"It's my cane. I have a shattered hip."

"That's a hell of a cane, son. Why is it sticking in the intruder's chest?"

"He pulled a second gun from behind his back and tried to shoot us. Instinct kicked in."

The older deputy approached Ralph's body, carefully stepping around the blood while leaning over to get a closer examination. He then placed his fingers to Ralph's wrist.

"Whose house is this?" asked the younger officer.

"Mine."

"What's your name?"

"Jackson Fabacher. That's my brother, Marcus, and this is my roommate, Logan."

Logan extended his hand toward the deputy. "Nice to make your acquaintance, officer." The deputy didn't extend a hand towards Logan. "It's cool," he said, retracting his hand.

"Jackson, you've had a busy week," spoke the heavier deputy from the kitchen.

"Yes, sir. It's been a little hectic."

"May we lower our hands?" Marcus asked.

The officer returned to the living room, holstering his gun as he said, "Yes, you may." The other officer lowered his gun, yet it remained in his right hand.

"Is anyone else in the house?"

"No, sir. Just the three of us," Marcus answered.

I was momentarily taken back to Hank's living room, watching through the attic floor as police officers asked all-too-familiar questions while examining a dead body.

"So, what exactly happened here?"

"A little while ago," Marcus began, "a loud noise woke me up. I came out of the guest bedroom and heard fumbling in the kitchen. I thought maybe the back door was left open and a raccoon or another wild animal had snuck in and knocked something over. When I turned the lights on, I saw this man lying on the floor, covered in blood. I kicked away the gun he was reaching for then asked who he was. He didn't say anything. I grabbed my cell phone, and when I went to call the police, he reached into his pants and pulled out another gun. That's when I instinctively stabbed him with my cane."

"You definitely stabbed him. Looks like you got him right in the heart. No one here recognizes this man?" asked the heavier officer.

"No, sir," Marcus answered first.

I shook my head. "No, sir."

"What about you?"

"Nope. I don't know any gangsters."

I watched Marcus' jaw clinch as Logan's answer was five words too many. My brother appeared just as furious as me.

"Gangster? How do you know this man is a gangster?"

"Look at him. If that man's not Italian, then I'm Aretha Franklin. His track suit, the slicked-back hair, the rings on his fingers. The only thing missing from his ensemble is a bowl of spaghetti and meatballs."

"And if he is Italian…what was your name by the way?"

"Logan Besthoff."

"If he is Italian, Mr. Besthoff, how do you know he's a gangster?"

The lengthy pause provided ample time for me to reconsider telling the truth to the deputies.

"He's wearing a black track suit. Does that out-of-shape, piece-of-shit look like he's running in a track meet anytime soon? Plus, he had two guns. What kind of intruder carries two guns? By the way, I never caught your names, officers."

"I'm Officer Maroney," the heavier officer answered before pointing to his partner. "That's Officer Hoffman."

"Pleasure to meet you, gentlemen. Is it possible for Deputy Hoffman to put his weapon away, Deputy Maroney? I think it's obvious that we're not a threat."

Maroney nodded at his partner, who then placed his gun in his holster.

"And is it possible, officers, to turn your lights and sirens off?" I imagined several neighbors already huddled at the base of my driveway. "It's 5:00 in the morning and I'm sure my neighbors would like to go back to sleep."

"Inform the station that we're going to need the coroner. And kill the sirens." As Officer Hoffman stepped outside, Maroney again approached the dead body. "So, what you're saying is this man slipped and shot himself?"

Marcus still appeared cool and collected as he told him, "Yes, sir."

The police sirens went silent. Maroney leaned over to more closely inspect the floor. "Is this yellow liquid some kind of…soft drink?"

"That's my piss."

Maroney turned around. "Urine?"

Logan, sticking his chest out like a conditioned Marine would in front of his drill sergeant, nodded with a proud grin upon his face. "Yes, sir."

"Why is your urine on the kitchen floor, son?"

Logan was increasing my anxiety, so I answered for him. "When he gets drunk, he sometimes sleepwalks and urinates in places that aren't toilets."

"Be sure to put that in your report, officer—" added Logan, "that I saved the day."

Officer Hoffman re-entered the house as Officer Maroney asked my brother, "Why do you have a sword hidden inside your cane staff?"

"Twenty years ago, my brother and I were held up at gunpoint. I was shot in the hip. I've had to use a cane ever since. A friend said he could construct a special cane for protection. I never thought I would actually get to use it."

Dr. Blanchard helped me to understand that my brother's accident wasn't my fault. She also helped me realize that Marcus' injury could have been much worse. While two police officers stood in my house and a dead body lay on the kitchen floor, I realized that if the accident never took place, my brother, Logan, and I may very well be dead. "It's a good thing you had it. Where were the two of you during all of this?"

"I drank heavily tonight, hence my piss on the kitchen floor. I slept through all of it."

"And you?"

After swallowing, I told him, "I was asleep also."

"You didn't hear the gunshot?"

"No, sir. I had a couple of drinks tonight, so I slept pretty soundly."

The young deputy stepped closer, just a few inches from my face. He looked up and down as if inspecting me for something. "Do you have a rabbit's foot in your pocket?"

"He's just happy to see you, officer."

Hoffman ignored Logan's remark as I commented, "I don't understand."

"You're a very lucky person, Jackson."

"How do you mean?"

He stepped back. "A week ago you were believed to have been dead. Now, less than three days after being declared alive, a man carrying two guns is found stabbed to death in your kitchen?"

"Crazy, huh?" Logan remarked.

"I agree that it seems a bit bizarre, but the two incidents have no relation to one another. I have no idea who this man is or why he broke into my house."

"Just a coincidence perhaps?"

While looking away from the officer, I noticed a blinking red light beneath the kitchen table. The cell phone Marcus knocked out of Ralph's hand was hidden behind one of the thick legs of the table. A message most likely awaited the dead hit man. "Yes, sir, just a coincidence." I began to make my way across the living room towards the kitchen table.

Deputy Maroney held his hand up to me before I could step into the kitchen. "Hold it right there, son."

"I need to sit down. The dead body is making me light-headed."

"We can't have you interfering with the crime scene. Why don't you take a seat on the couch. In fact, why doesn't everyone take a seat on the couch."

Soon after the three of us sat on the couch, a bald man in civilian clothes walked through my front door. He introduced himself as Detective Jeremiah Kohl. He asked the three of us more of the same questions, receiving the same answers we gave the deputies. He examined the scene much more thoroughly than the police officers did, taking blood samples and pictures. Neither he nor the other officers had yet to see the blinking cell phone.

Shortly after the coroner arrived, so did the man that raised me for nearly three decades. "Are y'all okay?" he asked out of breath upon running into the house. Marcus was the first to hug him. Logan was second. I was a hesitant third, only doing so to avoid inquisitive stares from the law enforcement officials in my house. "What happened?"

"Hello, Mr. Fabacher. Detective Jeremiah Kohl. I'm a big fan of your work with the D.A. over the years." The two shook hands. "According to your sons and Mr. Besthoff," he pointed towards the kitchen, "that man broke into the house, slipped in Mr. Besthoff's urine, and shot himself. He then tried to pull out another gun, but your older son stabbed him with the sword hidden in his cane."

"Who is he?"

"No one seems to know. We'll know in a few hours, though, who the mystery man is. In the meantime, we need to get these three to the station to get their statements on file."

"Jesus!" Logan exclaimed, throwing his hands in the air.

Both Marcus and I sighed. It was nearing 6:00 in the morning. The last six-and-a-half hours were the most mentally exhausting hours of my life. I just wanted to lie down in my bed.

"Jeremiah, the boys have had a long night. Is going to the station all that necessary? It seems like their statements have already been given."

Detective Kohl looked at the three of us before subtly nodding. "I guess we have enough information for the time being."

"And until we know who this mystery man is, I want all three of their names withheld from the media for safety reasons. We've had an eventful last couple of days and would like some privacy in this matter."

"Yes, sir, Mr. Fabacher."

Andrew handed the detective a business card. "Thank you for all your help, Jeremiah. As soon as you find out who this man is, please give me a call." The two shook hands. Minutes later, the coroner, Ralph's body, the detective, and deputies were gone. On his way out, Detective Kohl returned Marcus's cane to him.

The man I had trouble calling Dad held his cell phone up to his ear while telling the three of us, "Y'all look exhausted."

"I can barely stand right now I'm so tired," Marcus said as he stood from the couch with Logan's assistance.

"Everything's okay, honey," Andrew spoke into the phone. "No one is hurt…No one knows who he is…Some hoodlum probably." He then looked at me. "He's fine…Hold on." He handed me the phone. "Tell your mother you're okay."

I didn't grab the phone, instead placing my mouth to it while saying, "I'm okay. Go back to bed." I was still too upset with her to speak as if everything she told me had been forgotten. Even though she was my real mother, I didn't want to hear her voice at the moment.

"I'll see you when I get home…I love you too." He hung up. "If anyone feels uncomfortable sleeping here, you're more than welcome to sleep at our house."

"I don't care if someone was killed in the kitchen an hour ago. I'm falling asleep as soon as my head hits the pillow. Saving lives is exhausting." Logan yawned while stretching his arms overhead. "Hopefully the invasion of the Italians is over with for the night. I'll see you kids in a few hours." Logan walked to his room, shutting the door behind him.

"Jax, are you okay?"

Instead of answering him, I walked to the cell phone still hidden beneath the table. A text message awaited Ralph on the cheap-looking cell phone. *'Is it complete?'*

"Is that the phone I knocked out of Ralph's hand?"

"Yes, and a text sent at 4:48 asks 'is it complete?'"

"That's probably Vincent."

"I thought y'all didn't know who the man was."

Marcus gave a subtle nod while looking at me. "Tell him. He can help us."

I didn't want to get him involved, but Marcus left me no choice. "When I was in Las Vegas, I unknowingly had sex with a married woman. Turns out that she was married to a mobster, and the dead guy in the kitchen was his right-hand man."

"When were you in Las Vegas?"

"After my wedding."

"I thought you said you drove north."

"I lied," I told him with a shrug of my shoulders. "Oops."

After a lengthy exhale and a run of his hands through his salted hair, he asked, "Why didn't you tell the detective?"

"What are two police officers and a detective from the small town of Madisonville, Louisiana going to do about a Las Vegas mobster? Plus, I didn't like the idea of word getting out that I slept with a married woman. I don't want my dirty laundry aired out for everyone to see. I guess hiding adultery runs in the family." The comment was a bit harsh, but I was still very bitter about my parents' past. I imagined the bitterness would last for quite a while, possibly for the rest of my life. "Now, what should we do about the text?"

The elder male in the room extended his hand. "Give it to me. I'll run a trace on the number and see what turns up."

"Should we respond to it first?" I asked Marcus, as if he was the only person in the room. "If we text back 'yes', then Vincent won't know right away that Ralph is dead."

"I agree. Dad, what do you think?"

"I don't like the idea of playing games with a mobster who wants to kill my son. Let me talk to some people. We'll get to the bottom of this real quick." His hand still awaited the phone.

I pointed to the kitchen. "What do we do about the blood?" As they peered into the kitchen, I stepped behind them and quickly texted 'yes' into the phone.

"Where's your mop?"

"In the laundry room," I answered after deleting my text once it went through. "Here you go." I placed the phone in his hand.

"You two try to get some rest. We have a big day ahead of us. I'll clean up then go home and get some rest myself."

"Thanks for coming over, Dad." The two embraced. Marcus appeared to have already forgiven him.

"And for how long have you been carrying a sword around inside your cane?"

"A couple of years."

"I'm glad you had it."

"Me too." Marcus then hugged me, tighter than he ever had before. "Be strong, bro. I'm here for you."

"Thank you." I suspected Marcus left to give the two of us some alone time.

"It's been a rough week for you, Jax. Your mother and I are so—"

"You and mom's relationship was one of the very few that I thought was real. I was obviously wrong."

"It is real, and it's better than it ever has been. The way we act around one another isn't fake or made up. I love your mother as much as I love you and Marcus." Barely able to stand, I took a seat on the couch as he continued. "Marriage isn't always happy. Your mother and I went through a very difficult time, and we made it out together. That dark time in our lives made what we have now even more special. We both forgave each other long ago."

"You're not my real dad." A feeling I hadn't felt since my senior year of high school started to overcome me. My cheeks felt tight and my jaw began to tremble, but as soon as the physical traits of someone on the verge of a good cry came on, I stopped them, not ready to end my streak. "Why didn't y'all tell me the truth?"

"We tried to on several occasions, but we got…scared." He sat next to me. "Plus, we didn't want you to feel any different from your brother. We also didn't feel that it was necessary for you or Marcus to know the truth about our indiscretions towards one another. Dominick, the man whom your mother mistakenly shared a moment of passion with, was a horrible person. We didn't want you to know who he was even though he was your biological father. Truth be told, Davis reminded me a lot of Dominick."

"I feel betrayed right now. The two people in the world that I trusted the most and never would have thought would lie to me did. I feel like I can't trust anyone now." I watched as he slowly lowered his head. I knew he felt ashamed, but that didn't make me feel any better. I stood from the couch. "After the wedding, I'm going to convince Delain that we should move away from here. I no longer feel safe in this house. It's in our best interest that she and I start our new life together some place far away from here."

He was slow to nod. "Okay."

I hit him where it hurt the most. The heartache he and my mom bestowed upon me hours earlier had just been reciprocated. "I'm going to rest up. I'll see you at the cathedral later today. I'll smile and pretend that our family isn't fucked up beyond repair." We didn't exchange hugs after what could only be described as the most grievous couple of hours of my life. I shut and locked my bedroom door. As I lay in bed, the calming effect the Xanax was supposed to elicit wasn't enough to make me believe everything would be okay. I still feared that Delain was hiding something from me. I feared the truth would be revealed about my parents' past. I feared Vincent would again come after me once he discovered the death of his partner. I feared I could still be arrested in Davis' death. I feared that escape was impossible.

Saturday

Chapter 79

A three-mile run under eighteen minutes, 100 push-ups, 200 sit-ups, 50 burpees, 50 pull-ups using the frame of the hotel door, ten minutes of jujitsu, a five minute plank, and a half-mile jog to a nearby health store satisfied Mitch's workout needs for the morning. The lack of fitness equipment wasn't a deterrent for Mitch; he felt just as energized as he did following most workouts in the gym. During his leisurely walk back to the hotel from the health store, he drank a high-protein smoothie. After showering, he sat at the desk in the hotel room, glancing over his notes from the previous day's investigation. He knew he was close to discovering the truth, and wasn't giving up. A thorough investigation at Hank's house the previous afternoon revealed no new evidence or clues as to who the mystery man may have been. While in the attic, Mitch combed over a particular area where white insulation was scattered about the plywood floor. His only thought was that the mystery man was perhaps buried beneath the insulation when the police officer entered the attic. After thirty minutes, Mitch couldn't take the heat any longer. He was quite impressed that whoever was in the attic during the middle of the day was capable of withstanding the heat for what must have been several hours.

Mitch glanced outside his hotel window at the passing cars. Inspiration soon struck. He pushed his notes to the side and grabbed the exterior pictures of Hank's house, taken by the police hours after they first responded to the 911 call. Something in the pictures was no longer outside of the house when Mitch visited the day before. It was time for another visit to the Mobile Police Station.

The officer in charge of the case, Robert McKenzie, wasn't the friendliest and most cooperative officer that Mitch had the pleasure of working alongside. He seemed almost offended that an F.B.I. agent was asking him questions about a case that had been closed. Any question Mitch asked, Robert answered with the same response: 'It's in the report.

Read it and you'll have your answer'. Years of martial arts taught Mitch to remain calm, almost Zen-like, in both his professional and personal life. Very rarely did he lose his cool.

Mitch spotted Robert typing on a computer in his office. Robert's eyes glanced up at him before returning to his computer screen. Mitch stuck his head into the office after knocking on the open door. "Can I borrow two minutes of your time, Officer McKenzie?"

"I'm not sure why you're still here, Agent Hennessey. The case is closed. The girls are safely at home, and the bad guys are dead. There's nothing more to investigate." He resumed typing.

"Yes, sir. I just have one question, and then I'll be out of your hair forever."

"Is that a promise?"

Mitch smiled. "Yes. When is—"

"Excuse me," an officer spoke upon sticking his head into the office. The pimple-faced officer looked as if he was fresh out of rookie school. "Spud, I need your signature on this paper."

"Not now. And stop calling me that."

"I apologize, Robert."

The young officer ducked out of the office as Mitch continued. "When is the last time, Officer McKenzie, you or any other officers have been at Hank's house?"

"Last Sunday."

"Did Hank's—"

"I thought you said one question," Robert said with the tone of someone who was being greatly disturbed.

"Please don't interrupt me again, Officer McKenzie," Mitch calmly spoke.

Robert stopped typing. He jumped to his feet, finally making eye contact with the F.B.I. agent. "This case is complete," he emphatically told him. "There is nothing else to investigate, Agent Hennessey. Everything is in my goddamn report!" His yelling incited the other officers in the station to glance towards the office.

"Stop yelling, officer," instructed a still calm Mitch. "You are being insubordinate to a federal agent. If you raise your voice at me again, you'll be lucky to get work as a crossing guard. Now, I'm going to ask you another question. You are going to give me an answer without raising your voice. Did Hank's truck get towed from his house?"

Robert's eyes remained squinted at Mitch as he answered, "I don't know."

"What can we do to find out the answer to that question, Officer McKenzie?"

Robert hastily picked up the phone from his desk. After dialing a number, he shot an intense stare at Mitch until speaking into the phone, "Tater, it's me. Were you able to get to Hank's truck yet?...Ok." He hung up. "He said they're gonna go get it later today."

"Tell him not to waste his time." Mitch turned around and began his walk out of the police station.

Robert followed. "Why not?"

"It's not there."

"What do you mean?" he asked, hurriedly walking behind Agent Hennessey.

"Someone stole it."

"Who?"

"The third person in the house at the time of the shootout." Mitch had a theory that the truck may have been somewhere in the vicinity of New Orleans, since Hank's blood was found in Davis' house nearly twenty-four hours after he was killed. The person of interest in Davis', and now Hank's, death couldn't have been dumb enough to continue driving in a murdered man's truck, Mitch assumed.

Robert ran in front of Mitch, stopping him in his tracks. "A third person? Are you sure?"

"Positive."

"How could you possibly know that?"

"You went into the attic, correct?"

Robert nodded. "I scanned it twice from the ladder."

"You should have looked harder."

"Someone was up there?"

"Yes."

"That's impossible. There was nothing up there but a couple of small boxes."

"And a man who killed someone less than twenty-four hours later." Mitch used great restraint in subduing the urge to punch Robert's bulbous nose for allowing the killer to escape a crime scene, and then murder one of his closest friends.

"What does this mean?"

"Case reopened."

"It's my case. I'll take it over again."

"This case is no longer in your jurisdiction. It now belongs in the hands of the F.B.I. Thank you for your help, Officer McKenzie." Mitch stepped around the concerned officer. "I'll be in touch if I need something."

While on his way back to the hotel, Mitch's cell phone rang. "Agent Hennessey," he answered.

"Mr. Hennessey?" The coarse voice sounded vaguely familiar.

"Yes?"

"Mr. Hennessey, this is Blanche McGovern—Rebecca's grandmother. You were at our house yesterday."

"Yes, ma'am, I remember who you are."

"You said to call if my granddaughter had anything else she needed to tell you."

Mitch lowered the volume on the radio. "Yes, ma'am. Did she remember something?"

"No, she didn't remember anything new."

"Well, is everything okay?"

"I'm not sure."

Mitch was starting to wonder if the elderly woman was becoming senile. "Can you explain what is going on, Ms. McGovern?"

"I'll try. My granddaughter was just watching the news with me. It was a recap of the week's stories. When a particular segment came on, Rebecca began to scream, but not in a scared kind of way. It was more of a happy scream." There was a pause.

"Ms. McGovern?" Silence ensued. "Blanche, are you there?" Mitch then heard what sounded like the opening of a squeaky door.

"Is that him?" another female asked. The voice may have belonged to Rebecca. "I told you not to—" The call ended. Mitch threw his phone onto the passenger seat. Lights flashed on the dashboard of his black Chevy Tahoe as he slammed on the gas pedal.

Chapter 80

With a glazed look in her eyes, Delain watched the elevator doors open on the fourth floor of the Doubletree Hotel. In less than twelve hours, her wedding was to take place. Before she could walk down the aisle, she needed something from an ex-boyfriend. If she couldn't find what she needed, there might not be a wedding. The doors began to close. She stuck her foot forward, reopening them. She wasn't ready to confront the man that had been a regular fixture in her thoughts since the last time she had seen him, but time was running out. "Crap," she mumbled as she stepped onto the carpeted hallway.

After knocking on the door of room 407, she hid her trembling hands in the back pockets of her jeans. While waiting for the door to open, she recalled the dramatic breakup with Tyler. It was the only time she had seen him cry, and the only time she had seen the temperamental side of him. Delain again put her right hand up to the door, only to notice a 'privacy please' tag hanging from the knob. *What if he thinks the maid is knocking on the door?* Again she knocked, louder than before. "Tyler, it's me." After placing her ear to the door, she heard what she believed to be Tyler's knees cracking as he approached the door. *He's just waking up.* Tyler's knees always cracked for the first few steps he took in the morning. She stepped back, returning both hands to her pockets. *Deep breaths!* The door opened. Tyler, wearing nothing but a pair of black boxer briefs, stood before her. His torso was much more defined than she remembered. Gone was his shaved chest and slight hint of love handles. Instead, there was a light layer of chest hair along with a chiseled midsection that lacked any hint of fat.

"This is a nice surprise," spoke a grinning Tyler. His voice was raspy, his right eye was shut, and his hair stuck up in the back.

"I hope I didn't wake you."

"You didn't. I was just…"

"Waking up?"

His smile widened. "Maybe."

"Is it okay if I come in?"

"Of course." He stepped to the side. She anxiously walked past him.

"I'm sorry to come over unannounced."

He shut the door. "Please don't apologize for that. You can visit anytime you want." Tyler stepped into the bathroom, emerging with a toothbrush in his hand. "I need to brush real quick if that's okay."

"Of course." As water ran in the bathroom sink, Delain cast a wandering eye around the hotel room. A pair of panties on the ground, a wine glass on the nightstand with lipstick on it, or an empty condom wrapper in the wastebasket might incite a bit of jealousy. It didn't appear that he had company the night before. She felt relief with her discovery.

The water shut off. Tyler stepped out from the bathroom. "Sorry I don't have much to offer you." He grabbed from the nightstand a small paper bag. "Chocolate chip cookie?"

"No, thank you. Tyler, I stopped by because…" She found his body to be quite distracting, "do you think you can put a shirt on?"

"Oh, I'm sorry." He grabbed a white t-shirt from his suitcase. "I hate wearing shirts to bed."

"I know you do. It looks like you've been working out pretty religiously."

"A little bit." With his arms stretched overhead, Delain could see the 'v' indention of his lower abdominals as he slipped into the shirt. Tyler was, hands down, the sexiest she had ever seen him. His body, his hair, the sparkle in his blue eyes, the vertical lines on both sides of his mouth as he grinned, even his collarbone was sexier than she remembered. "Exercising was a great stress relief while my mom was sick."

"Again, I'm sorry to hear about her passing."

"The loss of a loved one is never easy, but I've had to do it a few times in my life. I'm starting to learn how to handle it."

She was certain he was referencing their breakup as well. "Can I sit down?"

He grabbed the chair from the desk and set it next to her. She removed both hands from her pockets before sitting down. "Should my stomach have knots in it right now, Chrissy? Because it does. Huge knots." He sat at arm's distance from her on the queen-sized bed.

"That makes two of us. What time is your interview today?"

He glanced at the clock on the nightstand. "A couple of hours."

"That's good." The uneasiness she was experiencing prompted her to gaze around the room until finding something to talk about. "How's the view from up—"

"Chrissy, there's no need for small talk. Why are you in my hotel room…on your wedding day?"

Delain attempted to, but couldn't look at him. Instead, her glance was aimed at the orange suitcase on the floor of the hotel room. She knew the suitcase quite well, as she purchased it for him before their first trip together. Delain opted for orange because black was the most common suitcase color. An orange suitcase stood out, just as she thought Tyler did among every other man she dated leading up to him. "Closure."

"I'm sorry?" After perking up on the bed, his smile dissipated. "You? You're the one who needs closure?"

"Yes."

"Don't you think I'm the one who needs closure? You're the one who left me. And for the record, I don't believe you just fell out of love with me in a weekend. I know you're not telling the truth."

For his own well-being, she was determined to not let him discover the truth; at least not until after she was able to claim Caleb as her own. "I felt that way for a while. I just didn't want to hurt you. I should have told you sooner. I'm sorry for that."

"You came here just to tell me that?"

Engaged in eye contact, she told him, "Yes."

He nodded several times, almost in a sarcastic manner, as if he didn't believe her. "Okay. Then I guess we went shopping for engagement rings a week before you broke up with me because you weren't feeling the love. I could see how emphatically happy you were with every ring you tried on. I know you were madly in love with me, Chrissy. Something happened to you right here in this city."

She tried her hardest not to breakdown in front of him.

"If you want closure, then tell me right now you still don't have feelings for me."

Unable to tell him what he asked, Delain shook her head side to side.

"What? You don't have feelings for me?"

She cleared her throat before saying, "I don't."

"You don't what?"

"I…I don't have feelings for you."

"Stop fumbling your words. Say it like you mean it," he demanded, his tone becoming more assertive. "Say 'I no longer have feelings for you, Tyler Bennett.'"

Her hands began to tremble once more. "I no longer…have…" A sick feeling overcame her, "feelings for…you."

"Say my name, Christina. Say the whole phrase with my name."

"I just told you."

"Say it again." He rose to his feet, his cheeks flustered. "Christina Delain Foster, tell me you don't have feelings for me, and that our two years together meant nothing to you."

She had no choice but to say it. "I no longer have feelings for you, Tyler Bennett." She wanted to cry in front of him. The clinching of her jaw was the only thing preventing her from completely losing it in front of the man she, apparently, still cared deeply about. Delain stood from her chair. "I need to go."

Tyler grabbed her hand before she could walk away. "'There were times when I thought, I'd never find true love. That's when I would look up, and pray to heaven above. Lord, please send me someone, who will always be true. And make me want to smile, on days I am blue. A man with passionate kisses, that always make me tingle. With an outgoing personality, who loves to mingle. Adventurous and fun, and never a bore. Who will always give me butterflies, when he walks through the door. But more important, Lord, beauty that is deep. Who understands why *The Notebook*, will always make me weep. Well, Lord, you listened, and brought Tyler to me, and I promise to love him, forever plus eternity.' Does that ring a bell, Chrissy?" He had recited, without error, the poem she had written for him.

"Yes."

"You wrote that less than a month before you told me you didn't want to see me anymore."

Delain was merely seconds away from balling in front of him. She removed her hand from his grasp, kept her head down, and walked towards the door. Her intentions didn't involve leaving the hotel, but crying in the hallway. She reached for the door handle. Tyler grabbed her right arm, swung her around, pushed her against the door, and then forcefully placed his lips against hers. She could have easily pushed him away or demanded that he stop kissing her. Instead, she cradled the back of his head with both hands. Intense feelings from the past resurfaced, reminding her of a love that was stronger than any relationship before it. She didn't want to stop kissing him. He stepped back. "Tell me again you don't have feelings for me, Chrissy."

"I can't."

"Why?"

She could no longer lie to him. "Because it wouldn't be true."

"I never stopped loving you. I'm not letting you go this time."

"I'm getting married tonight."

"No, you're not."

Their lips again met. His kisses were just as she remembered—intense and full of fervor. As Jackson came to mind, she nudged him away. "I shouldn't be doing this." Tyler leaned forward to kiss her a third time. She turned her head, despite wanting to continue kissing him.

"Remember yesterday when you asked me what my mom said about you right before she passed away?"

"Yes," Delain told him, staring hypnotically into his eyes while awaiting the answer.

"The drugs the doctors gave her for the cancer made her have these very vivid dreams. The doctors called them hallucinations. She called them visions. The last vision she had was one of you and me. It was Christmas morning. We were gathered around the tree with our son. She could see in our eyes how madly in love we were with one another. She said I would find you again, and that we would wed."

"But..."

"But what? Do you think it was just a coincidence we ran into each other yesterday...or something else?"

"I don't know," a confused, scared, and guilt-ridden Delain spoke. "I don't know what to do."

"For starters, I think you should at least postpone the wedding. You're not ready to get married tonight. I know it and so do you."

"But..."

"But nothing. You're in the arms of an ex-boyfriend in his hotel room on the day of your wedding. We both know you shouldn't be getting married tonight."

She found it impossible to disagree with him.

"Why are you marrying someone when you still have strong feelings for me?" She couldn't answer. "Does he make you laugh? Does he make you feel beautiful? Do you feel safe in his arms?"

The answer to each of his questions, especially the latter, was a resounding 'yes'. Delain recalled how Jackson came to her rescue inside Davis' house, how special she felt on the night of the proposal, and how he remained engaged to her even though he was certain she was dumping him at the altar. She was again reminded of how much she truly did love him. "Very much so."

"I made you feel all of those things too, didn't I?"

"Of course. You did everything right."

"Evidently not. He must have something over me for you to want to marry him. What is it?"

"Nothing."

"Is he better looking than me?"

None-too-pleased by his question, she asked, "Tyler, what kind of question is—?"

"Is he loaded?"

"What?"

"Is he rich?"

Quickly bypassing 'none-too-pleased', she became outraged to hear Tyler suggest such a thing. "I can't believe you just said that."

"I'm sorry. You're not a gold digger. I don't know why it came out."

With clinched jaw she told him, "You know I would never date someone for money."

"Then why the hell are you marrying this guy?! Something is going on, damnit! Tell me!"

"I have to go." She tried to open the door. Tyler pressed his hand firmly against it. "Please let go, Tyler."

"No," he calmly said. "You're not leaving here until you tell me what the hell is going on."

"What's going on is that I'm marrying someone today who would never suggest I would date someone for money. Can you please remove your hand from the door?" While awaiting an answer, her phone vibrated. She retrieved it from her pocket.

"Is it him?"

Delain nodded.

"Why don't you answer it, and tell him where you are?"

Delain grew tired of Tyler's condescending behavior. "I'm politely asking you again to please move so I can go."

His hand remained on the door. "Everything we've been through, and you're just going to leave it like this?"

"Tyler, I'll admit that after seeing you yesterday, I spent all last night and this morning thinking about you and what might have been if we stayed together. You and I had something special. I wouldn't exchange those memories for anything. However, Jackson and I have been through a lot together, and I can't just throw all of that away. I do care about you very much, but I just realized how madly in love I am with my fiancé. I am going to marry him this evening."

"So that's it? Just like that?"

"Yes."

"Kiss me again and tell me you don't feel anything."

"Tyler—"

"Just kiss me, and if you don't feel anything then it's over between us for good."

She leaned towards him, planted her lips against his, and pulled away seconds later. It was as if she had awoken from a trance. She felt something—and it was exactly what she had hoped to find.

"Anything?" he asked.

She nodded. "Closure."

"So, you're done with me?"

"I am, Tyler. I'm sorry."

He let out a deep breath, shaking his head back and forth, before stepping back from the door. "Then I guess I won't mention the other reason I thought you might have tried to contact me shortly after you left me the first time." Delain ignored his comment to avoid any further conversation while opening the door. She wasn't curious to know what he was referring to. "Since you never mentioned having one, I'm assuming you never got pregnant."

With one foot out the door, she stopped in her tracks. Her gaze wasn't directed behind her where Tyler stood, but instead down the hallway. Curiosity had finally gotten the better of her. "What are you talking about?"

"Nothing."

She slowly turned towards him. "What are you talking about, Tyler?"

"You won't tell me your secrets, so I won't tell you mine."

Delain grew paranoid that he somehow knew about Caleb. If she lost her cool and tried to force information from him, it would only confirm that a baby was indeed involved. "I have no idea what you're talking about. Goodbye, Tyler." With each step she took towards the elevator, she hoped he would reveal what he knew.

"On the night you broke up with me, we had sex, remember?"

She turned around. About twenty feet separated them. "Yes."

"I wore a condom that night."

"Yes."

"Before putting it on, I poked a hole in it. I thought if I got you pregnant, you would come back to me. But, I guess we never made a baby together."

A paralyzing sensation overcame Delain. Her thoughts began to waiver. *Maybe Caleb wasn't born premature. Maybe he was in fact a full-term baby whose weight was slightly less than the average newborn. Maybe Davis isn't the father!* "You thought you impregnated me?"

Tyler nodded. "For months, I waited for a call from you telling me that you were pregnant—that along with an explanation of why in the hell you suddenly left me."

This changes everything! "No, we didn't make a baby together. Goodbye." There was only one person she wanted to see, and she needed to see him immediately.

"I still love you, Christina!" Tyler yelled as she hastily walked down the hallway. "Uno!"

She hurried to the elevator. Once inside, she grabbed her cell phone. Jackson answered immediately. "Baby, where are you?" she frantically asked.

"Home. I know its bad luck to see the bride before the wedding, but we need to—"

"I need you, Jackson. I need you now," she cried into the phone. "Please come to me."

"Are you okay?"

"No."

"Is someone after you? Are you in danger?"

"No. I just need you right now."

"Where are you?"

"In the city."

"Go to your house. I'll be there soon."

"I love you so much, Jackson. I don't want to be without you. Please hurry."

Chapter 81

Tyler grabbed his cell phone from the nightstand. Two missed calls from an unknown number appeared on his screen. Before he could dial John's phone number, there was a knock on the door. "You came to your senses, Chrissy," he mumbled to himself. Upon opening the door, Tyler sighed. It wasn't the person he hoped for, but the person he was about to call. "What are you doing here?"

"I've been following Christina. When she showed up here I called you. Why didn't you answer?"

"I didn't realize the ringer was turned off. I must have accidentally silenced it."

"It's a good sign she came here on her own will. How did it go?"

"It started great. She told me she still cared about me, and we kissed. Then," running his hands vigorously through his hair, he told John, "it was like she snapped."

"How do you mean? You didn't accidentally call her Delain, did you?"

"No. I told her I didn't believe she just fell out of love with me. She pretty much agreed. I asked why she left me, but she couldn't give me a straight answer. Something happened, and she's not telling me."

"That's when she snapped?"

Tyler shook his head in disgust. "No. I made a stupid comment that maybe she was marrying this Jackson guy because he was rich. She got upset at me for suggesting such a thing."

"Then what?"

"I blocked the door. She told me she found closure with me and that she was marrying Jackson tonight. I let her go."

"That was the last thing you two talked about?"

Tyler shook his head, embarrassed as he told him, "As she walked away, I confessed to poking a hole in the condom the last time we had sex. I thought telling her would show her how deeply I cared about her. She stopped in her tracks to tell me we never made a baby together. That was the last thing she said."

"I heard that part in the hallway," John said upon lowering himself into the chair.

"It's over." Tyler punched the bed in anger. "I blew it with the 'marrying for money' comment. She's never been about money. That's one of the reasons I loved her so much." Again he punched the bed. "Goddamnit!"

"Relax, Tyler. It's far from over."

"Far from over? John, she just told me she's marrying Jackson tonight, and that she found closure with me. It's over."

"Is she married yet?"

Tyler fell backwards onto the bed, placing his hands over his face. He didn't have to close his eyes to visualize Christina's distraught face after he made the comment that, he was certain, pushed her away forever. "No."

"Then stop whining. We still have the upper hand."

"How can you possibly think that?"

"Trust me. We do."

"Now you're sounding just like Christina. You're hiding something from me too? What is it?"

"Tyler, I can't tell you yet. It's for your own well-being. I need you to trust that everything will work out."

Tyler sat upright. "I'm tired of being the only one that doesn't know what the hell is going on. I'm paying you a lot of money, John. I want to know right now why you're so optimistic she and I will end up together."

John leaned forward, inches from his client's face. "You will soon know everything that I have learned. Until that moment, stop whining like a four-year-old brat and let me do what I'm damn good at doing." John stood from the chair. "I have to see what her next move is. I'll call you soon. Turn your damn ringer back on."

As John walked past him, Tyler asked, "Can you at least give me something right now that will keep me optimistic."

"They will not marry one another tonight."

"How do you know?"

"Because I never lose."

Chapter 82

"Gentlemen, I apologize for calling a meeting so abruptly, but I have something of great urgency to discuss." Mitch clasped his hands together as he stood in the dining room of the Fleur-de-Leans. The other six members of the krewe sat before him in the same booth they had occupied every Friday afternoon over the last five years.

"Mitch, I do hope this urgent meeting of yours has great importance," Charlie spoke. "Mrs. Guichet is none too thrilled that I had to delay our trip to the Gulf Coast."

Judge Broussard spoke next. "He's right, Mitch. We have never met on a Saturday afternoon. I hope you have some Earth shattering news."

"I do, Your Honor. Thank you again, everyone, for your promptness in meeting here today. And thank you, Scott, for letting us use the restaurant. I know you're busy trying to get everything up and running."

"It's okay. I needed a break anyway."

"Gentlemen, I'll get right to it. As you all know, Davis' body was found in his garage on Monday morning. The autopsy showed that he died of a heart attack. Before his funeral two days ago, Tiffany called me over to her late father's house. She brought to my attention a few peculiarities in the house. First, there were fresh scratches on the headboard of his bed. Secondly, duct tape in his garage was scattered about the shelf. As we all know, Davis was very particular about keeping things clean and organized."

"That's an understatement. The man was obsessive compulsive," Percy spoke.

Scott cleared his throat before adding, "He was like that ever since childhood."

"There were markings on his headboard and duct tape was out of place. So what?"

"I'm not finished, Redmond. The good stuff is still to come. Next, Tiffany pointed out that a large kitchen knife was found under Davis' living room couch."

Charlie put his hand on Scott's shoulder while saying, "Scottie and I were there the night little Thomas pulled the knife from beneath the couch. We were a bit perplexed. Isn't that right, Scottie?"

"I did find it odd that his kitchen knife was under the couch."

"It is odd indeed, but there was something else that Tiffany brought to my attention. In the garage, on the base of the doorframe, she discovered blood. It was just a small amount, but enough to be noticed if you were looking for it. Since foul play wasn't suspected in Davis' death, no one thought to thoroughly search the house or garage. Luckily, Tiffany knew her father very well. She had a feeling something happened the night of his death—and her feeling turned out to be right."

"What are you saying, Mitch? That Davis may have been murdered?" the judge asked.

"Once I'm done telling the six of you what I have learned over the last few days, we can all come to our own conclusion." Mitch placed his hands on the table while leaning forward. "My forensics guy went back to Davis' and took a sample of the blood from the door frame. Using CODIS, he found who the blood belonged to—a man from Mobile named Hank Bowery."

"Hank Bowery? Are you referring to the man that was on the news earlier in the week for having a sex dungeon in his basement?"

"Yes, I am, Charlie."

"How is that possible? Are you saying my brother was connected to that horrible human being?"

"No."

"Then what on God's green Earth are you telling us?" Charlie asked.

"Hank and another man named Cliff Robertson were shot and killed in Hank's house in Mobile. Their deaths were determined to have occurred less than twenty-four hours before Davis' death. That means Hank could not have been in Davis' house around the time of his death."

"Then are you saying that he was in Davis' house before his death?"

"No, Roger. According to statements from neighbors and local residents who knew Hank, he never left his house. He was a recluse. Groceries were delivered to him and he worked from home."

"Then how was his blood in my brother's house?"

"There was a third person in Hank's house at the time of the shootout. That third person happened to get Hank's blood on his shoe. A day later he was in Davis' garage, and while wearing the same shoe, stubbed it against the doorframe on his way inside."

With his arms folded against his chest, Redmond asked, "Why would someone from Hank's house be in Davis'?"

"I'm getting to that soon. Now, I believe there was some sort of struggle inside Davis' house, hence the knife under the couch. Also, I think someone was handcuffed to the bed frame."

"Davis was handcuffed?"

"No. There were no signs of bruising about his wrist. However, my forensics guy discovered tape residue—most likely the duct tape in his garage that never found its way back to its proper location on the shelf—on the cuffs of the shirt Davis was wearing the night he died. Also, I discovered duct tape residue on the steering wheel of Davis' Ferrari. I believe the person that was at the shootout in Mobile, bound Davis inside his car just moments before he suffered a fatal heart attack. The person then walked inside Davis' house, stubbing his toe on the way in. I suspect there was another person involved as well—a woman."

Percy cleared his throat before asking, "Why do you think that?"

Mitch stood upright. "Follow me, gentlemen." Once all six were standing next to the bar, Mitch pointed to two cameras. One was aimed in the direction of the bar entrance. The other aimed towards the cash register. "I looked at surveillance from last Sunday night. Davis talked to many customers that night, but there was one in particular that stood out. The video is black and white, and I could be wrong, but she looked to have either red or a medium brown hair color. The interaction between Davis and the woman looked to be very suggestive. It wasn't until I saw footage from the outside camera that my hunch about the woman was confirmed. She got into Davis' car with him less than two hours before he was determined to have died."

"Maybe the woman that left here with him was the same person from Mobile."

"That's a good thought, Roger, but the other person in the shootout in Mobile was a male. I spoke with one of the two young women that were held captive in the basement dungeon. She never told the police there was a third person involved in the shootout. When I talked to her, she eventually confessed that another man was there, and he was the one that actually rescued her and the other girl. He wore a ski mask, so she couldn't see his face."

"Why would someone not want to be recognized as a hero?" Redmond asked. "I would have wanted my face all over the news for rescuing two women."

"Because the person didn't want to be recognized. Maybe this person wanted everyone to believe he was much farther away."

"How far away?" Scott inquired.

"Out west."

"How do you know that?"

"Well, Percy, because he didn't want to get caught."

"Who?"

Mitch glanced at Scott as he told the group, "Jackson Fabacher."

"The runaway groom?" Roger asked.

"Yes."

Percy laughed, as did the judge and Charlie. Mitch noticed that Scott's immediate reaction was one of disbelief, as he shook his head side to side several times.

"No way. Jackson would never do that."

"Are you saying that the son of Andrew Fabacher—former assistant to the D.A.—murdered Davis?"

"I have reason to believe he may responsible for Davis' death, Charlie."

"You think that young man, who comes from an upstanding family, faked his death just so he could come home to murder his former fiancée's father, only to reappear two days later in Arizona?"

"I know it sounds crazy, Charlie, but the girl whose life he saved in Mobile recognized his voice on a newscast. Her grandmother said the young girl's back was to the television when the report aired, and when she heard Jackson's voice, she repeatedly screamed 'that's him!' The young girl was certain Jackson was the one who saved her, and she didn't want her grandmother to tell me. She was worried harm would come to him if his identity was revealed."

"I almost forgot," added Charlie, "he also had time to run to Mobile and discover an underground sex dungeon—shooting two men in the process—before killing Davis with a heart attack, and then get back out west in two days unnoticed." Charlie let out a belly jiggling laugh. "Thank you, Mitch. I needed a good chuckle today."

"I agree with Charlie," Scott spoke. "I know what Jackson did at the wedding to my niece was a bit over the top, but he's not a violent person. He stayed with my wife and me in Colorado for a few days. He's a good kid. I could never see him orchestrating this elaborate scheme."

"I know it sounds ridiculous, but all of the evidence points to him. Friday afternoon he leaves the Denver airport and reappears Wednesday in an Arizona gas station. So far, no one has yet to come forward to say they saw Jackson on any of those days, except for the young girl that places him in Mobile early Sunday morning."

"You have a young, traumatized girl who thinks she recognizes his voice," spoke Judge Broussard. "That's seems to be the only evidence you have of him being in Mobile."

"Think about it, Judge—he knows Davis, so it's not that unlikely that he unknowingly transferred DNA from Hank's house to Davis' house."

"Why was Jackson in Mobile in the first place, Mitch? How would he know about the sex ring going on there? And why would he want to kill Davis? And who is this mysterious woman you claim was in Davis' house at the same time Jackson was there?"

"I don't know how he knew about the sex ring, and I don't know who the woman is. As for a motive to kill Davis—"

"Mitch," Percy interrupted, "show me the videos from that night." As he stood, so did Scott and Redmond. "Guys, why don't y'all wait right here while Mitch and I look at the videos? No sense in all of us huddling up in that tiny office. We'll be right back."

The two stepped into the kitchen. Percy spoke first, at a low decibel. "Scott is new to this organization. Until we find out if he's going to be a long-term member, maybe we shouldn't let him know about some of our previous…endeavors."

"You're right. But do you think Jackson found out the truth about his friend, Mikey?"

"If Jackson was indeed with Davis the night he died, Davis would have never confessed to what he did."

"You don't believe Jackson was at Davis' house?" Before Percy could answer, Mitch's phone rang. While glancing at the screen, he told Percy, "It's a 251 area code."

"Mobile has a 251 area code."

"Yes, it does." He put the phone to his ear. "Agent Hennessey."

"Agent Hennessey, this is Officer Tim Mitchell with the Mobile Police Department. How are you doing?"

"Fine. What do you need, Officer Mitchell?"

"Well, sir, we just got the fingerprint analysis back from inside Cliff's truck."

"And?"

"We found several fingerprints on the passenger door handle, along with a Denver Broncos hat."

"Were you able to find a match with the fingerprint?"

"Yes, sir. You were right."

"How was I right, officer?"

"One of the fingerprints we found belongs to a man named Jackson Fabacher."

Mitch lowered his phone, pressing the 'speaker' button. "Officer Mitchell, could you tell me again the name of the individual whose fingerprints you found inside Cliff's truck?"

"Jackson Fabacher, sir."

Percy's eyes grew large.

"Good work, Officer Mitchell. I'll be in touch." He hung up.

"Cliff was the other man who was found dead in Hank's house, correct?"

"Yes," Mitch spoke with a smirk. "And Jackson was in Denver last week. That could explain the hat too. Do you believe my story now, Doc?"

"Shit," Percy mumbled. "I can't believe it."

"Let's go tell the others."

Percy followed Mitch to the bar. With hands high in the air, Mitch told the others, "We got 'em! Jackson's fingerprints were found inside the truck of the man that was killed alongside Hank Bowery in Mobile. After killing Hank and Cliff, Jackson transferred Hank's DNA into Davis' house the night he was murdered!" Mitch slammed his hands on the bar.

"Are you positively certain?" Judge Broussard asked.

"Percy, can you back me up on this?"

"It's true, Judge. We just got confirmation from the Mobile Police Department."

"What do we do now?" Mitch asked the group. No one spoke. "Do we arrest him?"

"Jackson killed my brother?"

Mitch nodded. "I'm sorry, Scott."

"You can't prove that someone killed another man by giving him a heart attack."

"Charlie, Davis was bound to the steering wheel of his own car. He couldn't get to his nitroglycerin pills, which were two feet away in the glove compartment."

"Are you 100% positive that Davis was duct taped to the steering wheel? And if so, is Jackson Fabacher the one who did it? Do we know who the mysterious woman is and if she was even in Davis' house at the time of his heart attack? Do you know if perhaps she bound Davis to the steering wheel?"

Mitch already knew the answer to all five questions, and it was the same for each—no. "But there's blood from the Mobile crime scene there."

"And that's about all the evidence we have—that and a traumatized young girl who may or may not be telling the truth. Besides, with his father's track record and connections with the D.A.'s office, I'm inclined to believe that Jackson will not be found guilty in a court of law, let alone even be prosecuted. Judge Broussard, will you back me up on this one?"

"Charlie's right, Mitch. Davis has had heart problems in the past. You can't prove that if Jackson was indeed in his house, that he gave him a heart attack. Based on the information you have at this point, he won't be convicted."

"What about the blood from the shootout in Mobile?"

"If it comes out that Jackson did in fact save the two girls' lives, do you think a jury will convict him of second-degree murder?"

"So, we just let him get away with what he did, Judge?"

"No, but first we make sure everything you just presented to us is accurate. Secondly, we find out about the mystery woman Davis left here with that may or may not have been in the house when he died. For all we know, she may have driven Davis to a heart attack by performing some sort of sadomasochistic act involving a kitchen knife and duct tape or handcuffs. Perhaps Jackson showed up after the fact."

"And what if we discover that Jackson was there at the time of Davis' death, and was the cause of his death?" Roger asked.

"Well, if it's true that Jackson did in fact cause Davis' heart attack, then…we take matters into our own hands," the judge suggested. Does everyone agree?"

"I do," said the judge's nephew, Redmond.

Percy Weller was the next to speak. "Davis has done so much for everyone at this table, including me. I'm in."

"Me too," Roger added.

"I spent the last three days investigating all of this. Of course I'm in."

Two men had yet to cast their vote. Charlie rubbed his belly as he spoke, "Gentlemen, do y'all feel that we are getting to old for these shenanigans?"

"Davis' murder doesn't require justice?"

Charlie chuckled before saying, "You didn't let me finish, Redmond. Do y'all feel that we are getting too old for these shenanigans? Because I don't think we are. Count me in."

Six sets of eyes were cast upon Scott. "I miss my brother dearly. If it's true that he was driven to a heart attack, I think the person involved should be punished. Let's make it unanimous."

Chapter 83

Delain's front door swung open before I could take the keys out of the ignition. I hurried towards her. It was apparent she had been crying. Her eyes were red and puffy.

"What happened?" I shut and locked the front door behind me.

She lunged forward, latching her arms desperately around my neck. "I feel horrible."

"About what?"

"I don't want to lose you. I thought that might have happened today. You mean so much to me, Jackson. I realize that now, more than ever."

Revealing to her the catastrophic events that took place since we last saw one another suddenly took the back burner. "What happened today?"

"I'm going to tell you everything right now."

"Should I sit down?"

"Let's both sit down." She guided me to the couch. "Even though I already told you some of this information, I'm going to start from the beginning."

I grew worrisome, anticipating something that might be hard for me to take.

"You look…exhausted," she told me, reaching for my hand.

"It was a long night. I'll tell you in a minute what happened."

Firmly holding onto my hand, she began. "When Davis blackmailed me into dating him, I was already in a serious relationship with someone."

"Tyler."

"Yes. We loved one another very much—so much so that we talked about marriage. We even went looking at engagement rings together a week before I came down here for the bachelorette party. When I accidentally killed the man outside of Davis' restaurant, my whole life changed. I didn't want to, but I had to breakup with Tyler for his own safety."

"Hold on. I could have sworn on our first date that you said Tyler died in a car wreck."

She shook her head. "I never said that."

"Lainey, you said there was a car wreck."

"There was—mine. I had to break up with him because of the guy I killed with my car."

On the one hand, I was relieved she didn't lie about his death. On the other hand, I grew even more apprehensive about the fact that she was talking about him one day after Caroline said they had run into each other. "I see."

"I apologize. I must have said it in a way that was misleading. I didn't mean to trick you, but I'm sure you now see why I couldn't tell you the whole truth on our first date."

"I do."

"So, after I ended things with Tyler, I didn't see him or have any communication with him for nearly three years—that is, until I saw him yesterday at the airport. I have to be honest with you, seeing him again caused some feelings to resurface. I didn't feel like myself last night, and I want to apologize for that too."

"I knew something was wrong."

"I had a feeling you might think that. When we got back to my house from the party, I told Caroline I was exhausted and needed some sleep."

"Where is she, by the way?"

"At her aunt and uncle's. She's coming back over here to help me get ready for the wedding in a little bit. Where was I? Oh, so when I was lying in bed, all I could think about was the chance meeting I had with Tyler the day before my wedding. I started to wonder if fate had brought us together again."

I took a deep breath. It wasn't easy hearing the truth. "And…?"

Delain grimaced as she said, "And…this morning I went to visit him at his hotel."

"In his room?"

Her mournful eyes remained locked with mine. "Yes."

I took another deep breath, exhaling before saying, "I see."

"I know it's not easy to hear, but I had to find out something."

"What?"

"If I still had feelings for him."

While picturing her in a hotel room with a former lover, I grew nauseous. I had already lost my parents. I wasn't prepared to lose another loved one.

"After a few minutes of talking to him, I got what I needed."

"Which was…?"

"Closure." She partially grinned. "I finally reached closure with him. When we were talking, I thought about you, and how safe and loved I feel when I'm with you. Baby, I have no doubt in my mind that I want to be with you. There's no one else but you. I love you so much, Jackson Fabacher."

I stood from the couch. With my hands resting atop my head, I began to pace the living room. "I don't know what to believe right now. I feel like I've been on a roller coaster ride with you all week. There were moments, like in the coffee shop with Brittany, that I felt you truly loved me, and then last night it seemed like you didn't want to be with me or anywhere near my family. How do I know you're telling the truth?" She stood from the couch. "I want to believe you but with everything—"

Grabbing the sides of my face, she kissed me. Davis' death wasn't on my mind. Neither was my parents' dark and disturbing secret, my twin brother, the dead gangster in my kitchen, nor the incident in Mobile. My thoughts went blank as Delain kissed me in a way she had never done before. Every nerve ending of my body tingled, which preceded the most relaxed, calming sensation I had ever experienced. Delain—I had no doubt—was telling the truth.

She looked me squarely in the eyes. "Do you now believe that I'm madly in love with you?" There was no smile on her face or any hint of doubt in her expression. She knew what my answer would be.

"Yes."

"I love you, Jackson. That's the God's honest truth."

"Don't you mean 'uno'?"

She shook her head. "No. Uno was a dumb way of saying how I truly feel about you. I love you with all my heart."

"I love you just as much." It was time to fill her in on what had happened since we last saw one another. "I have something to tell you as well—two things actually."

With concerned eyes, she squeezed my hand, pulling it closer to her. "What is it?"

"I don't know how to say it, so I'm just going to come out and say it. Last night after you left, I found out that I have a twin brother."

She shook her head, half-heartedly smiling while saying, "What?"

Stone-faced, I told her, "I'm not joking."

Her bottom jaw slowly dropped, while the grip on my hand eased up considerably. "What?" she again asked.

"My mom had an affair with a man nine months before I was born. She had twins. The man, an artist my mom met while working at the museum, threatened my parents into taking my twin brother back home. They claimed they didn't have a choice. My unknown twin knocked on my parents' door last night after you left."

Shaking her head, she said, "You're not joking."

"I wish I was. I hate my parents right now, and I have no desire to speak to them now or possibly forever."

"Baby," she pulled me as close as I could get to her. The embrace, despite what I was going through, again calmed me in the same way as her recent kiss.

"Unfortunately, that wasn't the only dramatic part of my night. About 4:30 this morning, a gunshot woke me up. My brother and I snuck into my kitchen to find a man bleeding all over the floor. He accidentally shot himself. He was coming to kill me."

She again looked on in disbelief, her mouth again hinged opened. She shook her head while attempting to say something.

"It's a little hard to believe, huh?"

"Quite hard to believe."

"I know. I barely believe it, and I witnessed it all happen. Last night was, hands down, the worst damn night of my life."

"Who was the guy coming to kill you? Was it related to Davis?"

"No." Since she had confessed the truth to me, I felt it fair to reciprocate. "When I left New Orleans after the wedding, I ended up in Vegas. One night after a few drinks, I slept with a married woman, but I didn't know she was married until after we had sex. Not only that, she just so happened to be married to a mobster. I left Vegas thinking her husband didn't find out, but he did and when he saw me on the news, he put the pieces together. The man he sent here to kill me was his right-hand man."

Delain appeared frozen for several seconds before moving her lips "Where is he now? Jail?"

I shook my head. "He tried to pull another gun on me, but Marcus killed him."

Again, she grew speechless. Tears began to trickle down her cheeks as she placed both hands over her mouth. She then compassionately hugged me. Her reaction left no doubt in my mind of how deeply she cared for me.

"How's that for some wedding day drama?"

Her crying grew heavier. "You could be dead right now."

"I know." She hugged me with every ounce of strength in her body.

"I'm sorry you had the night from hell. I'm so thankful nothing happened to you."

"And I'm glad you got closure."

"How are we going to be able to concentrate on the wedding tonight?"

"We're not."

She stepped back. "What are you saying?"

"We can't pretend that nothing out of the ordinary happened to us this week, and then go through with a wedding ceremony."

"You don't think we should get married?" She appeared upset.

"I love you to death, but I don't want to be around people that lied to me for almost thirty years. The man who I thought was my dad isn't my dad. He's just a guy that raised me and pretended to be something he wasn't. My mom's not the sweet, nurturing, and honest woman I thought she was. With everything that has happened, I just want to go away—me and you."

"When?"

"Now. I want to get in my car with you and leave this city."

"And do what?"

"Start over. I can't be around here anymore. I no longer trust my parents, and I don't feel safe in my own home. That panic attack I had yesterday morning in your bathroom was one of three, maybe four, that I had in the last couple of days. I need to get out of here. I have about $5,000 saved up. Let's go away together and get away from all the madness and drama and lies."

Her momentary silence instilled hope that she was contemplating getting on board with my newly-minted plan.

"Just you and me on the open road, Lainey. You can pick where we go."

"Before I can give an answer, I have to remind you why you and I met in the first place, or more importantly, *who* was the reason you and I initially met."

"Caleb," I answered.

She nodded. "Today's his birthday, by the way. He's two years old."

After wrapping my arms around her, I could hear her sniffling. "I'm sorry you're not with him on his birthday. Let's go away together and come up with a plan to get him back. I promise you'll get him back very soon. It looks like Davis' death isn't drawing any suspicion that foul play was involved. We need to somehow get a DNA test of Caleb and then we can prove he's your son."

We stepped back from one another. I wiped the tears from her cheeks with my thumbs as she asked, "How do we do that? We need someone who knows the law that can figure out a way to do that."

I knew someone who was very knowledgeable of the law, but I didn't want to speak to him.

"What about your dad?"

"I will talk to him soon and see what he can do. Until that time, why don't you go pack a couple of bags? I'll go home and do the same, and then we get the hell out of here."

Delain placed both hands on my face. My grandmother's engagement ring pressed against my right cheek as she told me, "I love you, Jackson." The few seconds she hesitated in giving an answer had me second guessing my sudden spontaneity. "When I'm with you, I feel like nothing bad will happen. I want to be with you, no matter where it is. Let's go away together."

A wave of euphoria overcame me as she pressed her pouty lips against mine. Besides Marcus, she felt like the only family I had left. It was just her and me; us against the world. I couldn't wait to leave. "I'm going to run home, pack some bags, and grab my money. We'll use cash, so we can stay hidden for as long as possible."

"I have about $3,500 saved up too. I'll go get as much as I can. This is kind of exciting," She flashed an eager smile.

Despite what had happened recently, I strangely felt happier than I had in some time, mostly because I was certain Delain honestly loved me to the point that she was willing to run away with me and start a new life. "I know. I'll be back in less than two hours."

"Where are we gonna go?"

"I don't know yet. We can decide that once we get in the car. I'll be back soon." As she kissed me, I felt needed, wanted, and more importantly, loved. I knew we were making the right choice. "I love you, Lainey."

"I love you too, baby. Hurry back. I'll start packing."

Chapter 84

While driving down the street leading to my house, I cast a paranoid eye upon every vehicle I passed. Much to my delight, it appeared the media were no longer around, and had yet to learn about the dead gangster on my kitchen floor. Much to my dismay, Logan's truck and cherry-red Mustang sat in the driveway. Wasting precious seconds by explaining to Logan the adventure I was about to embark with Delain was the last thing I wanted and needed to do. With the engine still running, I removed the house key from my key chain and quietly inserted it in the front door lock. I gently cracked the door. Logan wasn't in the living room, and after pushing the door halfway open, I could see he wasn't in the kitchen either. What was in the kitchen, however, was the lingering reminder of an indiscretion, along with the realization that I was only alive because of a fluke. Just as a football fan may call it luck that his team won on a fifty-yard Hail Mary pass with no time left on the clock, it was luck that I was still alive because of a puddle of urine left by my roommate. I was still trying to process how I had cheated death at least twice in the last eight days; three times if I included the shootout in Hank's house.

I peered around the living room corner, down the hallway. Logan's bedroom door was open, yet the arrhythmic sound of water falling in the bathroom tub alluded that he was showering. I grabbed two suitcases from beneath my bed, filling the first with various pants and shirts from my closet. There was no time to see if the articles of clothing matched one another, and no time for folding. The second suitcase I filled with items from my dresser drawers, including socks, underwear, t-shirts, and shorts. Enough space remained for a toiletry bag, athletic shoes, boots, and my laptop. With two pillows underneath my arms, I carried the suitcases to my SUV. There was one last thing I needed to do before leaving.

On the dry erase board magnetized to the refrigerator, I wrote the following message: *Logan, there will be no wedding tonight. Due to recent events, I feel it is in my best interest to leave town. I hope you understand. Please tell Marcus and the guys the news. I'm sorry for everything –Jackson.* While grabbing a bottled water from the refrigerator, the running water in Logan's bathroom shut off. I darted out of the house, locking the front door behind me. As I backed out of the driveway, I glanced at the clock. It was 2:25. At about 3:15, Delain would be sitting next to me, holding my hand as we began our new life together.

Just before 3:00, my phone rang. Not wanting to explain to Logan why I was leaving, I ignored his call. Immediately, he called back, and once more I ignored it. As I exited the twenty-four-mile bridge crossing Lake Pontchartrain, a text message appeared from Logan. *'Call me back! It's a goddamn emergency! Two men were just here looking for you!!'* I nervously placed the phone to my ear.

"Where the hell are you?" he feverishly asked.

"In my car. Why?" Delain's house was less than ten minutes away.

"Two F.B.I. agents were just at the house looking for you."

I began to panic—so much so that I began to shake. I pulled into a gas station and put the car in park. "What did they look like?"

"One was black and the other white. Agent Parker and I think the other's name was…"

"Agent Williams."

"That's it! You know them?"

"I talked to them a few days ago. What did they want?"

"To talk to you. I said you weren't here and they asked where you might be. I figured you were either at your parents' or Marcus' house, so I lied and told them the last place I thought you might be on your wedding day."

"And that would be…?"

"Your fiancée's."

I silently cursed Logan while backing out of the gas station. I had to get to Delain's quickly. "You told them I was getting married today?"

"It kind of slipped out. They had guns. I cracked under the pressure."

"How long ago did they leave?"

"Eight seconds before I called you. They high-tailed it out of here. They really want to find you, Jackson. What do you think they want? Is it about Ralph?"

I was certain it was because the agents had found some irregularities with my alibi. "I don't know." Davis' death then came to mind. My palms began to sweat on the steering wheel.

"They asked me several questions about you."

"Like what?"

"How long I have known you. What kind of person you are. If I had any contact with you while you were presumed dead."

"How did you answer the last question?"

"The truth—no."

"So, judging by the last place you thought I might be right now, I take it you didn't see the message on the refrigerator."

"What message?"

"I wrote on the dry—"

"'Logan, there will be no wedding tonight. Due to recent events, I feel it is in my best interest to leave town. I hope you understand. Please tell Marcus and the guys the news. I'm sorry for everything –Jackson.' What the hell, dude? I understand and agree you should back off on the wedding, but why are you leaving town again?"

"I can't tell you right now, but I will soon."

"Does it have to do with the F.B.I. agents that were just here?"

"Maybe."

"Shit! What's going on? Should I be concerned?"

"No, but I think it may be safer if you stay with your sister for a little while until things blow over."

"What things?"

"I can't tell you yet. Just do me a favor and tell Marcus I'm leaving town for a little bit."

"If you're trying to avoid those F.B.I. guys, you may want to get rid of your phone. I've seen movies where they can trace it to where you are or where you're going."

I wasn't sure if it was possible to trace my phone, but it was probably a good idea. "I'm sorry to just leave like this, but Delain and I need to get away. I'll call you tomorrow from a pay phone to see if anything new has developed. Keep your phone close by tomorrow afternoon."

"What about your wedding? What do I tell people when they ask why it's cancelled?"

"Just say it's cancelled, but you don't know why. I need a couple of hours head start away from these F.B.I. guys."

"You're starting to freak me out a little bit, Jackson."

"I'm sorry."

"Don't be. It's about time I get some excitement in my life again. First, a dead mobster in the kitchen, and now some secret thing you got going on involving the F.B.I. I hope you can get me involved in this." Logan seemed to be in high spirits on the other end of the phone, while I had become the most paranoid than any point in my life.

"You never know. You may already be involved."

"You just made my balls get a little tingly, dude. Please get me involved."

"I gotta go, Logan. I'll call you tomorrow. Don't forget to call Marcus."

"I'm calling him now, Outlaw."

I memorized Logan's number before throwing my phone into a canal that ran parallel with the road. Delain's house was three minutes away. In five minutes, we would be on the road together.

I inserted the spare key into her front door, but it wasn't necessary. It was already unlocked. Delain wasn't waiting in the living room with suitcases in hand as I thought she might, and she wasn't in the kitchen either. "Lainey, we have to go now!" I screamed from the bottom of the stairs. There was no answer. I ran upstairs, shouting her name along the way. Still, no reply. I pushed open her bedroom door. It was empty. My stomach tightened as I hurried into the bathroom. "Delain!" The bathroom was empty as well.

It didn't take long to realize I was the only person in the house. I was certain she didn't leave on her own accord. It then hit me what happened—Vincent had found and kidnapped her! The only way I knew to contact him was the cellphone Marcus knocked out of Ralph's hand. I had to get it from the man that had raised me. As I hurried downstairs, a piece of paper hanging on the back of the front door caught my eye. Two words were written on the paper in black ink. Two words consisting of seven letters and one apostrophe. Two words that let me know everything she said was nothing but a lie. I said out loud the two words as I grabbed the piece of paper from the door. "I'm sorry." There was no explanation—just an apology, and a pathetic one at that. No longer believing she had been kidnapped by Vincent, I picked up the kitchen phone to call her cell phone. It was turned off. I slammed the phone back onto its receiver. "Shit, Delain. What the hell are you up to? I need you."

My left arm grew numb as I walked back into the living room. There was no time to wait around for Agents Parker and Williams. The thought of partaking another road trip by myself didn't sit well with me, but I had no other option. Before I could make it to the front door, an intense pain in my chest forced me onto my knees. It was happening again. Breathing was nearly impossible. Everything in the living room began to spin. I fell onto my back, gasping for air. Not long after succumbing to another panic attack, a set of hands touched my cheeks. I couldn't see who they belonged to. The person leaned forward. I soon recognized the blonde hair and the mismatched eyes.

"Are you okay? What's wrong?" Caroline asked.

What felt like a cool breeze brushed against me, bringing with it the sudden realization that I was going to be okay. I managed to breathe deeply.

"Jackson, talk to me."

"I'm…fine."

"Are you sure?"

I focused on her eyes. They had begun to water. "Don't cry," I told her while attempting to smile.

"Seeing you like that makes me want to cry. What are you doing here? You're not supposed to see the bride before the wedding?"

I remained on the floor. Her left hand held the back of my head. "There isn't going to be a wedding."

"What do you mean?"

"Delain left."

"Where did she go? Her car is here."

"I don't know. All she left was this note." I handed it to her.

"'I'm sorry.' Sorry about what?" Using her own t-shirt, she wiped at the sweat that had gathered on my forehead.

I wiped at a lone tear trickling down her cheek with my thumb. "Sorry for running away, I guess."

Caroline retrieved her phone from her pocket. "I'm supposed to meet her here to help her get ready." She put the phone to her ear. I already knew Delain wasn't going to answer. "It's going straight to voicemail. Should I leave a message?"

"Don't worry about it. You won't hear back from her anyway."

"How do you know that?"

I sat up. My heart was still beating rapidly. A light pink dress lay on the floor next to Caroline. "Two hours ago, she told me how much she loved me and knew I was the one she was supposed to be with. I believed her. I told her I didn't feel safe around here and wanted to go away. She said she wanted to come with me. I told her to pack some bags and I would go home and do the same. When I got here a few minutes ago, she was gone. All that was left behind was that note. She tricked me."

"Why don't you feel safe around here any longer?"

"Some things finally caught up to me."

"What kind of things?"

"The kind of things that make you need to leave town."

"Where are you going to go?"

"Not sure, but some place far away from here."

"You're just going to go away and not come back?"

"I don't know. Two F.B.I. agents showed up at my door a little while ago. Logan said they want to talk to me. I'm certain it's concerning—shit!"

"What?"

"They're probably going to be here any minute." With Caroline's assistance, I climbed to my feet. "I have to get out of here now."

"By yourself?"

"I'm afraid so."

"Do you want company?" Caroline had one of those rare smiles that made you momentarily forget about all the negativity in your life, no matter how shitty of a day you were having.

"I can't ask you to come along, Caroline. The F.B.I. is looking for me and a pissed off mob boss wants me dead. I can't get you involved."

"Hello! I'm already involved!" With a confused look she asked, "And what do you mean a mob boss wants you dead?"

"It's a long story." Next to her pink dress was a suitcase. "What if the F.B.I. agents are coming to arrest me?"

"Then I suggest we get the hell out of here now and be extra cautious on the road. Jackson, what do you say we embark on an adventure together?"

Her response was exactly what I wanted to hear. "Let's go."

Made in the USA
Coppell, TX
02 March 2021